Lizzy Harrison Loses Control

PIPPA WRIGHT lives in London and works in book publishing. You can find her on twitter at www.twitter.com/troisverres

PIPPA
WRIGHT

Lizzy Harrison Loses Control

PAN BOOKS

First published 2011 by Pan Books
an imprint of Pan Macmillan, a division of Macmillan Publishers Limited
Pan Macmillan, 20 New Wharf Road, London N1 9RR
Basingstoke and Oxford
Associated companies throughout the world
www.panmacmillan.com

ISBN 978-0-330-52171-0

1 3 5 7 9 8 6 4 2

A CIP catalogue record for this book is available from
the British Library.

Printed in the UK by CPI Mackays, Chatham ME5 8TD

dear Sally - happy birthday and here's the book my friend Pippa wrote. See if you can spot me inside! lots of love Sal Mal forever + a day xxx

To Julia and Jo,

for everything

Acknowledgements

Huge thanks and love to . . .

My sister Julia Nicholls, the first person to know I was writing a book, and the most encouraging voice of all. Thank you for support, friendship and twenty emails a day. I don't know what I'd do without you.

My best friend Jo Paton for her endless patience and thoughtfulness. And for coining the ever-useful decision-making question, 'What Would Mariella Frostrup Do?' which always leads one in the right direction.

Cath Lovesey, for film premieres, fancy dress and your insistence on marking every possible book-related moment with celebratory cocktails. Most of all, thank you for the suggestion, when I was struggling with over-ambitious subplots, to 'just be funny'. I hope you laughed.

Harrie Evans, Rebecca Folland and Liz Iveson. Fabulous friends through thick and thin (you're the thinnest), thank you for huge support and reality checks as I descended from rational publishing professional into paranoid aspiring author.

Thank you to my agent Andrew Kidd, whose advice, encouragement, sense of humour and excellent gossip have made me grateful a thousand times over that he agreed to be my agent.

My whip-smart editor, Jenny Geras, who is mistress of walking that tricky line between confidence-boosting flattery and constructive criticism. Our shared references, from Heather Shimmer lipstick to Bagley's nightclub in King's Cross, have made working together a total pleasure.

Sally Riley at Aitken Alexander, for placing me with the crème de la crème of international publishing. I couldn't have dreamed of a better list of foreign publishers.

Jane Southern, literary scout extraordinaire, for encouraging her publishers to buy my book, and then offering me a job. I'm enormously grateful for both.

Thank you, too, to Sophie Hopkin, Jo Roberts-Miller, Suzy McGrath, Nic Boddington and Lisa McCormack for being lovely friends, always.

Lots of people were amazingly kind and helpful when I lost my job in the middle of writing this book. Impossible to thank everyone, but especial gratitude to the following: Helen Manders, Lucy Vanderbilt, Sarah Ballard, Georgina Moore, Carly Cook, Sarah Hunt-Cooke, Kate Walwyn, Rachel Clements, Francoise Higson, Eugenie Furniss, Simon Trewin, Sheila Crowley, Frederika van Traa. And Dan at Smile Bank for extending my overdraft when the computer said no, and promising to buy the book for his girlfriend. I hope you did so she can see your name here!

And lastly thank you to my parents, Janet and Alan Wright,

who may not have always agreed with my decisions, but have always supported them. Alan, remember this is a novel and not an autobiography, don't read anything into Lizzy's dad being dead. I swear I will try to write something with submarines in next time, just for you. Janet, I know you have never lived on an ashram, but you are still very wise.

‘If you ask me, Mary,’ continued Flora, ‘I think I have much in common with Miss Austen. She liked everything to be tidy and pleasant and comfortable about her and so do I. You see, Mary,’ – and here Flora began to grow earnest and wave one finger about – ‘unless everything is tidy and pleasant and comfortable all about one, people cannot even begin to enjoy life. I cannot *endure messes*.’

Cold Comfort Farm,
Stella Gibbons

1

The train seems to have been stuck just outside Victoria station for ages, which gives me a chance to read my just-purchased copy of *Hot Slebs* in the half-inch of space that's opened up under the armpit of a lanky tweed-suited commuter. (Tweed. In June. I ask you.)

Before you judge me for reading *Hot Slebs* at the relatively advanced age of thirty-three, may I point out that when you work in the world of celebrity PR, Wednesday morning is crunch time – *Hot Slebs* goes on sale and your clients had better be in it. And, crucially, in the right place – not with a big yellow arrow pointing to cellulite, wayward body hair or a mysterious bald patch; not on the 'What Sort of Outfit Do You Call This?' or 'Who Wore It Worst?' page. You want them to have been 'accidentally' caught at a children's hospice on a secret visit, or spotted sneaking out of a rock star's hotel room in the early hours, or carefully primped and flashing their veneered smiles on the red carpet. When

I open my *Hot Slebs*, I'm just checking for any nasty surprises. It's *work*, okay? (But have you *seen* the state of Jodie Marsh lately?)

Suddenly I realize that Mr Tweed seems to think I'm using *Hot Slebs* as an excuse to squeeze a little closer to him. He smiles encouragingly and winks at me from under a greasy hank of red hair that's falling into his face. Trying to convey outraged indignation while not actually making eye contact with him, I wriggle into the space to my right, earning a venomous look from the large woman wedged up against the window. No chance to open the magazine now, but if I close one eye and squint, I can just about make out my horoscope in her paper. *Libra: you will become close to a tall stranger*. Translation: *Libra: you will find your body pressed against that of a lascivious tweed-suited commuter with a ginger comb-over*. The woman flicks the paper aggressively in my direction with a sharp tut, spotting that I have broken rule number forty-two of the commuter code: Thou shalt not be caught openly reading another's literature.

Clearly I need to be more subtle as I crane my neck in the direction of the fat paperback novel being read by a blonde woman who is somehow managing to read avidly while listening to death metal at full volume. Judging by the swarthy model on the front, the book is a romance, which seems a little incongruous given the soundtrack. I don't even try to read it over her shoulder. After all, romance is not exactly my strong suit these days, not even the fictional kind.

I mean, have you ever noticed that the modern romantic heroine can be, not to put too fine a point on it, a bit useless? Every book seems to open with an incident designed to show us just how adorably scatty she is. And how desperately appealing that is to all the men she encounters. Whoops, I dropped my overstuffed handbag on the pavement, and who should help me pick up the four hundred lipsticks and shoes that fell out but a gorgeous man who fell in love with me, the end. Oh no, I had to strip to my underwear in front of the dishy doctor and it turned out that I was wearing knickers that said 'Tuesday', but it was Friday! So mortifying! Then we got married. Uh-oh, the dreamy boss that I was hoping to impress with my business brain seems far more keen on my cleavage – if only I could stop my shirt buttons from popping open all the time, perhaps he wouldn't fall so desperately in love with me.

Does this happen to you? Because when I drop my handbag, the only men who rush to pick it up are after the contents of my wallet rather than my hand in marriage. Granted, I do live in Peckham. I wear matching underwear every day, and not once has it made my doctor declare his undying love for me. But then, my doctor is a fifty-something Asian gentleman approximately four and a half feet high, so perhaps that is a good thing. And let's establish right now that both of my bosses are women and that, if I was going to go there, I hope my standards would be considerably higher. Especially when it comes to Jemima.

I can't help but wonder how being adorably scatty pays the mortgage. My bosses just want to know that I've booked the car with the blacked-out windows for Alice Mannering's photo shoot at eleven; they don't care how cute and winsome I was while arranging it. Tell me – how do these romantic heroines function in a world where bills must be paid, bosses must be placated, appointments must be kept? Does their laundry magic itself into the machine while they're simpering elsewhere? Does their cat (they *always* have a cat, because they're *single*, you see) feed itself? Pay its own vet's bills? Sometimes just keeping on top of everyday life feels like a full-time job. How do these ridiculous child-women actually cope outside the pages of a book?

The train starts moving at last and inches along to stop at the platform, where we all spill out of the carriage on to the concourse. Because I carefully chose my spot on the platform and my place by the carriage doors, I'm at the ticket barrier before the mass of commuters catches up and clogs the machines. Would a dippy romantic heroine have planned ahead so wisely? No, she would not. As I glide efficiently through, I glance behind me at Blonde Romance-Reader. She is, of course, squashed in the middle of the crowd. The large newspaper-wielding woman pushes past her, Blondie drops her handbag, and the contents spill out over the platform. Four hundred lipsticks and a pair of shoes? Check. Mr Tweed races to her aid and she beams at him prettily. A conversation begins. Clearly the two of them are tragic lunatics. They deserve each other.

2

I'm always in the office by eight-thirty. Carter Morgan PR doesn't officially open until nine, but I like to have time to get myself organized before the day begins. Computer on, phone messages checked, post opened, invitations responded to, list of tasks for the day drawn up ready for Camilla Carter's arrival. The other PAs tend to swan in well after nine, clutching their temples, grimacing cheerfully about late nights and hangovers, and sneaking off to Pret in pairs to load up on stomach-settling tuna sandwiches, crisps and cokes. But this quiet time in the morning settles me for the chaos ahead. The stillness of the office is soothing – no phones ringing, no shouting across the partitions. I need this time to function like other people need a double espresso or three cups of PG Tips. To be honest, I could probably come in much later and still have half an hour before Camilla turns up, time-keeping not being one of her strengths these days, so I'm not expecting to see that there's already someone in her office, head bent low, rummaging through the desk drawers.

I peer in through the door. With a skirt that short and legs that long, there's no way it's my boss, but I say, as loudly and sharply as I can, 'Camilla?'

There's a loud bang as someone hits their head hard against the underside of the desk. Good. It serves you right, Jemima Morgan.

'Lizzy!' she exclaims as if it's a tremendous, nay delightful, surprise to see me. As if this is not the second time this week that I've caught Camilla's business partner and so-called friend snooping in her office for no apparent reason.

She straightens herself up and smooths down her blow-dried helmet of glossy black hair. It's so precisely blunt-cut it always reminds me of the snap-on hair of a Lego figurine, though I'm fairly sure that's not the look she's going for. I suppose you would have to say that she is technically attractive, in a tight, sinewy sort of way. One of our clients once referred to her as 'stunning – like a kick in the bollocks', and that is probably the best description I have ever heard of her somewhat aggressive looks.

'Was there something I could help you with, Jemima?' I ask. 'Camilla won't be here until nine-thirty. She's got a breakfast meeting at the Wolseley.'

Between you and me, I'm fibbing here. The only

breakfast meetings Camilla attends these days are with her three children and the nanny, but it's best to set up an excuse now in advance of her inevitably late arrival. 'I know where all her files are if you're after something important.'

Jemima smiles with all the toothy warmth of a crocodile. 'Really, it's nothing. I was just after a nail file, and I'm sure Cam always keeps one about, doesn't she?'

I look down at her immaculate manicure.

'I wouldn't know about that – sorry,' I say. 'Perhaps I could pop to Boots and get you one?'

'Oh no, I wouldn't *dream* of asking you to do that – I can get Mel to do that when she gets in. Whenever *that* is. You know what she's like.' Jemima rolls her eyes and places a confiding hand on my arm. 'If only she would take a leaf out of your book, Lizzy – you're so wonderfully organized. I mean, poor old Cam simply wouldn't be able to cope without you at the moment, would she?'

'I'm sure she'd cope just fine,' I mumble non-committally, as I suspect this is less a compliment to me than a dangling of bait to see if I'll join in with a bit of Camilla-Carter's-lost-the-plot-lately chat, Jemima's specialist subject.

'Well, we could all do with a loyal PA like you onside, Lizzy; I just hope she lets you know you're appreciated. You're behind her through thick and thin, aren't you? Even when things are . . . well, even when things are . . . like they are.' She casts a glance over the office as if the very sight of it is painful to her, but I know I've got nothing to worry about. Camilla's in-tray is carefully sorted in clear plastic folders. Her diary is open at this week, and matches up to her electronic diary (she at least knows where she's *meant* to be). The flowers on her desk are fresh. The magazines on her side table feature her clients prominently on the front covers. It's calm, clean and serene. On the surface.

'Everything's just fine, Jemima – why wouldn't it be?' I ask, picking up papers from my desk and pretending to sort them in the hope that she'll stop angling for me to lay into my boss.

'Well, if you ever need a chat about . . . well, how you're coping with poor Cam, you know where I am. Girl to girl. Just to get things off your chest. Confidential, of course. Camilla need never know.'

She gives my arm a final squeeze and totters out of the door on her five-inch heels. As if I'd confide in her about anything. I'd feel safer sticking my head in a lion's mouth.

Jemima leans back into the office momentarily. 'Do tell Camilla the planning meeting's going to be in my office today.'

'Okay, will do.'

'By the way,' she says casually as she leaves. '*Ghastly* about Randy Jones, isn't it? Saw it in *Hot Slebs*, poor lamb.'

Oh God, oh God, oh *GOD* – how have they found out? I knew I should have checked through the whole magazine on the train. I grab the *Hot Slebs* out of my bag and start flicking through the pages as I turn my computer on. And there it is on page twelve. They don't need a big yellow arrow for this one. No jokey headline. The truth is there's no circle of shame big enough to contain the grainy mobile-phone image of Camilla's hottest client slumped on the floor of a Holloway bedsit with an empty syringe hanging from his left arm and an unconscious teenage model draped across his lap.

It's not like we didn't know about this. Randy had come to in the early hours of Sunday morning and, panicking, had instantly called his manager. Some might say he should have called an ambulance first, but some do not know the depths of self-absorption of your average celebrity. Anyway, it turns out Randy was right to call Bryan Ross. Within four hours the model was in hospital, two paramedics were celebrating an unexpected cash windfall in exchange for their silence, and Randy was in a Croydon rehab centre with high, high walls and fabulously discreet staff. Most people don't even know the place exists. First thing on Monday morning Camilla had issued a press release announcing that Randy had been hospitalized for 'exhaustion'. It was the third time this year, and the press was bound to be suspicious, but Randy has a major US tour lined up for September; we can't afford for his relapse to be made public.

Camilla took Randy on when he was a struggling comedian living in a Hackney squat, but a brief stint on a reality show (and an even briefer 'relationship' with a co-star) turned him into a tabloid darling famed for his outrageous behaviour. His story of triumph over a serious substance-abuse problem was part of the legend of Randy Jones. I say substance when really I mean substan*ces*. Back in the day, Randy would no more limit himself to abusing just one substance than he would limit himself to just one woman – alcohol, pills, powders: he'd take pretty much anything that was offered. But as his star rose, he became a clean, mean comedy machine whose crazy stunts were fuelled by nothing more than being high on life. So his public thought. But really, anyone who actually says they're 'high on life' is deeply suspect, don't you think? The truth is, Randy is on so much prescription medication he practically rattles like a maraca. And every now and then, when the legal stuff doesn't quite take the edge off his manic moods, he finds himself back in the welcoming embrace of the 'friends' he claims to have left behind. One of whom has just shopped him to the press.

How is Camilla going to get him out of this one?

It's nine-twenty when she lurches in, blonde hair flying. She appears to be carrying two handbags, one Bob the Builder rucksack, a bulging Marks & Spencer's carrier bag and a paper bag from Starbucks containing (from the look of the stains on the outside) a spilled coffee and some sort of greasy pastry. It may sound like a lot, but, believe me, she's travelling pretty light today.

'Hello, Lizzy!' she exclaims, trying, and failing, to swing the rucksack back on to her shoulder. 'Here already? Course you are – I could set my watch by you! If I was ever here before you, that is, ha-ha! Bit late this morning getting Cassius off to nursery. Oh, bugger.'

She glances down at the Bob the Builder rucksack, which has now slid down her arm all the way to the floor.

'Oh, bugger, bugger, *bugger* – I've got his bloody buggering rucksack. No wonder he cried so much when I said goodbye – I thought he was stretching out his arms for a hug, but of course it was his packed lunch he was after. I've got to call the nursery straightaway. Sorry, Lizzy, how are you?'

'Morning, Camilla. I'm fine, thanks,' I say to her retreating back. As she throws the bags on to the floor of her office, I spot something white on the back of her pink wool dress – baby formula? Yoghurt? Please God let it not be something revolting relating to her ridiculously fertile husband, Jeremy, whom we all call the Sperminator since Camilla popped out three children in just two years. But no, it looks like it's probably baby sick from one of the twins, and I must remind her of it before she races off to her nine-thirty meeting. If she even knows she has a nine-thirty meeting.

She's on the phone before she's even sat down and, without being asked, I punch in the number for the courier company – the trip to Cassius's nursery with bag or toys or lunch is one that they already know well.

'Morning – bike from Carter Morgan PR to Onslow Gardens, please.'

'Morning. That's got to be Lizzy, right? Bumblebee Nursery, is it, Lizzy? Delivery for young Muhammad Ali?'

'Hello, Dave – ha-ha! Yes, it's for Cassius,' I say, laughing politely. This is a conversation we've had a thousand times before. My role is merely to feed him his lines.

'Highly appropriate destination, ha-ha. Does he sting like a bumblebee?'

'Oh, very good, Dave. I don't think bumblebees sting, do they? At least, not when they're hungry, which he will be if we don't get this bag delivered.'

'Ah, lunch, is it? Well, we can't have the young fella starving, can we? What's he got today then? I Ham the Greatest sandwiches? Ha-ha! Geddit? HAM the greatest!'

'Ha-ha! Oh, that's a good one, Dave,' I say (and indeed perhaps it was when I first heard it – about six weeks ago). 'Will you send a bike straightaway?'

'Course we will, Lizzy, don't you worry. Don't want

any kind of tummy rumble in the jungle, do we, eh? Eh?'

'Ha-ha, absolutely not. Thanks, Dave, have a good day.'

He is exhausting.

As I put down the phone, Camilla swings out of her office, Bob the Builder rucksack in hand. 'Lizzy, could you . . .'

'Bike's on its way, Camilla.'

'God bless you, Lizzy.'

'And here's a baby wipe. I think there might be something on the back of your dress.'

She spins round to inspect her rear and dabs at the mysterious stain. 'Oh, good Lord, what next? Thank God you noticed, Lizzy – you really are an absolute lifesaver. Now, what's first on your wondrous list for the day?'

'You've got the planning meeting in five minutes, just moved to Jemima's office. Should be out by eleven. No lunch today because I've booked you in at the dentist for twelve-fifteen. Book signing for Eliza Evans at Selfridges at four – taxi will pick you up from here at three-thirty so you can see her before she goes on. Taxi will collect you at five to take you for drinks with Tom Porter—'

'Tom . . . ?' Camilla looks blank.

'Porter. Isobel Valentine's new agent? To discuss how to spin her pregnancy? You remember – it's triplets, but she doesn't want to admit it's IVF and wants a "my miracle babies" story?'

'Of course, of course – right. Tom Porter,' says Camilla, still looking a bit confused. I've got to allow her this one as Isobel Valentine gets through agents like other people get through packets of chewing gum.

'But before you get on to any of that, you're probably going to want to see this.' I hand her the copy of *Hot Slebs*, open at page twelve.

'Brill-o-pads, Lizzy, what would I do without you?' says Camilla, racing out of the door with the magazine in her hand. Almost immediately I see her stop in the corridor.

'Bloody buggering bollocks.'

As Camilla stomps down the corridor, frowning at *Hot Slebs*, I notice Jemima's PA nudging her friend to point out the stain that Camilla hasn't quite managed to remove from her skirt. I distinctly see her mouth the word 'Sperminator'.

You wouldn't think it to look at her this morning, but there was a time when Camilla Carter was the most formidable PR woman in the business. Her stable of celebrity clients could be relied upon to be in the papers for all the right reasons – My Fabulous Wedding, My Baby Joy, My Oscar-Winning Role, My Selfless Charity Work. She seemed like a cheery Malory Towers captain of games, all heartiness and hockey sticks, but when crossed she was a one hundred per cent scary head girl. Features editors quaked at her call. If you pissed off one of Camilla's clients, she'd withhold access to all the others until you promised her the sun, moon and stars. She'd insist on copy approval for interviews, make-up artists who charged a thousand pounds an hour, helicopter rides to and from photo shoots. It was easier to pull the offending story before it ran and save yourself the grief.

And it wasn't just the press who obeyed her every order. Spoiled celebrities who strayed from the pre-approved Carter Morgan publicity path were read the riot act. They stubbed out their cigarettes, looked shamefacedly down at their shoes and called her 'Miss' as if they were back at school because they knew they owed Camilla Carter everything.

It was thanks to her that coverage of Isobel Valentine's Fabulous Wedding hadn't included a single mention of the best man's spectacularly drunken speech (culminating in a toast so obscene that the groom had punched him backwards into the wedding cake).

It was thanks to her that Damien Elliott's Baby Joy was unmarred by the revelation that Damien had demanded a paternity test after his wife had admitted shagging not only her personal trainer but also the gardener, driver and pool boy. (Really, who even has a pool boy when they live in Cheshire?)

It was thanks to her that the press faithfully reported

the racy ladies'-man exploits of cinematic action star David Mortensen, when most evenings found him happily at home in the company of his long-term male lover and their two toy poodles.

But these days it was thanks to me that anything got done at all.

Camilla has always been one of those women whose seemingly chaotic exterior belies astonishing organization and an ability to leap from one idea to the next in a way that leaves lesser mortals agape. But a ludicrously early return from maternity leave has meant that, lately, her chaotic front isn't covering a cunning strategy or a trademark Carter master plan. It's only covering more chaos. She's slipping, and we all know it.

And no one more so than Jemima. In the three short months Camilla was away on maternity leave, Jemima hovered around her clients like an Armani-clad vulture. If Camilla is the talent of the operation, Jemima is the naked greed and ambition: Carter Morgan is merely a stepping stone to establishing the world-dominating conglomerate that will be Jemima Morgan PR. She'd think nothing of finding an excuse to force Camilla out and get her manicured talons on her glittering client list.

So far Jemima has persuaded three of Camilla's clients to be looked after by her 'temporarily'.

'Just while poor Cam gets back on her feet – it would help her out so much if you'd agree, sweetie. You know she'd never say so to you, but all those children of hers are so *demanding*, and I know you wouldn't want to add to her worries.'

And now she's got her fangs into Camilla's clients, there's no way she'll let go without a fight.

In the four years I've been Camilla's PA, she's worked me like a dog, but taught me everything she knows. To Jemima's horror, Camilla chose to employ me – the disillusioned pushing-thirty journalist from the Croydon *Examiner* – over the hordes of ferociously confident twenty-two-year-old graduates who battered on the doors of Carter Morgan each summer. Camilla always claimed she was after maturity and experience over rapacious ambition, but I think she took pity on me when I admitted that my journalism-school dreams of a career on a glossy magazine had come to a shuddering halt in a cul-de-sac of regional flower shows and church fêtes. She parachuted me straight into glamorous parties, introducing me as a rising star; she passed on presents from grateful clients and insisted I took the credit for anything we'd worked on together. When my boyfriend Joe left me two years ago, she arrived at my flat with ice cream, a DVD of *Miss Congeniality* (in a box set with *Miss Congeniality 2*, but I wasn't feeling *that* bad) and an insistence that I take the week off. In short, she inspired something Jemima wouldn't ever understand: loyalty.

I'll do whatever it takes to help Camilla because I

know that, underneath that light crusting of baby sick, she's still every bit the tough and brilliant PR of legend. But she isn't exactly helping herself. At the moment she's less *I Don't Know How She Does It* than *What In The Name of Arse Is She Doing?* I don't think she had a clue the Randy Jones rehab story was out until I waved it under her nose. I hope she realizes it isn't just his career that's in the balance here. It's hers too.

By the time she returns from her meeting, it's clear that it's going to be a fairly hideous day. I've already fielded fourteen phone calls from irate journalists who had faithfully reported Camilla's 'exhaustion' line, only to be proven spectacularly wrong by the *Hot Slebs* photographs.

'I'm going to make you a cup of tea, Cam, to give you strength,' I say. 'You're going to need it when you see how many messages I've got for you about Randy Jones. Just let me know when you want me to hit you with them.'

'Urgh. Thanks, Lizzy,' she says with a grimace. 'I'll take the tea, but hold the messages for now. I'm going to be working on a new press release for Randy, so I'm not taking any calls this morning. Just answer "no comment" for now, and I'll get back to people with our official statement later.'

She seems calm, but when I take in the tea a short while later, I can't help but notice that she's slumped in her chair looking grey with tiredness.

'Is there anything I can do, Camilla?' I ask, hovering in the doorway of her office. 'Break Randy Jones's legs? Have him sectioned? Buy biscuits?'

Camilla smiles weakly, sighs and pushes her chair away from the desk. She rubs her temples with the heels of her hands, and then places her palms flat on the desk and takes a deep breath.

'Lizzy, I simply don't know what line to take on Randy this time,' she says, looking at me blankly. 'He's used up chance after chance, and I don't know how many more excuses people are prepared to swallow. I don't know how many more excuses I can be bloody bothered to make up, to tell you the truth.'

I've never seen Camilla like this before – she's always the one with the plan, with the cheesy lines about 'challenges' and 'opportunities' where others see doom and disaster.

'Well,' I start, trying to think of something. 'He's in rehab now, so he can't do anything dreadful for a while, at least. Don't you always say that this kind of thing blows over as soon as the next big story hits? Can we announce Isobel's triplets yet?'

Celebrities would be appalled if they knew how we trade them in for favours like a complicated game of Famous People Top Trumps – I'll trade you one exclusive interview with X for a first photo shoot with Y's baby, plus a set of staged paparazzi shots with Z and his new girlfriend. But Isobel's triplets story is good news, and the unspoken rule is that one bit of bad news is worth several good – even three babies can't be more interesting than Randy's latest fall from grace.

'We've already tried it, Lizzy. We've been through every single client, and no one has anything that's going to knock Randy out of the headlines. All we can hope for on that score is for some other celebrity disaster over the next week or so. Come on, Katie Price.' Camilla laughs without cracking a smile.

'What does Bryan think we should do?' I know Randy's manager, a no-nonsense northerner, will have very definite opinions on how this should be handled, even if he leaves the actual handling to Camilla. He can't stand the press since being described by one journalist as an 'overprotective Svengali in a flat cap'. Once Bryan had looked up the word Svengali in a dictionary he was extremely offended. In fact he is absolutely the right manager for a charmer like Randy. Bryan is completely unimpressed by Randy's winning ways, and, far from being twisted round Randy's little finger, he would happily snap it like a twig if he thought it was in Randy's best interests.

'Bryan thinks that we have no choice but to hold our hands up and say we lied. We admit it all, and then work on building up a new story for a post-rehab Randy.' Camilla looks exhausted at the thought of it.

'Post-post rehab, I guess,' I say tactlessly.

'Thanks for reminding me,' Camilla says. 'Well, I'd

better get started, so can you just close the door for the moment and stick to the "no comment" line until I say so.'

Back at my desk I see the light flashing on my phone – four more messages.

Message one: What is going on with Randy Jones?

Message two: Will Camilla call me urgently about Randy Jones?

Message three: I need to speak to someone about Randy Jones.

Message four: Darling? Darling! It's Mum here! Why is your phone always busy, darling? I'll call you another time. Lots of love.

As much as I love my mother, it's as if she possesses a maternal sonar that means she always gets in touch at moments of high stress and inconvenience. Even though she's currently ensconced in a Himalayan ashram on her annual meditation retreat, it seems she has detected my panicky mood from across the snowy mountaintops. It's a minor blessing that I wasn't around to take her call, or I'd have been subjected to a half-hour monologue on how deep breaths will change my life.

The phone rings again. A man's voice speaks.

'I want to speak to someone about Randy Jones, right now, and I'm not taking any of your no comment bullshit.'

Today is a bad day.

3

The doors of the office close behind me at seven. I take a few deep breaths and feel my shoulders slowly sinking down from under my ears, where they've been hunched for most of the day. Mum would be proud. I'm trying my best to shut the door on my bad day, too, and start the evening afresh.

For once, the British summer is helping. It's one of those beautiful early summer evenings as I walk to the French bar in Dean Street. Soho feels slowed down by the sunshine – everyone's got all the time in the world to get to where they're going. The pavements, usually inhabited only by clusters of disgruntled smokers, are set up with small tables, flickering tea lights, linen napkins. Everyone is captivating on nights like this: the gorgeous boys holding hands on Old Compton Street, the wizened man on a stool outside the Italian wine shop, the woman singing out of a top-floor window to no one in particular.

It feels like the whole world is young and fascinating and full of possibility. Anything might happen.

But what is actually happening is that I'm meeting my best friend, Lulu, as I do every Wednesday night.

Lulu and I first bonded over twenty years ago at the side of a rainy rugby pitch, forced by our parents to watch our loser brothers throw themselves around the field in the drizzle Sunday after Sunday. After three consecutive weeks of casting covetous glances at Lulu's ever-changing array of legwarmers (I had only one pair, in muddy brown – thanks for nothing, Dad), I bravely sidled over to her, bridging the formidable two-year age gap between my flat-chested twelve and her vastly sophisticated fourteen. I shyly admired the pink streaks in her hair and a friendship was born. So far it's survived university (for me), hairdressing college (for her), an ill-advised attempt at flat-sharing in the late Nineties (Lulu's respect for personal property being of the 'what's yours is mine' school), and countless drunken evenings out with the once legendary Spinsters' Social Club. Membership of said club has been sadly depleted in recent years by the traitorous departure of four of our number to the Dark Side of loved-up coupledom and, in three cases, the arrival of babies. Not that Lulu and I have anything against babies. Who doesn't love babies? Especially the babies of one's dearest friends. But as Lulu says, until the children are ready to take their turn buying rounds, they're not going to add anything to a girls' night out.

The crowd at the French bar is spilling out on to the street, resting drinks on the window sills, lighting Gitanes. There is many a battered Camus paperback being enthusiastically brandished in conversation, there is many a Gallic shrugging of shoulders, there is almost certainly not one single actual French person here, but we are all trying to project a little *je ne sais quoi*, and on this beautiful night we might just get away with it.

I can't see Lulu outside, so I squeeze my way into the tiny bar. Mirrors on every wall make it seem more crowded than it is, but even in all the reflections I can't see her. Mind you, Lulu is not the easiest person to spot in a crowd. Not only is she only five foot two, but she has a habit of changing her hair at least once a month, so you spend ten minutes looking for a Paris Hilton-style blonde with extensions, only to realize she's the gamine waif with the jet-black pixie cut. Her excuse is that it's her profession, but you've got to wonder about someone who can't commit to a hairstyle for longer than four weeks. Finally I spot her in a far corner, reflected in three mirrors, all the better to show off the latest look.

'Well hi there, Shirley Temple,' I say as I slide into the booth beside her. 'Love the new do – you look gorgeous.'

'The perm. Is back,' Lulu proclaims, as if announcing the Second Coming, and shakes her new copper curls in the manner of a dressage pony. She and her bouncy locks have managed to get us half a small table (quite an achievement) and a bottle of rosé. I grab a glass gratefully.

'Cheers! Here's to the resurrection of the permanent wave. It takes years off you.' This is not strictly true, Lulu being one of those petite waifs who already looks as if she has a fountain of youth installed in her home, but she's obsessed with her age and I know it's what she wants to hear.

'Seriously, do you think it makes me look younger? How young exactly? Twenty-nine? Twenty-eight from a distance? Maybe if I was in candlelight?' Lulu glances in each of the mirrors; the nearer she gets to thirty-five (still two months away), the more determined she is to pass for under thirty. In Lulu's version of the Underground Railroad, being mistaken for someone in her twenties is a passport to the hallowed shores of Youth and all its associated privileges.

'I've never seen you look younger,' I say. 'Forget twenty-eight, you're like a foetus in a wig, Lulu, I swear.'

'Oh, honestly,' she scoffs. 'Twenty-eight, though. Really?' She looks away from the mirror in time to see me down my glass almost in one.

'So, crappy day at the office? Let me guess: Randy

Jones, your desperate housewife of a boss and some unauthorized photographs.' She shakes her curls sympathetically.

'You read *Hot Slebs* this morning, then?'

Lulu rolls her eyes. '*Everyone* reads *Hot Slebs* on a Wednesday morning, like I have to tell you that. Darling, I did feel sorry for you when I saw the pics, but it is all quite fascinating, isn't it? Tell me eeeeeverything.'

I'd like to say Lulu is entirely motivated by concern for my welfare, but it must be acknowledged that her reputation as the most in-the-know salon owner in Chelsea earns her a lot of extra tips. And as long as she spends those on Spinsters' Social Club wine and snacks, as she usually does, I think it's a fair exchange.

'Well, his US tour's been put on hold – the insurance depended on him being drug tested each week and there's no point doing that now it's quite clear he's not drug-free. His manager's gone mental, Camilla's lost the plot, and Jemima's blatantly hoping the situation will get worse so she's got an excuse to get rid of Camilla.'

'But what happened to the underage model? Is he in the Priory? How long's he staying in?' Lulu needs the specifics for her tips. She's not about to waste her time on tedious office politics between Camilla and Jemima.

'Well, it turns out the model was actually just heavily asleep and slightly dehydrated, no overdose involved, so all's well on that score – 'scuse the pun. Randy's in some secret rehab place, but he checked in voluntarily, which means he can leave any time he likes.'

I drain my glass and slam it down on the table. Interesting how alcohol helps you let go even better than deep breaths on the office doorstep, I note. One to discuss with Mum some time.

'I'll bet you he checks out within a week,' I say.

'And when he does, I'll be right there waiting for him, if you'd just give me the address.' Lulu signals to the waiter for another bottle of wine. 'Putting aside his teeny-weeny substance problems, you have to admit he's absolutely sex on legs.'

'Urgh! Honestly, Lulu,' I shudder, 'you'd want to give him a good wash. Really, what is sexy about an all-pervading odour of stale fags and BO?'

'Fwwwaawwr, I bet he'd be filthy – you're just way too uptight, Harrison.' Lulu is gazing off into the distance, and I can't tell if she is contemplating her new curls in another mirror or dreaming of jumping the bones of Randy Jones.

'Lulu, it's not uptight to expect a man to take a shower once in a while, especially when that man likes to wear the same skintight jeans, sans underpants, for months at a time.'

I sound prim even to myself, but really, Randy Jones, heartthrob to millions, is pretty unappealing in the flesh. Even more so because he's entirely convinced of his own gorgeousness. If a dog looked at him in the street, he'd think it fancied him. He likes to stand just a *little* too close to any woman under seventy (he's not an ageist) so he can hit them with the power of his personality. Unfortunately it's the power of his armpits I tend to notice first. You'd think that someone as obsessed with his appearance as he is (Randy being no stranger to the make-up counter) would consider washing more often, but he's like some Elizabethan courtier who covers up his body odour with yet more perfume rather than risk his health by taking a bath. Sometimes I think his insistence on smelling like a builder after a sweaty day on site is an intentional contrast to his campness, as if the manly stench of his pits somehow cancels out his penchant for Cuban heels and eyeliner. Though if there are any doubts about his heterosexuality, the fact he's never without a glamour model on his arm should be enough to disprove them, one busty blonde at a time.

Lulu sighs wistfully. 'I'd still do him. Dirty jeans and stinky pits and all.'

'Yeah, just think of the tips you'd get with *that* piece of first-hand information. Probably enough to cover your treatment at the clap clinic afterwards, eh?' I snigger into my wine glass.

'Jeez, Harrison, do you always have to take all the *fun* out of it? Can't I even have a fantasy shag without you insisting that I get a virtual STD? Don't go imposing your lifetime sex ban on me.'

Ouch. That one's a little below the belt. The dark-haired man whose table we're sharing looks up with raised eyebrows and then, seeing my furious face, straight back down at his paper. (*Le Monde*, *naturellement*. Fake Frenchman, I bet.)

'It's not been a *lifetime*, Lulu,' I hiss. 'It's two years since I split up with Joe – doesn't your precious break-up equation say that's acceptable?'

Lulu is pretty strict about the fact that you can only mourn a relationship for a period of time equal to half the length of the relationship itself. It's a useful equation for forcing you to get a grip – especially when your relationships tend to be short ones, like Lulu's. But five years with Joe grants me a permitted mourning period of two years and six months.

'Darling, that's a *maximum* possible time for getting over a break-up, not the minimum requirement. I mean, two years? You're practically a born-again virgin.'

'Two years is not that long in the scheme of things, Lu,' I hiss.

'In the scheme of *what*?' exclaims Lulu. 'In the scheme of a convent? In the scheme of a weirdo agoraphobic who hasn't left the house in twenty-four months? In the scheme of someone who really should be back in the saddle by now?'

Lulu's voice is getting louder and louder, and the dark-haired man has blatantly stopped reading his paper to listen to us.

I hope that right now you're thinking, 'Who is this so-called best friend who's being so mean to Lizzy?', but I'm pretty sure that what you're actually thinking is: 'Two *years*? Twenty-four *months*? What the hell is wrong with this woman?' So I'd like to take a moment to reassure you that I'm a perfectly normal thirty-three-year-old woman in all respects. I'm not morbidly obese; in fact, breaking up with Joe helped me lose about ten pounds on the tried and tested misery diet (none better), and I've kept it off ever since. My hair isn't shaved into anything terrifying, it's standard issue PR-girl highlighted blonde to my shoulders. Piercings in ears only, and I'm entirely free of tattoos. I'm five foot seven in heels and, as I'm rarely out of them, I like to think of that as my real height, despite evidence to the contrary.

I've had dry periods before – who hasn't? But even for me, this is a record. And in contrast to Lulu's love life, it looks even worse. Lulu is in and out of relationships as often as she changes her hair. People who don't know her – well, okay, *women* who don't know her well – are inclined to think of her as a bit of a slapper, but she'd be horrified to know it. In fact she's the most romantic person I know. Each new man is The One, every encounter a dazzling adventure, even if it only lasts a few weeks. And it only ever does last a few weeks. I am in awe of her faith in love and possibility and hope. But right now she's pissing me off.

'Lulu, I wish I was more like you,' I say, and I mean it. Sort of. 'But I'm just not. You can hardly pop out for a pint of milk without meeting someone new and wonderful. My life is different. It's complicated.'

She snorts as she pours more wine. 'Complicated how, Harrison? You're single, you're gorgeous, you're smart and funny. You're in need of a shag. Why exactly is this complicated?'

'I don't meet new people like you do, Lulu, really I don't. They don't come into my salon and sit in my chair and tell me about their love lives and ask me out on dates. I don't live with my twin brother and meet all of his friends every five minutes. I work in an office full of women! I live alone! But I'm trying! It's not my fault I haven't met the right man yet.'

And it's not. It just seemed that at the moment when all of my friends finally settled down, Joe and I split up. And almost overnight my carefree twenty-something existence of rocking up to weddings every weekend and hitting festivals in vast groups suddenly turned into an endless round of christenings and birth-day parties for the under-fives. Don't get me wrong – like I said, I love children; but it just seems wrong that the last time I got kissed by a male of the species he was two years old and covered in strawberry ice cream.

Suddenly Lulu lunges across the leather banquette and grabs my handbag. She shoves her hand in and grabs my baby-blue Smythson diary (a gift from Camilla) and brandishes it above her head triumphantly. My stomach lurches. Don't worry, it's not a confessional deep-thoughts sort of diary – as if I'd keep one of those in the first place, let alone carry it around in public. We're talking a day-planner here – but I'm still not sure I want my weekly schedule to be held to account so publicly.

'Right, let me *seeeee*,' says Lulu, opening it at random. 'Spinsters' Social Club on Wednesdays?' She flicks through the diary. 'Yup, I knew it! You've actually put this in your diary as a date for the *entire year*. Already. It's *June*, Harrison.'

'Of course I have!' I protest, 'We *do* meet every Wednesday – we have for ever. Why wouldn't I put it in my diary?'

'Because –' Lulu thumps the table a little too vigorously. How many glasses has she had now? 'Be*cause* you haven't even considered the possibility that anything in your life might actually *change*. I mean, where might you be in six months? Where might I be?'

'Lulu, don't get hysterical – you're my best friend, I'm making time for you in my diary because I want to see you. Why's that weird?'

'It's weird because – ' She thumps the table again. Oh dear, she's definitely hit her four-glasses-plus ranting stride now. 'Be*cause* you've also put in your Monday night yoga class to the end of the year, your Tuesday night babysitting, and your Thursday night Italian lessons. What kind of a control freak are you?'

The dark-haired man has now given up any pretence of reading the paper, Lulu looks at him for back-up and waves the diary in his direction. 'I ask you, is this normal?'

'Eet ees a leetle strawnge,' he says with a Gallic shrug – a real one. Either he's truly a Frenchman or he's doing a very good impression of one.

'When I want your opinion, I'll ask for it, *Monsieur*,' I snap, turning back to Lulu, who's beaming at him gratefully, glad to have an ally in the annihilation of my life. 'So I have a full life, Lulu – I'm busy, I'm out there, I'm trying to meet people. Can't you see that?'

'No you're not. This isn't a diary, it's an activity chart. You're filling your life with stupid classes and meetings because you're scared of opening yourself up to randomness, to any encounter you're not in charge of.' Lulu flicks the diary shut and throws it on to the table. I snatch it back before our French interloper can pick it up.

'Oh fuck off, Mrs Freud,' I say, trying to defend myself. 'I could meet a man at yoga – there are quite a few good-looking men in that Monday-night class, I'll have you know.'

Lulu looks at me with pity. 'Harrison, I've been to yoga classes. I'm here to tell you, darling, that you deserve better than some earnest wispy-bearded youth who's a bit too much in touch with his feminine side. And besides, you hate the smell of patchouli oil.'

She has a point.

'Don't you see, darling, that this isn't normal?'

'Lulu, it's perfectly normal. I don't see why you're picking my life to bits like this. I like my life just fine the way it is.'

'Do you, though?' says Lulu, leaning across the table with sudden urgency. '*Do* you? Because I've been thinking for a while that these Spinsters' Social Club evenings aren't doing us any good at all. I mean, do you really want to be meeting up every Wednesday for ever and ever to discuss being single?'

'Of course not.'

'Then we need to do something about it, Harrison. And when I say *we*, I mean *you*.' Lulu pushes the table away and stands up, holding her glass above her head for emphasis. And spills a bit of rosé on the white shirt of the *Le Monde*-reader, but he doesn't seem to object; indeed he's looking at Lulu with frank admiration. 'Because it's time we got you a man, Lizzy Harrison!'

'Thanks for telling the *whole bar*, Lulu,' I hiss, pulling her back into her seat before the group of curious businessmen behind us get any ideas. 'What exactly do you want me to do about it? Start hanging out in bars on my own, talking to strangers?'

'That,' says Lulu, sitting up sharply, curls bobbing, 'is not a bad place to start.'

'Oh, honestly,' I scoff. 'I'm not going to go out on the pull on my own like a low-rent prozzie. What do you take me for?'

'You'd never be low-rent, darling,' says Lulu, patting my hand reassuringly as if I'm genuinely concerned about where I'd fit in in the hierarchy of prostitution. 'You'd be high-class all the way, but the point stands. You *do* need to talk to strangers, to loosen up a little, and you're never going to do that if you're always in your safe little groups for yoga or Italian or any of the other things you're filling that stupid diary with.'

'It's not about safety,' I protest as Lulu fills my glass again. How many have we had now? 'I'm just doing things I like.'

'That's what *you* think,' says Lulu, her words of great wisdom only slightly slurred. 'But *I* know that you're stuck in a rut, and I'm here to get you out of it. You need to loosen up, Harrison, take a few chances, let go a little!'

She rises to her feet once more. 'Elizabeth Harriet Harrison – ' more gesturing and wine-sloshing, but our neighbour is too interested to object – 'you are going to take my advice and learn to lose control!'

The Frenchman looks at her rapturously. Clearly she speaks of what she knows, as there isn't a great deal of control to her movements right now.

And then she falls off her chair into his lap.

4

I wake at five a.m. with the dry-mouthed morning horrors.

In my twenties I would routinely complain about hangovers as I scoffed a bacon sandwich and conducted a party post-mortem with my housemates, a slight ache in my temples and possibly a little queasiness in my stomach – nothing that couldn't be cured with a cup of tea, and a medicinal ginger beer if things got really bad. But my thirties are different. I woke on the morning after my thirtieth birthday party with an absolute conviction that I was the worst person in the world. Everything I had ever done was a disaster. Everything I would ever do would be appalling. I knew, without entirely remembering what I had done, that I had completely embarrassed myself at my own birthday party. Hadn't I insisted on making a speech, even when Joe had tried to tell me I was too drunk? Hadn't I actually *cried* at some point during said speech (the details of why were escaping me)? Hadn't I then insisted on dancing on a table for two hours? Hadn't I fallen off? What *else* had I done? No doubt all of my friends were ringing each other to laugh about me and to arrange to meet up later, without me, to laugh some more. The fear of it pinned me to my pillow like a two-hundred-pound weight. Luckily Joe had been next to me in bed that morning, bleary-eyed and sleepy and not at all bothered by my horrors.

'It's just hangover paranoia, Lizzy,' he'd mumbled into his pillow, throwing a reassuring arm around me. 'Everyone gets it – just go back to sleep. You were fine, you were fun. Why shouldn't you get pissed at your own birthday party?'

He was right, of course, but when the evil fears have you in their grasp, it's hard to be rational. And now that I live on my own, there's no warm body to prod awake for a promise that I'm not awful. And the fear of still being alone two years after Joe left is threatening to send me into another tailspin. I try to rationalize with my hung-over self. I am not a bad person. I may have got drunk, but I am far too uptight to have got up to anything really regrettable. As Lulu always says: 'Did you throw up on the kindly driver who was trying to wake you up at the last stop on the night bus? No, you did not. Did you get thrown out of a bar for having sex in the toilets? No, you did not. Did you flash your boobs at Gordon Ramsay while dining in one of his restaurants?

No. Have I done those things when drunk? Yes, I have, and I am not an awful person either. So get a grip.'

Thank God for Lulu, I think. She always makes me feel better about myself. Except . . . hang on, yesterday night is beginning to come back to me.

We moved on to a third bottle of rosé, I remember that bit. And Lulu insisted she was going to change my life by making me lose control or something. And (ouch, my head – shouldn't have tried sitting up) I seem to recall that I actually *agreed* to it. Such is the power of wine on an empty stomach. Then we staggered out of the bar, and I must have been really drunk by then because for some reason I keep thinking there were three of us at this point. I have a vague memory of slipping down some black metal steps to land at the feet of a vast (and vastly unimpressed) doorman at a karaoke bar on Poland Street. I look under the duvet at my right thigh. Oh yes: manoeuvre verified by an array of delightful bruises. I remember he refused to let us in, my gymnastic display notwithstanding. From there it's getting blurry, so I resort to the last-ditch tactic of the truly obliterated of memory – reconstructing one's evening via receipts. My handbag is on the floor by the side of my bed and I reach gingerly down for my purse. Contents: three twenties and a flurry of receipts.

Cashpoint at 11.30 – £100. Ah yes – the stage in the evening when one feels generous and loaded, no matter that it's the week before payday.

One receipt from Kettner's at midnight – a bottle of champagne? What were we celebrating?

One taxi receipt. Thank God I retained enough self-preservation to get home safely.

And one scrunched-up cocktail napkin wedged right down at the bottom of my bag. I unfold it and smooth it out on my pillow. Large, loopy handwriting – mine, I realize, with a combination of surprise and foreboding – spells out:

> *I, Lizzy Harrison, do hereby agree with Lulu Miller that I need to lose control in future. Because I am way too uptight lately, and Lulu knows what is best for me.*

On closer inspection, that last line is in Lulu's handwriting.

It's followed by my scrawled signature, slightly blotched by . . . champagne? Tears? And is accompanied by scratchier writing in a different hand at the bottom:

> *Witnessed by: Laurent Martin.*

Laurent Who?

The Frenchman from the bar?

The *Le Monde*-reader whose lap Lulu fell into?

How did he end up in Kettner's with us?

Try as I might, I can't remember the very end of the evening. But hangover or no hangover, my morning routine is too firmly ingrained for me to deviate far from it, and I force myself out of bed. The early waking means I can get ahead of myself. Admittedly, my morning run is more a gentle stagger around Peckham Rye. With frequent stops. My usual egg-white omelette ends up being a bit closer to a fried egg sandwich. But I'm at my usual spot at the station on time, even if it's taken a bottle of ginger beer to ensure I can get on the train without feeling sick.

And I'm still at my desk at eight-thirty. But this morning Camilla's to-do list comes second to emailing Lulu with one word.

From: Lizzy Harrison
To: Lulu Miller

Laurent?

As her salon doesn't open until eleven and she spends most of her time on her feet instead of longing for distraction at a desk, Lulu is a rubbish email correspondent, so I'm not expecting an answer from her until much later in the morning. But her BlackBerry must be on as I get a reply straightaway.

From: Lulu Miller
To: Lizzy Harrison

Honh-hi-honh. He's still here, darling. Will call you later.

Au revoir.

At nine-thirty Camilla sweeps in, mobile clamped between ear and shoulder, on the phone to the nursery once again. 'His violin? I'm so sorry, Mrs Paton – I realized as soon as I got to the office. I'll get it to you straightaway. Thank you so much for letting me know.'

She casts me an agonized look as she deposits a violin case on my desk, and, *plus ça change*, I'm straight on the phone to the courier company.

'Morning, Lizzy – what's young Master Ali mislaid this time?'

'It's a violin, Dave.' I'm hung-over, tired and impatient.

'Ooooh, I hope he won't be threatening the other children with violins, Lizzy! Geddit, violins?'

'Brilliant, Dave, quite brilliant,' I snap rudely. 'You should be on the stage. But seeing as you're not, could you just get on with sending a bike, please.'

There is a hurt silence at the end of the phone. God, why do I have to be such a bitch?

'Actually, Lizzy, I *am* going to be on the stage. Bet you didn't expect that, did you? No, you think I'm just some figure of fun on the end of the phone, counting out my days in a dead-end job. Well, thanks very much.'

That was unexpected.

'God, Dave, sorry,' I mumble shamefacedly. 'Bit hung-over this morning and I shouldn't be taking it out on you. Are you really going to be on stage? Wow, that sounds great!' Guilt makes me sound about three hundred times more excited than I feel.

More silence. I think he's torn between letting me know he's upset and a longing to reveal all. Showbiz wins.

'If you really think that, Lizzy, then why don't you come along? Next Wednesday, comedy night at the Queen's Arms in Balham. I'm the first on at seven.'

I take a deep breath and prepare to decline politely, but there's a note of plaintive hope in the voice of this man I've never met. My resistance is low. And I hear myself saying, 'I'd love to, Dave, I really would. Thanks for the invitation and good for you. I'll see you there.'

I hang up, safe in the knowledge that Dave has no idea what I look like, no way of contacting me except on my work number, and can easily be fobbed off with an excuse. ('I was there! At the back! Waving, didn't you see me? Honestly, you were brilliant!'). There is no way on earth I actually mean it.

And anyway, I always see Lulu on Wednesdays, and once she's sobered up I know she'll stop going on about this losing control rubbish and get back to downing the rosé as normal.

5

I've been giving Lulu's rant some thought over the last week and, in my weaker moments, I have to admit that she isn't completely insane. While my friends are moving on, getting married, having children, getting brilliant new jobs, I am still exactly where I was two years ago, and not making any effort to change. Don't get me wrong – I like my life; but will I still like it in another two years? Maybe I do need to shake things up a little – perhaps join an online dating agency? Attend a few singles nights? Hang out at gallery openings or other smart places to meet cultured, attractive single men? Imagining myself, champagne glass in hand, holding a group of gorgeous men spellbound with a witty anecdote, I am beginning to see that there might be something to be said for making a few changes to my well-ordered routine.

But it's a surprise to find myself standing on my own in a queue outside a suburban pub near the lower reaches of the Northern Line. For a Peckham girl like me, this neighbourhood holds no fears, but the situation itself fills me with dread. How have I let Lulu talk me into this? The evening that stretches out in front of me holds, of all things, the debut appearance of Dave the Comedy Courier.

'But this is perfect!' Lulu exclaimed when I called her for a Frenchman post-mortem (big nose, big hands, big everything, apparently) and made the tactical error of mentioning Dave's comedy gig as a brief aside.

'Have you ever met this man?'

'Of course not, Lulu – he's just some courier I talk to on the phone,' I sighed, wishing I'd never raised it in the first place.

'Then for all you know, the man of your dreams is at the end of that telephone line. You're going. I was going to tell you that I can't make Wednesday anyway, and this is the perfect way to get you out of your rut. You will go to a comedy evening and you will meet new people without me.' She was all righteous decisiveness and bossiness. It was infuriating.

'Without you? No way. If I'm going, you're going too,' I insisted, attempting to boss her back. 'How else will you know if I've obeyed your command? And you can't really make me go on my own, Lulu – come on.'

'I will be working on improving European relations that evening, Harrison, specifically between the French and the English, but I can assure you I have spies everywhere, so don't even *think* of piking out. You promised you'd make an effort: here's your chance to prove it. My next appointment's here – got to go.' And the line went as dead as my hopes of a good night out.

In an effort to look (a) unapproachable and (b) as if I have a legitimate reason for being at the comedy show alone and am not just a saddo with no friends, I have come in costume. Not like a giant bear or anything – be realistic, I'm looking for anonymity here. My long hair is twisted up into a chignon, and my only-on-a-contact-lens-free-Sunday glasses are perched on the end of my nose to give me a studious look. I'm carrying a small notebook and am attempting to give off an air of weary indifference as if I'm a jaded habituée of the comedy circuit, here to cast judgement on fresh blood. A pencil skirt, modest heels and a blouse complete the picture. I'm thinking efficient, businesslike and definitely in journalist/critic mode. My fellow queuers are evidently thinking 'weirdo librarian' and I've noticed a few odd looks. Like I care. I'm doing this to show Lulu that I can be as spontaneous as the next person, but she's insane if she thinks I have any intention of actually speaking to anyone.

We shuffle into the pub and, quite unexpectedly, it turns from unassuming boozer to cavernous theatre once inside. There's a balcony running around the top of the room, and large tables are set up in front of a proper stage with floodlights and a microphone. I suddenly feel a pang of pride for Dave-the-courier; this is a real comedy showcase, not the two-bit suburban pub I'd imagined. Pride is swiftly followed by a rush of nerves on his behalf as I see the size of the audience: there have to be at least two hundred people here. And more are streaming in – big after-work gangs of suited men pushing to get to the tables at the front, while others head straight for the bar at the back where a harassed barmaid is pouring pint after pint into plastic glasses. A few girls seem to have come with boyfriends or husbands, but there aren't many women here at all, and those that are have dressed up to the extent of putting on their best fleece and jeans, so I feel more conspicuous than ever. I'm just trying to work out where to hide when a voice in my ear slurs, 'Exshelllent dishguise, Misshhh Moneypenny.'

I roll my eyes as I turn round, looking as forbidding as possible.

'I *beg* your pard – oh! Dan!'

Lulu's twin brother grins at me as he runs a hand through his black hair. You'd hardly believe the two of them were related, let alone twins. To Lulu's intense annoyance, Dan got all the tall genes and towers over her (and me) at six foot two. Lulu believes, with irrational indignation, that if Dan hadn't hogged all the available height in the womb, she might have been granted a crucial few extra inches. And while she changes her hair constantly, he's had the same tousled curly mop since he was at school – not so much a style as a complete lack of one. Ever since she bought her first pair of haircutting scissors, Lulu has itched to give Dan a new look, but he has firmly resisted her every attempt. During our teenage years it was a source of great shame to Lulu and me to be seen in Dan's uncoiffed company, but right now I'm so relieved to see someone I know that I'm beaming at him as if he's George Clooney.

Suddenly I remember Lulu's email. 'Ah, I *seeeee*. Lulu has spies everywhere and you're it tonight, right?'

Dan looks a little confused and starts looking around the pub. 'Lulu? Is she here? I didn't know she was coming tonight – I thought she was out with her new French bloke. I'm just here with the boys.' He gestures over to a table of beery rugby-shirted men, exactly the people I'd have guessed he was with.

I'm not sure I've ever seen Dan in anything other than a rugby shirt or sober work suit. Ever since Lulu and I first met, Dan has been in the background of our friendship, never-changing, rugby-shirted and style-free. When he left university, Lulu took it as a personal affront that he chose to pursue a career in corporate law. 'Like he's not square enough with the rugby and the hair don't, he has to go for the most boring career he can find. I mean, doesn't he stop to think how badly this reflects on me, him constantly hanging out with such losers?' Not that that stopped Lulu from shagging half Dan's colleagues over the years. ('Better to shag them than have to listen to them, Harrison – you can't imagine how dull they are.')

'Well, it's great to see you, Dan,' I say. 'Especially if Lulu didn't send you here to spy on me.'

'Spy on you? Why would she do that? She didn't even know I was coming here tonight. Are you up to something interesting, then? *Should* I be spying?' He tilts his head towards mine, and though his face is perfectly serious, his dark blue eyes are definitely laughing at me.

'Oh, no, it's nothing interesting at all,' I stammer, sounding highly suspect. 'Lulu just thought it was important for me to come to support, er, a friend of mine who's doing a set here tonight. Moral support, that sort of thing.'

Dan raises his eyebrows. 'Moral support while dressed like a Fifties secretary, Miss Harrison? Who is he? Rock Hudson?'

'Ha! No! Er, that's to say, I don't really *know* him, he's more of a work acquaintance,' I explain. I don't want to come out and say that I'm here to see a man I've never met and know precious little about. So I go on the defensive. 'I mean, it's for my *job*, you know. So I'm dressed for *work*.'

'Well, whoever he is, you can't stand here on your own looking like you're about to take a letter. Why don't you come and sit with us? There's plenty of room and I promise not to let the boys be too much trouble.' Dan smiles and places his hand in the small of my back, propelling me gently towards his friends, who are rowdily refilling their glasses from the pitchers on the long table and grabbing greasy handfuls of chips from large white platters of lager-absorbing snacks that the management have provided more as insurance against drunkenness than out of any kind of culinary ambition. The men briefly look up as we approach.

'Lizzy Harrison, I'd like you to meet Bangers, Bodders, Johnno, Dusty, Paddy.' Dan gestures around the table to each man in turn, but I'm finding it hard to keep track. Quite why these grown men insist on using pets' names is beyond me, but they seem friendly enough as they shuffle up good-naturedly to make room for me to sit down next to Dan.

'Nice to meet you, Milo,' says one of them – Bangers? Paddy?

'Milo? Do you mean me?' I ask, baffled.

'Milo – as in Miles Harrison? Rugby commentator? You've really never heard of him?' asks the one with the Irish accent. I'm thinking he's got to be Paddy, these being fairly literal boys. He shakes his head and sighs, as if under great mental strain. 'Thing is, you've got to have a nickname to fit in with the boys tonight, Lizzy, and Harrison's just not giving me a lot to work with.'

'Ah, right, Milo it is,' I say. 'Thanks. Great. So what's your special rugger-bugger name then, Dan?'

'Er, you can just call me Dan, like normal,' he mumbles, grabbing his pint and fixing his eyes on the empty stage. 'I think the lights are going down – must be about to start.'

'Dan, you total liar, it's perfectly light in here. No excuses, dish it.'

Dan is valiantly ignoring my stare when Bangers shouts from the end of the table, 'Oi, Windy, pass the chips, will you?'

'Windy! Ha, no wonder you didn't want to tell me. Suffering from some digestive issues, are we?' I tease, and Dan's mouth twists into a smirk. He turns his chair towards me and is about to reply when Johnno interrupts, painfully earnest from across the table.

'Er, no, actually, Lizzy – I mean, ah, Milo, was it? We actually call him Windy because of the nineteen-seventies children's television programme *Camberwick Green*, which featured a character, in fact a *miller*, called Windy Miller. Windy Miller, Dan Miller, do you see?' He looks at me with the patient expression of a kindly teacher instructing the class dunce.

'Ah, right, I *think* I get it,' I say innocently, sipping my beer and avoiding looking in Dan's direction. Johnno seems well-meaning, so what's a bit of patronizing between new friends? 'Thanks so much for explaining.'

'No problemo, Milo, no problemo. Glad to help out,' Johnno says, settling comfortably back into his seat and proceeding to expand on his theme. 'Now you see, *Paddy* here gets his name because he actually comes from the *Emerald Isle*, also known as the *Republic of Ireland*, and people from there are sometimes called either Paddies or Micks. Some might say these are *pejorative* terms which—'

'Johnno, mate,' interrupts Dan. 'I think we might want another pitcher of lager before the show starts. Do you mind doing the honours?'

'No problemo, Windy, no problemo. Leave it in my capable hands,' says Johnno affably, and he heads over to the bar.

'Great bloke, Johnno, great bloke,' says Dan, watching as Johnno instantly strikes up conversation with a tall brunette in the bar queue. That's to say, he's doing most of the talking. 'Amazing winger on the pitch. Tedious as fuck off it, unfortunately.'

'Don't be mean – he's just trying to make me feel comfortable,' I laugh. 'At least he means well.'

'Yeah, he does mean well. I just wish he'd mean it a bit further away so I could talk to you properly.' He smiles at me over the top of his pint.

'Oh, really?' I turn towards him on the bench. 'And what do you think we need to talk about properly, Dan? What colour rugby shirts are in this season? Refereeing decisions in the Six Nations Cup? Which key is best for singing a rousing chorus of "Swing Low, Sweet Chariot"?'

'Oh, Lizzy,' says Dan with mock seriousness. 'Everyone knows you should sing "Chariot" in the key of C. But I think we should talk about you tonight.'

'What are you on about, you lunatic? I'm offering you the chance to talk about rugby but you'd rather talk about me? Whatever is there to discuss?'

'Where do we start?' he says, his twinkling eyes belying his stern tone. 'So many issues, so little time.'

'Issues? What sorts of issues?' I tease. 'Have you been talking to my therapist again, Dan Miller? You know that's terribly unethical.'

'Well, your therapist, by which I mean my bossy sister, is full of interesting revelations about her best friend.' Dan grins, and suddenly I'm feeling paranoid. What exactly has Lulu told him?

'Is she now?' I ask warily. 'And what might those revelations be, exactly?' Please, please, *please* let it not be anything about my status as accidental celibate – I hope some things are sacred between friends. It's not that Dan doesn't know I've been single for ages – of course he does; I see him all the time since I spend half my life at the house he shares with Lulu. But I'd rather he, and everyone else we know, imagine I'm up to all sorts of exciting antics offstage.

'Something about giving up on your Wednesday nights together in search of adventure – which I suppose is what brings you here. And what I want to know,

Lizzy Harrison, is just how much adventure can you handle? In Balham?' Dan chuckles into his pint glass at the very idea, which is fairly annoying as his idea of crazy adventure is probably of the 'wearing a pair of comedy breasts in public' variety. I am far more adventurous than he could ever be, I reassure myself, even if I don't look it tonight in my librarian number.

'Oh, I can handle plenty of adventure, Dan, in Balham or anywhere else,' I say, smiling at him sweetly. 'Can you?'

'Why don't you try me?' He turns on the bench so he's facing me, one thigh pressed against mine.

'Oh come off it, Dan! You? Adventurous? You've always been the straightest man I know. Except when you dress up in women's clothing, of course,' I say, though I don't really think this is a sign of latent homosexuality since I have yet to encounter the rugby bloke who doesn't grab any excuse to slip into a dress to amuse his friends.

'You and Lulu always did have a funny idea of what it is to be adventurous,' says Dan, his mild tone disguising a surprisingly effective barb.

'What's that supposed to mean?' I ask, stung.

'Well, just that if it doesn't fit in with *your* idea of cool, then it doesn't count,' he says.

'Dan, I'm in a dodgy bar in Balham dressed like Miss Moneypenny and you're lecturing me on being too cool for school?' I say, jiggling my desperately unattractive glasses on the end of my nose to make him laugh. 'Is this about your hair?'

'Yeah, it always comes back to the hair, doesn't it?' he chuckles. 'You and Lulu won't be satisfied until I've got myself some wanky boy-band directional fringe.'

'I'm just concerned those lovely curls of yours might get in your eyes on the rugby pitch,' I say teasingly, poking his thigh with a finger. 'Always looking out for your needs, Dan.'

'Oh, really?' he says, attempting an air of mystery. 'What needs might those be?'

'Dan,' I reply, 'your needs are very simple: sport, beer and birds. They haven't changed since you were a teenager, so don't go making out you're all complex and inscrutable.'

'Plenty of things have changed since I was a teenager,' says Dan, still aiming for gravity but fighting a losing battle against smiling.

'Yeah?' I laugh. 'Like what? Not your hairstyle, that's for sure.'

Before he has a chance to reply, Johnno reappears, stumbling back to the table with two pitchers of beer. He drops down on to the bench with a satisfied sigh, saying, 'Now then, Lizzy, ah, Milo, where were we? I think we were about to talk about how our friend Bangers got his name . . .' To my immense relief, the house lights dim almost immediately and a hush descends over the audience.

Dan leans over to whisper in my ear. 'I hope your friend is an entertaining one, Miss Moneypenny.'

Oh God, I hope so too.

The compère steps on to the stage, blinking into the lights. He looks surprisingly harassed for a man who's just introducing the acts, and there's a piece of paper in his hand which, even from this distance, I can see is covered with scribbles and crossings-out.

'Ladies and gennelmen!' he announces, squinting out into the audience. 'Welcome to the Queen's Arms comedy night, where we have three wunnerful acts waiting in the wings to entertaaaaaaain – ' a spotlight sweeps through the audience – '*you!*' The spotlight picks out Bodders at random from the crowd, pint half raised to his lips; he raises it above his head in acknowledgement as the crowd cheers and whoops.

'And for the rest of you,' the compère continues, 'we have three mediocre acts. Ah, just kidding – we're following our usual programme. Our first act will be Dave Diamond, a debut act, so I hope you're all going to be very kind.' The audience goes *awww*. Dave Diamond? Surely not. Is *anyone* here going by their real name tonight?

'After Dave we have our old friend Stanley Judd (cheers from the audience). I see he's got his fan club in tonight.' The spotlight roams the room again and stops on a small Jack Russell perched forlornly on a bar stool at the back of the room. Oh ha-ha, my aching sides. This is going to be a long night.

'And after Stanley, I'm delighted to say we have a surpriiiiise guest, ladies and gennelmen. I'm not going to spoil it by telling you anything except that he was a regular here once upon a time and, though he's gone on to greater things, ladies and gennelmen, he hasn't forgotten his old friends here at the Queen's Arms.'

Dan leans in again. 'So which of them is it, Lizzy? Who's your special friend?'

'Wouldn't you like to know?' I say pertly, stalling for time. I'm getting the impression Dan thinks I'm here to see some new love interest, and I'm not about to admit to anything that might incriminate me. 'Tell you what, have a guess once we've seen all three acts and I'll tell you if you're right.'

A woman from the table next to us glances over to glare in our direction with a hissed 'shush'.

'Such mystery, Lizzy, such mystery. I can see you would definitely be worth spying on,' whispers Dan with an amused smile.

'Welcome to the stage, puhleeezzze, ladies and gennelman, in his first appearance at the Queen's Arms, let's hope it's the first of many, the one, the only Daaaaave Diamond!'

The compère leaves the side of the stage as a very large man in a fez enters, patches of nervous sweat blooming under the arms of his blue checked shirt. His short hair is brushed forward and glistens with either hair gel or more sweat; it's hard to tell at this distance.

Dave shuffles towards the centre of the stage, clutching the microphone with white knuckles, as if it's a grenade that might go off if he relaxes his grip even a fraction.

Please be good, Dave the Comedy Courier, I think. Please, please be good.

Dave, who has gone an unpleasant shade of grey, gulps and shifts his considerable weight from left foot to right foot.

'Now then, now then,' he whispers into the microphone.

Oh God, an irony-free Jimmy Savile impression? In the twenty-first century? There is complete silence from the audience.

'Now then, now then,' says Dave again, a little louder. I can feel the mood of the crowd shifting already from amused curiosity to impatience. Loyally, and slightly insanely, I laugh as loudly as I can manage, even though I'm not sure if this is meant to be a joke. Bangers, Bodders, Johnno, Dusty and Paddy all turn round to stare in disbelief, first at me, and then at Dan for knowing such a peculiar person. Dave is clearly every bit as surprised as they are, and squints out into the audience to see his solitary fan.

'Now then.' Dave is valiantly, some might say ludicrously, going for a third attempt with the same opener when a streak of denim and flying blond hair launches itself from the wings, wraps its arms round Dave's legs and pulls them from under him. Dave's fez falls first, and his eyes open wide in shock as he crashes down on to the stage like a felled redwood.

'Bloody good tackle, mate,' shouts Johnno, leaping up from his seat. 'Bloody good tackle.' The rugby boys thump each other on the back, impressed for the first time tonight.

The streak of denim springs to its feet like a cat, smoothing its long, unbrushed blond hair away from a face so familiar the audience gasps. The fierce cheekbones are unmistakable. The famously full lips saved from looking girlish by a strong jaw. The dark lashes enhanced with a liberal application of mascara.

Randy fucking Jones. I might have known.

He grabs the microphone from poor Dave, who is still lying stupefied on the floor. The flustered compère has rushed on to the stage and is trying to help Dave up, while another man, I'm guessing act two, Stanley Judd, is gesturing furiously from the wings with a 'get him off' hand signal.

'Sorry about that, mate,' says Randy, as if apologizing for treading on Dave's toes or something equally inoffensive. 'Thought you might need a hand out here. Now, where was I?' He grins wolfishly into the crowd, who are on their feet cheering and clapping – they think it's all part of the act. Randy pulls at his tight denim jacket, which just meets the heavy leather belt that holds up his even tighter jeans. On anyone else, the preponderance of denim combined with long hair and cowboy boots would suggest a dodgy Seventies heavy-metal roadie, but somehow Randy's confident swagger and chiselled face make every other man in here seem hopelessly uncool in comparison. Still, I tell myself, I bet he stinks like a roadie, even if he's getting away with looking like one.

Behind him, Dave is helped up at last and ushered into the wings, crestfallen. I can hardly look at him for pity. You might argue that Randy saved him from comedy shame, but Dave deserved at least a chance to be crucified on stage in front of all of us. It's what he would have wanted.

'Where was I?' repeats Randy. 'Ah yes. Rehab, that's where, gorgeous,' he says, addressing a statuesque redhead at one of the nearest tables. 'Ever been?' He leans forward, trips on the heel of his own boot and nearly topples into her substantial cleavage. 'Ooops, nearly,' he laughs and staggers backwards to regain his balance.

'He's off his face, mate,' says Dusty under his breath. And he is.

Randy lurches about the stage, swinging the microphone from its cord and failing to catch it once, twice, three times. The audience laughs, assuming he's doing it on purpose, but it seems to me he's actually incapable of anything requiring coordination. I start scanning the room for anyone with a camera; we can't afford a repeat of last Wednesday's *Hot Slebs* photos, but everyone is still too surprised that he's here at all to bother with taking pictures.

'Rehab, rehab, rrrrrr*rehab*,' slurs Randy, rolling his 'r's for dramatic effect. 'As you can see, it works like a *charm*.' To the delight of the audience, he flings his arms into the air, throws his head back and poses like a rock star, waiting for the whooping to die down. I can't believe they're actually applauding him for being shit-faced. Do they think it's all a joke?

Randy's head suddenly drops forward and his voice becomes hardly audible. 'Like a charming little charm, a charming, charming, charm of a charm.' He hiccups. 'A veritable Prince Charming of a charm.' He hiccups again, then belches loudly, and I can see the compère and Stanley Judd exchanging glances at the side of the stage. 'A charmer of a charm,' Randy half whispers, half sings into the microphone, staring fixedly at the tips of his boots.

The audience isn't laughing any more, and nor is Randy. He hiccups for a third time and I realize, at the same time that the compère does, that he's not hiccupping at all. Randy Jones is crying.

Before I know what I'm doing, I'm on my feet at the front of the stage.

'Randy,' I hiss. 'Randy, it's me, Lizzy.'

He looks up, trying to focus, and sniffs loudly. 'Lizzy?'

Of course he's ever the pro and lifts the microphone to his lips first, so everyone can hear my name boom through the PA system. Thanks for that, Randy.

'Lizzy Harrison from Carter Morgan. I work with Camilla.' I'm trying to whisper, but the entire front row of tables is hanging on our every word.

'Lizzy!' Randy exclaims into the microphone again, looking up gratefully, but, I suspect, none the wiser about who I am. However, it seems the magical name of Camilla Carter has reassured him and he takes a huge step towards me, dropping the microphone and opening his skinny arms wide as if I have come to save him. Unfortunately his step forwards is, like so much of this evening, misjudged. His right foot catches the edge of the stage, and for a brief moment he hovers there on the very tips of his toes, arms windmilling desperately backwards. The audience holds its breath, as if Randy might actually defy the law of gravity and recover his balance. But it's not meant to be. I see his hands clutching helplessly towards me as he topples forwards, and the next thing I know, I'm flat on my back on the sticky pub floor with Randy Jones lying on top of me, clinging on like a baby monkey to the click-and-whirr accompaniment of a hundred mobile-phone cameras.

It seems I have fulfilled my task of losing control beyond Lulu's wildest imaginings.

6

On my way into work the next morning (via the appallingly late 9.27 from Peckham Rye, for reasons that will become apparent), I try to reassure myself that having your photograph taken in the company of the famous is an occupational hazard in the world of celebrity PR, even if you're a lowly personal assistant. Camilla wisely advised me when I first started at Carter Morgan to avoid standing next to celebrities when cameras were around. 'All the paparazzi want is a picture of the famous person. So as long as they get that they don't care how dreadful you look next to them, they'll use the picture anyway. And if you're really unlucky, they'll put in a "who's the ugly friend?" caption. Just get out of the way when you see the cameras.' But everyone gets caught out now and then; in her former job at a book publisher's, our account executive Lucy was photographed coming out of a West End nightclub with Peter Stringfellow and subsequently identified in the Sunday papers as the nightclub mogul's 'mystery brunette'. Even her own mother didn't believe she'd been there just to publicize his autobiography.

But the invention of camera phones makes it practically impossible to take Camilla's advice – you never know when you're being snapped, which is one of the reasons I usually keep way in the background at any kind of celebrity event.

So, I reassure myself, Camilla will understand that I never meant to get involved in Randy's latest adventure, let alone photographed as a participant. I'll confess everything the minute she comes into the office. Once I would have rung her in the middle of the night, but these days I know she needs her sleep; and ever since Cassius dropped her BlackBerry down the toilet, there's no guarantee she'll actually pick up an email before she gets to the office. It will be fine, I tell myself. She's bound to know already that Randy's checked himself out of rehab, and I'm sure she'll be glad I did the best I could for him last night. Dan and his rugby friends had elbowed the crowd of gawkers out of the way and pulled Randy and me to our feet, and the compère had led us into the wings.

'Are you okay, Milo?' asked Paddy. 'Do you actually know this character?'

'It's a work thing, Paddy, and it's fine, really,' I replied, trying to regain my composure, albeit a bruised, beer-spattered sort of composure, while Randy swayed unsteadily next to me, refusing to let go of my hand.

'A work thing,' said Dan grimly. 'They shouldn't put you in this sort of situation. What are you going to do with him now?'

'I've got it all under control, Dan, don't worry. I'm going to call Randy's manager, aren't I, Randy?' I lifted his lank locks out of his face and tried to get him to look at me. 'I'm going to call Bryan, right?'

Randy smiled uncomprehendingly in my direction and murmured, 'Bryan.'

'And Bryan will meet us at Randy's house and we'll put him to bed and everything will be much better in the morning. Won't it, Randy?'

'Better in the morning,' Randy mumbled into my hair, resting his head on my shoulder with a contented sigh.

The compère had called us a minicab, delighted to see the back of us, and Dan had helped me wedge the semi-conscious Randy into the back seat, securing him in place with a seat belt. Randy sat still, quietly drooling on to the front of his shirt.

'Do you want me to come with you?' Dan asked, bending down to look through the passenger window. 'Are you sure you're going to be okay?'

The minicab driver sighed loudly and revved the engine.

'Thanks, Dan, but I've already disrupted your

evening enough – I'm so sorry. Randy and I will be fine, honestly. You go back inside and join your friends.'

'Okay, but you take care, Lizzy, and get home safely.' Dan cast a final look of disgust at Randy's sleeping form before straightening up.

The instant Dan's hands left the car window, the minicab driver hit the accelerator with a screech of tyres. He looked back at us in the mirror, at Randy comatose on the back seat. 'Your friend better not be sick, lady.' Then he flicked the radio on at full volume. Belinda Carlisle blasted out of the speakers courtesy of Magic FM, and I opened the window and looked out into the night, letting the cool air flow across my face the whole way across London.

Randy was not sick and, in fact, slept for the entire taxi ride to Belsize Park, where a weary Bryan met us with a set of keys. Together we got Randy undressed and into bed, where he curled himself up like a child, whispering, 'Night, Mummy,' as we shut the door on him.

Instead of taking another hour-long cab journey back home to Peckham, I let Bryan persuade me to stay the night at Randy's. After all, there were three spare bedrooms, and I had to agree with Bryan that Randy shouldn't be left alone in his current state. Quite why it couldn't have been Bryan who stayed over I don't know; I was too tired to argue.

I was woken by the sound of Randy's housekeeper letting herself in at six-thirty this morning, and took my chance to make my escape. I did the best I could to tidy up my hair and wipe the mascara from under my eyes, but it was a distinctly ropey-looking secretary that looked back at me from the hallway mirror, and I despaired at my life.

Here you are, Lizzy Harrison, I thought, feeling like a horror and looking like one too. *You have just spent the night with a man once voted Shagger of the Millennium, and he didn't even try to lay a finger on you.* Even though he hadn't been in a fit state to lift a finger, let alone anything else, and even though I fancied Randy as much as I fancied hitting myself repeatedly on the head with a mallet, I felt as if it was a reflection on my man-repelling ways. If Randy, Mr Testosterone himself, hadn't even had a go, my nun-like vibes must be super-strength. *You are about to do the walk of shame without having anything to be ashamed of,* I berated myself. *But why do you actually feel ashamed of that?* I was making my own head spin as I stepped out into the bright June morning.

So perhaps you can forgive me for looking rather forbidding and frowny in the paparazzi pictures of me descending the steps of Randy's house emailed to Carter Morgan by a picture agency at eight a.m. Which is significantly better than the way I look in the mobile phone images from the same agency half an hour later, in which Randy seems to be groping me on the pub floor while a crowd of grinning people cheer us on.

With my glasses, chignon and shocked expression, I look like a scandalized refugee from a librarian's conference. But my uptight appearance is entirely at odds with the fact that my hands, in attempting to grab Randy as he falls, appear to be firmly and enthusiastically grasping his buttocks.

Of course I don't manage to get to the office until ten, having had to get home, showered and back into town, which has given the staff of Carter Morgan plenty of time to study all the pictures in minute detail. Thankfully it has also given Lucy of Peter Stringfellow fame time to text me a brief warning:

> Where are you???? Pix of you & Randy Jones all over the place this morning. What happened?? Jemima mental (more than usual). Proceed with caution.

'Nice one, Lizzy,' says Jemima's PA, sneering as I pass her. 'I didn't know you had it in you. Randy Jones's cock, that is.'

'Morning, Mel,' I reply as sunnily as possible. 'How nice to see you here before ten-thirty for a change.' It's pathetic, but I can't manage anything better.

By the time I've run the gauntlet of post-room boys, secretaries and account executives, I'm in no doubt that everyone, including the office cleaner, not only knows what's happened, but has invented their own X-rated version of events. Lucy gives me a double thumbs-up from her office as I pass, but it's clear from her sympathetic grimace that this is a sign of solidarity-in-shame rather than approval. Camilla is at her desk already, and Jemima hovers behind her chair while they both stare, stony-faced, at the screen of Camilla's laptop.

I stand in the doorway of Camilla's office.

'I can explain,' I offer feebly.

'Close the door,' snaps Jemima, stalking towards me on her spiky heels. 'Close the door and sit down right now.'

'Lizzy, don't look so worried,' says Camilla, looking at me with sympathy. 'I've spoken to Bryan Ross and he's told me what you did for Randy last night. Golly, it must have been awful. You did just the right thing, and Bryan and Randy are both very grateful to you.'

I'd be surprised if Randy is even out of bed yet, let alone aware that I dragged his sorry arse home from Balham, but it's nice of Camilla to say so.

'But the fact remains, Florence Fucking Nightingale,' says Jemima, viciously flicking a strand of her black bob back into snap-on hair formation, 'that these pictures of you and Randy are a total fucking PR disaster.' Guess she's not up for one of her cosy girls' chats right now. It didn't take much for that mask to slip.

'I'm sorry, Jemima, Camilla – I had no idea Randy was going to be there last night, and when he fell apart on stage, well, I just did what seemed right at the time.'

I can't believe I'm having to defend myself, like it was my choice to be wrestled to the ground by a pissed and sobbing comedian.

'I know you did, Lizzy,' says Camilla. 'No one knew Randy was going to be there; the absolute idiot checked himself out of rehab without telling anyone and went straight from Croydon to the Queen's Arms. He'd been drinking there since four in the afternoon; Bryan spoke to the landlord this morning.'

'I don't care *why* it happened,' says Jemima to me, ignoring Camilla completely. 'I just care that when we are doing our best to persuade his American promoters that they can rely on Randy, that rehab has worked this time, that he's not going to run out on his commitments, he is photographed drunkenly writhing on top of you on the floor of a public bar.'

'He wasn't writhing on top of me, Jemima. I was just . . . well . . . in the way when he fell off stage,' I protest, looking at Camilla pleadingly. 'Why am I being read the riot act here? None of this is my fault.'

'It's not about fault, Lizzy,' Jemima says slowly, as if speaking to a very backward child. 'It's not about what *happened*, it's about what it *looks* like. Are you so stupid that you don't understand how public relations works after all this time?'

'Now just hold on a minute, Jemima,' says Camilla, stepping in at last. 'I know you're jolly cross, but shouting at Lizzy isn't going to solve anything.'

Jemima glares at me. 'Fine,' she snaps. 'Then let's get on with it. Tell her the plan. She got us into this. Now she's going to get us out of it.'

She points towards Camilla's computer screen and the *Hot Slebs* website, which has the mobile phone pictures uploaded extra large. 'Getting Busy with Lizzy!' shrieks the headline.

'Look at this first,' she says, pushing me towards Camilla's desk.

'Oh God,' I groan as she clicks into the site for more detail.

> Reprobate Randy Jones escaped from rehab yesterday only to be captured on the run by this sensible-looking sort, also spotted leaving his house this morning. Our spies on the scene said Randy bellowed the name Lizzy from the stage at a comedy night until the lady in question appeared from the crowd. A tired and emotional Randy followed her home like a faithful puppy. Not your usual type, is she, Randy? Can this Buttoned-Up Blonde keep Randy on the straight and narrow where his usual buxom buddies have failed?

Are they calling me flat-chested?

'Camilla, I'm so sorry – I don't know what to say,' I start again. Jemima tuts loudly behind me.

'Don't be sorry,' Camilla says, gesturing for me to sit back down. 'Jemima and I have talked this through and we think this is just the angle we need to sort everything out. Randy *does* need someone to keep him on the straight and narrow. At least for a few weeks while we get him back on track.'

You're telling me, I think. But who'd be mental enough to take that on?

'And after last night,' interrupts Jemima, 'we've decided it's going to be you.'

I laugh nervously, but Camilla doesn't join in. She nods earnestly in agreement with Jemima.

I'd expect it of Jemima, but I can't believe Camilla's serious. For a moment I'm too surprised to answer, but my cheeks begin to burn.

'I – I don't know what you think happened between me and Randy last night,' I stutter, furious, 'but I can assure you both it was all strictly above board. I just helped to get him home. I mean, he isn't even going to remember any of this when he wakes up, and he's definitely not going to want me hanging around reminding him of what an idiot he's been.'

'Randy Jones doesn't have the first clue what's good for him,' barks Jemima.

'And you suppose I do?' I ask in disbelief.

'Not yet, of course not,' says Camilla, taking control of the conversation with a silencing glance at Jemima. 'But *I* do. I mean goodness, of *course* I know you didn't fool around with Randy, you're far too sensible for that.'

God, even my boss thinks he wouldn't shag me.

'But right now you're just what he needs,' she continues. 'The down-to-earth non-celebrity girlfriend who helps him turn his life around. I've spoken to Bryan and he thinks it's going to work.'

'You know I'd do anything to help you, Camilla,' I splutter, 'but I draw the line at being made to have a relationship with your lunatic client for the sake of his reputation. What about mine?'

'*Your* reputation?' Jemima laughs, throwing her hands into the air in exasperation. 'You're a single, thirty-three-year-old personal assistant! A failed journalist! A nobody! What reputation do you have to lose? Jesus, Camilla, I told you there was no point in even asking her.'

'That's enough,' says Camilla, and there's an edge to her voice that makes both Jemima and me flinch. I just got a glimpse of the old head-girl-in-charge. I instantly sit up straighter.

'Remember what Jemima said, Lizzy. It's not about what happened, it's not about what's actually going to happen. It's about what it *looks* like. Randy needs to look like he's making changes in his life, and you, Lizzy, can be a very visible sign that he's moving on from the topless models and reality TV rejects. I'm not asking you to do anything other than be seen out with Randy, be photographed doing wholesome things: going to the zoo, having picnics in the park – all innocent larks, you see?'

I thought this crazy idea must be all Jemima's, but

now I can see that Camilla's right behind her; I haven't seen her this focused since before the twins were born.

'Wh-what does Randy think about this?' My final line of defence. Surely Randy, the Shagger of the Millennium, is not going to be up for this? He pretends to take his lothario reputation with a pinch of salt, but in fact he's in deadly earnest. He's going to hate being stuck with the sensible girlfriend type – even if it's just in public – because in public is all that Randy really cares about.

'Randy will do as he's told,' says Jemima in tones of steel. And I can hear, as clearly as if she's said it out loud, what she also means: 'And so will you.'

'We're not asking you to do this for long, Lizzy,' says Camilla. 'Just while we get Randy's US tour back on track and get him some positive press for once.' Then her eyes soften and she reaches across the table and grabs my hand. 'Lizzy, try not to see this as a total disaster. You've been my PA for way too long; this isn't exactly the promotion I had in mind for you, but it's a step out of your usual role and I think you can do it. If you can handle something like this, then you can handle anything. Jemima and I were already talking about expanding your role once this is over.'

Oh, great. I wonder what my role will be expanding into after this. A threesome with Paul Daniels and Debbie McGee? Surrogate mother for Cilla Black?

I hesitate, wresting my hand out of Camilla's and back into my lap.

'I'm sorry,' I say, turning from Camilla to Jemima, who is pacing so vigorously behind me it's as if she's trying to punch a row of holes in the carpet with her spike heels. 'I don't want to be in the public eye like this. It's not what I signed up for when I came to work at Carter Morgan. I like the behind-the-scenes stuff. I'm just not a front-of-house sort of girl.'

'You can say that again,' Jemima huffs, stopping mid-pace for a moment. 'I *told* you she wouldn't do it, Camilla. It was a stupid idea. I'm going to call Bryan and tell him we have to think again.'

Camilla's shoulders droop and she takes a deep breath as she rests her palms on her desk. 'It *is* a stupid idea. I'm sorry. I can't expect it of you, Lizzy, and I shouldn't have asked. *I* will call Bryan, thank you, Jemima. Randy is still my client, and I will find another way around this.'

Jemima folds her arms in front of her like bull bars, but her tone suddenly switches to sweetness and light. 'Oh, Cam. It's too bad that Lizzy's let you down like this. I know you thought this was the best way out. But now that's not going to happen, don't you think it's about time you handed Randy over to me?'

Both Camilla and I start in our chairs, and Camilla's face reddens as if she's been slapped.

'I mean, you've got so much else going on, especially

at home, and Randy's such a *demanding* client. I'm not saying that I'd have handled things any differently up to now, but isn't it in Randy's best interests to have someone who's available to him at any time of night or day? And isn't it in *your* best interests, too, darling?' Jemima cocks her head to the side to convey sympathy, concern, compassion, but looks more like a snake fixing her gaze on her prey.

'That is a low blow, Jemima,' says Camilla in a quiet voice. *Come on*, I think, *stand up*! Have at her! It's time you put her back in her box, with a heavy, heavy lid on.

'I don't mean to be harsh, darling,' says Jemima. 'You mustn't take this personally. I'm just trying to put our client first, and I know that's what you want to do, too, isn't it? You know this makes sense.'

Camilla shakes her head slowly in disbelief, but I can see her beginning to weaken under Jemima's basilisk stare. She's probably been up half the night with the twins. There's a smear of puréed food on her elbow and the bags under her eyes are a louring purple. She's too tough to cry, but too tired to resist Jemima for long.

'*I'll do it*!' I hear myself shout, in a voice that surprises me just as much as it does my bosses, whose heads whip round towards me as if on coiled springs.

Shit. What did I say that for?

Camilla leans forward on her desk, eyebrows practically buried in her hairline with surprise (her roots need doing – must remind her). 'What? Are you absolutely sure, Lizzy? You don't have to do this.'

I do.

'I'm sure. I am absolutely positively sure,' I say, sounding more confident than I feel. 'You're right, Jemima. We all need to put the client first, and it was selfish of me not to realize that from the start. You can count on me from now on.'

Jemima bares her teeth in an attempt at a smile. 'Well. I'm glad I helped you to see sense.'

'Oh, you bloody marvel,' Camilla says, grinning at me gratefully. 'Lizzy, you complete and utter marvel. What did I ever do to deserve you?'

Jemima rolls her eyes. 'If I could just interrupt your love-in for one moment, we need to establish some parameters here.'

'Absolutely,' I say, turning to face her with what I hope is a look of compliant obedience. 'Fire away, Jemima.'

'Well. Okay.' Jemima is disarmed; nothing undermines a bully quite as much as agreeing with everything they say. 'This relationship has to seem genuine for it to work. I hope that's clear? One word to a single loud-mouthed friend, or even to your mother, and we may as well give up on trying to save Randy's career. Do you quite understand?'

'I understand,' I say, wondering how I'm ever going to get this past Lulu.

'Jemima's right, you know,' says Camilla, suddenly all earnest. 'As far as everyone outside this office is concerned, you are the new love of Randy Jones's life and he is yours. No one else can know this isn't true.'

And suddenly I think: what more visible sign can a girl give that she's losing control than getting involved with a celebrity shagger? This is practically guaranteed to get Lulu off her 'Lizzy Harrison needs to lose control' bandwagon with no risk to myself – I mean, it's not as if it's real.

'Absolutely. You can count on me,' I say, and I mean it.

And yes, I know what you're thinking – here we go, standard romantic novel plotline number three: heroine is forced into close proximity with man she claims to find unattractive. Her brittle defences overcome by his charm, she discovers she loves him, the end. We've all seen *The Proposal*. But let me remind you that I'm doing this for work reasons. I'm far too professional (okay, uptight) to consider getting into bed with a client in anything other than the metaphorical sense.

Besides, if I fail to live up to the romantic heroine role, Randy is hardly the classic romantic hero of every girl's dreams either – I don't recall Mr Darcy getting it on with a multitude of nubile Regency babes before settling down with Elizabeth Bennet. I mean, it's one thing to know your boyfriend has put it about a bit in the past, and quite another to have seen his penchant for bondage and outdoor sex detailed in breathless prose in countless kiss-and-tell exposés in the national press.

Not to mention that if Mr Darcy had personal hygiene issues, Miss Austen forbore to mention them.

7

I am in the middle of Hyde Park, hair frizzing in the light mist, wearing, over my T-shirt and leggings, a distinctly BO-scented blue nylon vest with a large white 72 on it, jogging furiously on the spot while being shouted at by a small, squat half-man, half-bulldog whose neck is significantly wider than one of my thighs. Thank you, Lulu. Thank you so very much.

I had thought that out of everyone I had to lie to about Randy Jones, Lulu would be the one to see through it in an instant, but instead of questioning how I'd gone in the space of one night from accidental celibate to new girlfriend of the Shagger of the Millennium, she'd taken it as a personal triumph.

'Seeeee!!! *Seeeee*??? Just one night away from the Spinsters' Social Club and already you are seeing the benefits! You're seeing Randy fucking Jones! You're *fucking* Randy fucking Jones! Oh my God, I am quite, quite brilliant!'

'Lulu! I'm not fucking him! Jesus! I spent the night with him, but in his spare room. Who do you think I am?'

'Well, just get over your nun-like self!' exclaimed Lulu. 'I mean, there's no escape for you now you're seeing Randy Jones; it's only a matter of time before he gets you into his bed. Get ready to say goodbye to your born-again virginity, Harrison! You can thank me later.'

So thrilled was she at this proof of her own wondrousness that she barely asked me a thing about it. Instead she was fired up with a crazed sense of her own power and influence, and on Monday night I got a call.

'I have a treat in store for you,' she crowed over the phone. 'A new exercise regime!'

'New exercise regime? Are you calling me unfit?' I protested with all the defensiveness of one who was always picked last for teams at school. I might have been useless at anything involving balls flying at my face, as Lulu used to say, but since school I'd learned to love exercise. Especially the calming, meditative qualities of yoga, where you can feel the knots in your mind unravel and smooth themselves out over the course of a session. My slightly bonkers spiritual journeying mother had to be right about some things. The fact that it keeps my stomach flat is just a bonus.

'We've already discussed this, or are you going to tell me your yoga class was miraculously full of attractive non-patchouli'd men tonight, Harrison?'

'No,' I said, feeling my post-yoga glow dissipating. 'So what kind of man-attracting exercise are you going to have me take up instead? Football? Rugby? I mean, I see your logic – what man can resist a girl in a gum shield?'

'You, Lizzy Harrison, have been signed up for a free trial class with British Army Bootcamp,' said Lulu, triumphantly. 'Wednesday night, Hyde Park, seven-thirty. You can't say you're not free because I know you're supposed to be seeing me, but I am officially blowing you out. Don't be late or they'll make you suffer.'

Well, I wasn't late (this is me we're talking about), but I'm suffering all the same.

The half-man, half-bulldog has been making us run from tree to tree to tree in some kind of appalling competition – surely my first actual race since I was at school. I was wheezing by the third circuit and feeling distinctly nauseous by the fifth. The constant shouts of 'Faster, number 72!' are less encouraging than infuriating. So now I'm slowing myself down almost to a walk – I mean, respect your body's limitations, right? – when suddenly Bulldog Man shouts '*Stoooooop*!' Oh, thank God.

'Blue Team, one of our number has stopped running. And that number is 72.'

The twenty other blue vest wearers groan and look at me with loathing. I have clearly done something very, very wrong.

'What does it mean when someone stops following instructions?' the instructor shouts, and I flinch away from the flecks of spittle.

My team members mutter something about burping; what are they on about?

'You have it. Twenty burpees, right now, courtesy of number 72,' barks Bulldog Man, the tendons on his neck standing out in fury.

Twenty what? Everyone around me throws themselves to the ground and starts doing an odd combination of squats and star-jumps.

'Number 72! Get down there NOW or I'm making it fifty burpees for everyone!' The instructor's voice has gone so furiously high that the end of his sentence can probably only be heard by his canine brethren. I expect to see them come bounding out from behind the trees in response to his call.

Number 47, who's leaping about next to me, grabs the leg of my tracksuit bottoms and physically drags me to the ground. 'Do you want to kill us all?' he groans. 'Just do the fucking burpees, 72!'

My previous memories of Hyde Park are all sunshine and the Serpentine Gallery, lazing with Lulu in the deckchairs until being chased out by the attendants for not paying; watching the rollerbladers on a Sunday afternoon; feeding the ducks with my two-year-old nephew. The usual London park activities. I never imagined that I'd find myself voluntarily face down in the mud, hauling my own body weight from horizontal to vertical and back again more times than seems possible. I'm sure I remember hearing about two women who were struck by lightning in Hyde Park once, and I glance hopefully at the sky for deliverance, but it threatens no more than a gentle mist.

The instructor divides us into two groups and the man next to me pointedly moves himself into the group in which I am not. Well, screw you, number 84. Number 28 smiles at me sweetly. 'First session?' she asks.

'That obvious?' I reply, with my best attempt at a smile in return.

'I threw up my first time, so you're doing really well,' she grins, pushing her fringe out of her face with her hand and leaving a streak of mud and grass on her forehead. 'It gets better, honestly – everyone hates the first one.'

'And they come back?' I wheeze as we start running again.

'Oh yes, it's quite addictive – you'll see!' She sprints ahead with a wave, leaving me at the back with a surprisingly fit-looking man who appears to be struggling as badly as me.

'First session?' I wheeze, inspired by kindly number 28 – pay it forward, people.

'First session back after a car accident,' he says, breathing heavily. 'I thought I'd be okay, but the cracked ribs are giving me a bit of trouble. I'm just hoping the press-ups won't be too much for my wrist – the plaster only came off last week.'

'Oh my God, poor you! Are you sure you should be doing this?' I ask in horror.

'Oh yes,' he grins cheerily. 'I can't be doing with sitting on my arse all day, despite what the doctors say.' And with that he overtakes me easily.

After that it seems churlish to complain in the slightest, so I keep running and leaping and trying not to cry at the back of the group, cursing Lulu all the while.

When the session finally finishes – how was that only an hour? It felt like a lifetime – I throw myself gratefully on to the grass, gulping huge breaths of air. My heart thuds not just in my chest but through my whole body; blood rushes in my eardrums. After a few minutes I feel able to sit up straight without seeing stars and, to my immense relief, I see a bottle of water being held out in my direction. I grab it with a muffled 'Thanks', and have gulped down half the bottle before I realize whoever gave it to me is still standing there expectantly. I squint into the drizzle.

'Hi, Lizzy,' says Dan. 'I was hoping I'd bump into you.'

'Dan?' I stumble to my feet, tearing off my nylon 72 vest as if that's suddenly going to make me look more presentable. 'Dan, I'm so glad to see you. I meant to call you to apologize for the other night,' I start. And then realization dawns. 'Hang on. How did you know I was going to be here? You *are* bloody spying on me for your sister this time, aren't you?'

'Ha! Spying! As if!' Dan laughs and good-naturedly pushes my arm in mock defence. I'm still feeling so ridiculously feeble that I'm forced into an ungainly stagger to keep my balance, like a cow with BSE. Oh yes, looking good. He catches hold of my arm to steady me and turns me to face him.

'You can't deny it, Dan. The only person who knows I'm here is your sister – she's the one who got me into this in the first place.' Despite my attempt at righteous anger, I could sob with relief to see a friendly face after running the gauntlet of the shouty instructor.

'Okay, this time I knew you were going to be here, but Lulu only thought of making you do this because she'd heard about it from me. I come every week – can't you tell?' He flexes his biceps like Arnold Schwarzenegger in the Mr Universe final.

'I don't know, Dan – you still appear to have a clearly defined neck,' I say, looking over at the pumped-up instructor for comparison, 'and you can actually put your arms down alongside your body instead of having them stick out to the side like Action Man's. I'd say you've got a long way to go.'

'How dare you?' Dan grins, looking down at me. 'My neck measurement's been growing weekly – the instructor says it's only a matter of months until it's just one seamless line from ear to shoulder. Anyway, I've been meaning to call you to find out how you got on the other night, but Lulu said you were fine and I shouldn't make a fuss about it. Did you get that wanker home okay?'

'Er, didn't Lulu say anything?' I ask, feeling a flutter of nerves. I had kind of assumed that once I'd told her about Randy I wouldn't have to tell anyone else. I thought the Mouth of the South would broadcast my 'new boyfriend' to everyone we knew and save me fluffing my lines or crumbling under questioning. And that the paparazzi pictures would take care of the rest. But I should have guessed that Dan wasn't a *Hot Slebs* reader.

'Well, yeah,' says Dan. 'She said everything was okay, but she didn't say anything else. It *was* okay, wasn't it? He didn't try anything on with you, did he? Not that he looked in any fit state to.'

'Oh, well, of course not. It's more that – well – I just mean that Randy isn't really a wanker. It's just that he's, umm . . . he's a bit messed up. But you know, he's a good guy really.' I can't quite look Dan in the eye.

'Really?' he says, his forehead creasing into a quizzical frown. 'He seems like a total arse to me. I was worried about you. Lulu said you were coming along tonight, so I hoped we'd bump into each other. Why don't we grab a quick drink? I know a good pub just round the corner.'

Perhaps it's the effect of all the unaccustomed exercise, or maybe it's Dan's look of gentle concern making me come over all funny, or perhaps I am finally losing it and descending into complete and utter paranoia, but suddenly it seems as if everyone around us is picking up on our conversation. Am I imagining it or are we surrounded by people whispering RandyJonesRandyJones RandyJones?

I'm not imagining it.

Cuban heels sinking into the turf, a cigarette dangling from his lips, a shiny gold leather jacket atop his usual tight denim strides, Randy Jones is prancing across the grass. And prancing with a definite purpose. Towards me.

'What the—' Dan swears under his breath.

'Lizzy!' shrieks Randy, breaking into a lolloping, girly run that would get him fifty press-ups from Half-Man Half-Bulldog, no questions asked.

'Lizzy?' says Dan, turning to look from Randy to me and back again.

'Lizzy!' shouts the photographer who leaps out from behind a tree. How the hell does he know my name?

'Lizzy, as in the girl from *Hot Slebs*?' says the girl behind me. Oh, Jesus.

'Lizzy!' shouts Randy again, as he swoops a leather-clad arm round my waist and swings me into a passionate embrace as if he is Rhett Butler and I am Scarlett O'Hara after she has rolled about in the mud for a bit with a nylon vest on. I feel my knees buckle obligingly into the semblance of a swoon to complete the picture – who knew I was such a ham? As he pulls me back upright, Randy whispers in my ear, 'Camilla told me you'd be here. Play along.'

Dan takes a stride towards us. 'Lizzy, what's going on here?'

'What's going on here, my good man,' says Randy, draping his arm possessively over my shoulders, 'is that I am going to take my girlfriend off somewhere a bit more romantic. Aren't I, babe?' He grasps my rear firmly in a manner that is definitely not part of our agreement.

'Girlfriend?' says Dan, turning to me, his face flushed with surprise.

'Er?' I want to tell Dan everything, but all I can do is look at him and desperately try to convey through facial gestures alone that this is not all it seems. But now it's his turn not to look me in the eye.

'Yes, girlfriend,' says Randy loudly, for the benefit of everyone listening. 'Ready to go, babe?' He squeezes my buttocks harder. I am really going to have to speak to him about that the second we are alone. But right now I have to play my part.

'Of course, darling, let's go,' I say, smiling up at him like the adoring girlfriend I've promised to be. Randy leans down to kiss me again, and this time I feel his tongue push insistently between my lips, the cheeky bastard – this isn't part of the deal at all. As we break apart, he stares so long and so deep into my eyes (waiting for the photographer to get his shot, I expect) that I feel my traitorous heart drop down to my stomach for a moment. It's been a long time since someone looked at me like that, even if he's just pretending. Then he flashes me a wink that no one else can see and spins us round to make our exit.

But of course our way is blocked by fifty nylon-vested fans mobbing him for an autograph, a photograph, a snatch of mobile phone footage, and who is Randy to disappoint his public? Half-Man Half-Bulldog turns out to be especially persistent, and is only persuaded to let us go when Randy has expressed great admiration for his rather unexpected tattoos of Eric Morecambe (left bicep) and Ernie Wise (right bicep) and has advised him on the best location for a Randy Jones tattoo, should Bulldog Man choose to add to his collection. (Don't ask.)

It takes us fifteen minutes to leave, and in all that time Dan doesn't come near us once.

8

We must make quite a picture striding through the park towards Notting Hill Gate – Randy the urban dandy with his blond hair tied back in a velvet ribbon that matches his gold leather jacket, and ruddy-faced me in tatty trainers, T-shirt and leggings. I try to tell myself that my unglamorous appearance can only help Camilla's mission to make Randy seem more wholesome, but I'm shallow enough to wish I wasn't wearing the T-shirt that proclaims 'Seize the Day', which I stopped wearing for anything other than exercise when Lulu helpfully pointed out that as 'the day' appeared in small lettering, the T-shirt appeared to invite passers-by to seize my breasts.

I beg Randy to let me get changed before we go out for dinner. Even though the work clothes in my bag are no match for his rock-star ensemble, anything's got to be better than what I'm wearing right now. But he says it will be fine for me to sort myself out in the toilets of the restaurant when we get there. Which isn't the most romantic thing I've ever heard – in fact it's downright ungallant – but he strides ahead, deaf to my continued protests that I'm far too dishevelled to be seen in public.

'Look, babe,' he says, finally halting his stomp towards the busy road ahead. 'Number one, you've already been photographed like this, so just deal with it, those pictures will be on their way to an agency already. Number two, no one's going to be looking at you when you're with me. I'm sorry but it's true.' I must be looking crushed because he softens his voice a little. 'Number three, you do actually look quite cute all flushed and messed-up like this, so let's have no more complaining, okay?'

Well that told me.

'Now hold my hand,' says Randy, 'and look like you're having a good time.'

I feel like half of London has stopped to point and stare at our ungainly procession through the park and down Kensington Church Street, so it's a blessed relief when Randy stops at last in front of a small town house that's been converted into a restaurant. He strides in confidently while I lurk behind him, trying to cover the 'Seize' written on my chest and pull the too-short T-shirt down over my bottom. The dining room is full of the kind of immaculately fragrant women who have probably had all their sweat glands Botoxed and last perspired in 1997, and I'm immensely self-conscious. Surely they won't let me in dressed like this? But the maître d' is all smiles, promising that of course it's no problem to find a table at such short notice, and indeed they would be happy to accommodate sir in the discreet corner that he's enjoyed before. Randy declines and indicates instead one of two small tables next to the window.

'Is sir absolutely certain?' asks the maître d' in confusion. 'That table is somewhat . . . exposed. Sir might find more privacy within the upstairs dining room.'

'Oh, we don't mind being exposed, do we, babe?' says Randy with a leer, slipping an arm round my waist and pulling me towards him. Now, at last, the maître d' actually sees me instead of being blinded by the glowing light of Randy's celebrity, and I hear a tiny, stifled gasp as he clocks my clothes.

'Would you mind very much showing me where I can get changed into something more suitable for dinner?' I ask in my poshest voice, trying to sound super-confident, as if absolutely everyone who is anyone these days effects a Wonder Woman-style transformation in the lavatories of expensive restaurants.

'Certainly, madam,' he says, regaining his composure with aplomb (and with relief, I expect, that I'm not going to sit in the window of his establishment splattered in mud).

There is only so much of a transformation one can

affect in a cramped cubicle, even if it is lavishly appointed with Molton Brown toiletries. I struggle back into my cropped jeans and replace my trainers with strappy sandals, but no amount of rubbing will get rid of the sock marks round my ankles. The Seize the Day T-shirt is consigned to the bottom of my bag (where I will forget about it until I see the 'Seize THESE, Randy!' headline on the *Hot Slebs* website the next day). I replace it with a fitted checked shirt and reattach my gold hoop earrings. There's no rescuing my hair after the mud and drizzle, so I smooth it all back into a ponytail and convince myself, after a quick application of blusher, mascara and lip gloss, that I look just fine.

Now, I don't want you to think that this is some sort of *Pretty Woman* moment, and that I've never been taken out to a posh restaurant before. Though I admit that I book more fancy meals for Camilla than I go for myself, I've done my fair share of wining and dining with clients. So don't worry, I'm not going to be picking up the wrong knife or drinking the water from the fingerbowl or flinging an oyster across the room in an adorably klutzy move. I speak fluent menu in all European languages: I can avoid tripe in Spanish restaurants, order cavolo nero with confidence and am not thrown into confusion by a quenelle. And if I'd known I was coming here I'd have made the effort to dress accordingly. Still, I reassure myself as I leave the loo, I might be the only woman in here wearing jeans, but Randy is surely the only man in London wearing gold leather on this warm June evening. Like he said, no one's going to be looking at me.

Randy is already tucking into a bread roll as I reappear at the table. With his mouth full he gestures for me to sit down as a waiter shimmers over to pull out my chair.

Randy swallows his huge mouthful. 'Okay, babe, I've taken the liberty of ordering a bottle of some pretty crazy sparkling mineral water, and I'm just warning you that I might be moving on to a cranberry juice with the main course – do you reckon you can keep up with me tonight?'

'Well, I'll do my best, Randy, but that cranberry juice is pretty strong stuff,' I say, allowing the waiter to drape a napkin across my lap. 'Maybe you should dilute it first?'

'Yup, yup, you're probably right. Thank God you've been appointed to look after me, otherwise who knows what kind of fruit-based trouble I'd be getting myself into?' Randy laughs. 'But go on, don't let me stop you from having a real drink if you want one.'

'Right, well, if you really don't mind, I might just do that.' The waiter appears magically over my shoulder, offering a wine list before I even have a chance to ask for it.

Randy grabs it out of my hand and starts flicking

through the pages with the same barely contained excitement and anticipation with which I used to power through *Smash Hits* circa 1986. 'Glass of champagne to start? Hmm? Then follow up with a nice light white for your starter? Then how about a rich, full-bodied, spicy red for the main course?'

'Er, I was thinking I'd probably just have a glass of rosé, to be honest,' I say, and Randy looks crestfallen. Clearly he was planning an evening of drinking by proxy.

'Not even one glass of champagne to toast our new relationship, babe?' he asks, making puppy-dog eyes. 'Are you saying you don't feel like celebrating our beautiful love?'

The waiter hovers a few discreet steps from our table, staring stoically into the middle distance, but I can practically see his ears vibrating with interest. I guess I'd better make it worth his while.

'Oh, darling, what was I thinking? Of course we must celebrate our love – I'll drink for both of us. But just one glass; I'm not sure any more is safe in, well, in my condition.' I rub my stomach meaningfully.

Randy nearly chokes on his mineral water, but then reaches across the table to kiss me full on the lips in front of everyone.

'Champagne!' he calls out. 'Champagne for the lady! We're celebrating!' I turn to the waiter, half expecting that he will have a glass in his hand already, but his magical anticipatory powers have run out and he is on his way to the kitchen like a mere mortal.

'Jesus, do you think anyone is actually buying this?' I whisper as Randy blows me an extravagant kiss across the table.

'Who doesn't want to believe in love, babe?' he says, rubbing his leg along mine.

Who indeed? The irony isn't lost on me that, at the point when my love life is splashed all over the newspapers, I don't actually have one. When Randy agreed to our fake relationship, he was surprisingly strict about how it would work, and Camilla told me to go along with it so that Randy felt like it was all his idea. We agreed that we would go out publicly twice a week only, as Randy wasn't all that keen on a social life now that he was sober, and preferred instead to stay in plotting his comeback. So to keep up appearances I'd stay at Randy's house at least three times a week where, he assured me, I'd have a private room of my own in exchange for passionate snogging on the doorstep each morning for the benefit of the neighbours.

So while Lulu is wildly congratulating herself on my new out-of-control life, I'm actually going to be more regulated than ever, albeit by someone else's schedule. I have to confess I've been slightly dreading it all, especially handing over all decisions on how I spend my time to a complete fruitcake who's just out of rehab, but so far Randy has been charm itself and tonight, our first official night out, is proving to be surprisingly good fun. So what if Randy spends as much time checking himself out in the mirror as he does looking in my direction? He's got standards to maintain, and anyway I'm perfectly happy sipping my champagne and listening to his plans for world domination (primarily addressed to his own reflection). So what if our meal is occasionally interrupted by the flash of a mobile phone camera pressed up against the window? Isn't that what we're here for, after all? Rather than resenting any of it, I tell myself what a great job Randy and I are doing rehabilitating his image.

And what a great job we're doing rehabilitating, in a smaller way, mine. Friends I haven't seen for years have suddenly got in touch 'just to catch up', and my stock has risen higher than ever in the office, much to the annoyance of Jemima's mini-me assistant, Mel. Everyone's astonished at my new relationship, and I'm astonished myself at how many people, now that I'm seemingly part of a couple, have chosen to tell me that they are so pleased it's finally happened for me. That they'd been so worried about me, that they'd all been keeping their fingers crossed for me, that it was good to see me getting out at last. It's as if I have recovered from some dreadful illness, not emerged from a period of singledom. I smile and blush and murmur thanks and just try to swallow all these well-intentioned congratulations without admitting anything that will get me into trouble when this relationship ends in just a few weeks, as it must.

'Don't you think, babe?' says Randy, waving a hand in front of my face. 'Are you listening to me?'

'Course I am, Randy,' I lie, having tuned out of his future plans at the point at which he was winning his second Oscar; this, crucially, being awarded for a non-comedic role and therefore opening him up to a new market which – didn't I agree? – was essential for the longevity of his career.

'Really? So what was I saying?' Randy demands like a petulant child.

'You were, er . . .' I try to mentally rewind the monologue. 'You were . . . Sorry, Randy, you're right, I was actually thinking that it's getting a bit late and perhaps we should be thinking about getting home.'

'Ah, well, I think I can forgive your mind wandering if you're just planning how quickly you can get me home.' Randy's leg snakes around mine in a practised manoeuvre that pulls my chair closer towards him.

The waiter glides over to clear away our plates and Randy grins up at him conspiratorially. 'The bill, please, mate, and can you order us a taxi? I have a young lady here who is very anxious to get home, if you know what I mean?'

'Certainly, sir,' says the waiter with an infinitesimal flicker of his eyelid that might or might not have been a wink.

As I get into the cab, a lone photographer appears, no doubt tipped off by Camilla, and I'm half blinded by the flash as he captures Randy leaping into the back. Randy wastes no time in grappling me into an embrace which is faithfully recorded from several angles before we drive off into the night.

But as soon as we're out of sight, Randy lets go of me and turns to the taxi driver to begin a conversation about football. Although his arm is draped proprietorially over my leg, and although he absent-mindedly strokes the inside of my thigh with his thumb, it's as if I'm no longer there. Randy pays the driver with an extravagant tip and leads me up the steps to his house, where he takes my face between his hands and lifts it up towards him. I can hear the taxi engine idling as the driver waits to see us into the house. Randy leans forward and kisses me softly on the lips, then wraps his arm around me as he opens the door. The taxi driver revs his engine and is gone. Randy drops his arm from my shoulders and he and I step into the dark hall of his house, illuminated only by an orange glow from the street lamps outside. We both stand very still for a moment. Then Randy abruptly flicks on a light and, as I stand blinking in the glare, he stomps up the stairs without a backward glance.

I hear a door slam upstairs and wonder what on earth I've let myself in for.

9

The next few Wednesdays pass without any dramatic incident at all, as I've persuaded Lulu that signing up to a life-drawing class is well within my remit of trying new things, and anyway, don't I have a boyfriend now? Lulu agreed with alacrity. I think she imagines I'll be sketching a hot young stud muffin with whom I can exchange fruity glances over an easel, and then perhaps he and I will (forgetting Randy) retire for a passionate fumble in the art supplies cupboard, so she'd be disappointed to see the rotund pensioner who props himself up in a chair for our artistic inspiration.

Our model may not have washboard abs or pumped-up pectorals, but it turns out to be oddly satisfying attempting to capture the soft lines of his lived-in body for an hour. He stares calmly out of the window as if it is perfectly normal for him to be seated, naked, in front of fifteen strangers, and seems to be lost in thought. The only sounds are the swish of charcoal on paper and a quiet murmur of voices as the teacher moves from student to student. I spend a long time drawing his hands, the veins standing up on the backs of them, the broken nail on his thumb, the way his fingers splay out at the ends. The teacher compliments my careful focus, and I don't admit to her that it's because I'm avoiding paying close attention to the drooping geriatric genitals that I have captured instead in a vague impressionistic scribble.

The class finishes and we all sit around drinking tea for a while with the model, George, now attired in a natty little quilted dressing gown like a portly Hugh Hefner.

When the tea is finished and we've all admired each other's sketches (I note I'm not the only one to have avoided precision in the region of George's groin), I gather my things, say my goodbyes, and head off to spend the night with Randy Jones as I have done for the last three Wednesdays.

Sometimes he picks me up from work and we go back to Belsize Park together on the 68 bus; not quite the mode of transport you'd expect of a sleb, but 'there's no audience in a taxi, babe,' says Randy, basking in the adulation of our fellow commuters. Once we walked all the way home through Regent's Park holding hands the whole way, and that got us into the 'Spotted' section of *New Stars* magazine. But what they don't spot is how quickly Randy drops my hand as soon as we're in his vast white stuccoed house. In public I am adored and caressed and kissed and pampered, but once the door is closed and we're at home (which we usually are), then it's down to business, and I don't mean dirty business.

To Randy, I'm the boring babysitter he has to tolerate to get his career back on track, but he's not about to pay me any attention unless someone else is looking. The truth is, on my nights with Randy I'm more often to be found watching television alone while Randy writes in his study than out on the razzle.

Tonight I let myself in and wander into the kitchen, where Nina, Randy's formidable Bulgarian housekeeper, is just putting her heavy woollen coat on to leave, even though it's about thirty degrees outside. She often stays late so she can complain to me about Randy, and today is no exception. Before I've put my bag down she's launched into a furious description of his latest outrage: a puritanical banning of all wheat and sugar from the house as part of his detox.

'Like it is the sugar, Lizzy, what makes him inject himself, is it?' She gestures me over to the larder and opens it a crack.

'Don't tell him, okay? Is for you and me only. He never come in here anyway.'

I peer in to see that an entire shelf is packed with biscuits of every variety, from posh Marks & Spencer's tubs of chocolate-covered shortbreads and flapjacks to only-in-an-emergency Rich Teas. It would take us a year to get through them.

'Wow, great, Nina. Thanks – what a treat,' I say, allowing her to press a chocolate HobNob into my palm with the elaborate subterfuge of a spy passing on secret papers in Cold War Moscow.

'Eat up, eat up. Serve him right for calling me Nina the Cleaner,' says Nina, puffing herself up like an outraged hen. 'I gots Cordon Bleu, Lizzy, Cordon *Bleu*. Not just cleaner.'

'You are absolutely not just a cleaner, Nina. You know how Randy loves to tease you! He doesn't mean a word of it – he'd be lost without you, and he knows it,' I say, attempting to smooth her ruffled feathers.

'You are good girl, Lizzy, very good girl. Randy is changed man since you arrive.' Nina gives me a lascivious wink and I instantly feel paranoid. She must know that I don't sleep in the same room as Randy when I stay over. After all, she's the one who changes the sheets. What on earth does she think our relationship's about if it's not about sex?

'You not like the other bad girls who stay here before.' Nope, I am the boring babysitter who Randy would love to be shot of, I think, feeling irrationally jealous of the wild, beautiful girls who've trooped through the house before me. I doubt any of them spent more time with the housekeeper than with Randy. Not that I particularly want to spend time with Randy, the moody bastard, but somehow being beneath his notice is worse than if I was fending off his lecherous advances every five minutes.

'Gosh, well, I wouldn't know about that, Nina,' I bluster. 'Where is Randy, anyway? In the gym?'

Randy has embraced his newly clean life with all the desperate fervour of a former addict, and these days spends hour after hour in his basement gym, either with his trainer or pounding relentlessly on the treadmill while watching DVDs of Richard Pryor and Bill Hicks on a loop.

'Of course in gym, where else?' says Nina with a shrug. 'He gots *muscles*, now, Lizzy, isn't it!' She nudges me with her elbow, and I blush, which she takes as encouragement. 'Go down to gym, Lizzy, feel the muscles! See that bad boy.' She gives me a little push towards the stairs.

'Great thinking, Nina, will do. Bye – thanks for the biscuits!' I sing in my best attempt at the breezy style of one who has a totally uncomplicated relationship with a totally normal person who will be delighted to see their honest-to-goodness real girlfriend appear in their private gym at any moment.

I hear the front door close as I descend the steps and, sure enough, Bill Hicks is launching into his JFK routine while Randy sweats on the treadmill in just his shorts and trainers. Nina's not wrong, I think – gone is the pasty, skinny boy of last month. The new Randy is toned, lean and wiry, and while he'd still look like a toothpick standing next to the Bulldog Man from army training, or even next to rugby-boy Dan, there's no denying he looks pretty fit. His dirty blond hair is pulled back from his face, and for once he's not wearing any make-up. Free of jewellery and leather and the ubiquitous denim, I see, for the first time, a hint of the attractiveness that has lured endless glamour models into his boudoir. I'm pretty sure he still stinks, though.

'Hi,' I say, hovering in the doorway. Randy turns from the treadmill for a second and grunts, 'Hi,' then turns his head back towards the screen.

'Were you thinking that we'd go out for something to eat tonight?' I ask, raising my voice above the din of the treadmill and the television.

'Already eaten,' says Randy, gesturing to a carton of protein shake that lies on the floor.

'Okay,' I say. 'So, er, I'll see you upstairs later?'

Rolling his eyes, Randy slows the treadmill down to a walk and puts the DVD on pause. 'Look, I've got Bryan coming round in half an hour to talk about saving the US tour, and I want to be in bed by ten so I can see my trainer at seven. So I really don't need babysitting tonight, okay? Just entertain yourself, would you?'

'Fine,' I snap. 'I will. Again.'

'What's your problem?' says Randy, stopping the treadmill completely and wiping his forehead with a towel. 'Do I have to maintain our fake relationship in the privacy of my own fucking home?'

'I'm not asking you to play boyfriend and girlfriend, Randy, I'm just saying that this isn't exactly a barrel of laughs for me, you know, and maybe you could just try treating me with a bit of sodding courtesy.'

He raises his eyebrows superciliously, 'Oh, right, so it's discourteous of me to allow you free rein to treat my home as your own, is it? Discourteous to let you eat my food, sleep in my house, use anything you like without asking?'

'I suppose you think it's fun for me to sit in your house night after night while you act like I don't exist? If you could just stop thinking about yourself for one second, you might realize that I'm only here to help you save your stupid reputation, and all I'm getting from you is grief.'

'Oh really?' snarls Randy, stepping off the treadmill and striding powerfully towards me. 'You get nothing out of this? So you don't get to tell your friends about how you're hanging out with the famous Randy Jones all the time? So you don't love being in the papers every day as the girl who's saved Randy Jones from being such a total loser? So you're not loving all the attention that's coming your way, oh sensible saviour of tortured comedian? Give me a break – you're getting plenty out of this.'

'Fuck you, Randy Jones, if you think I care about any

of that stuff,' I say, trembling with anger. 'I'm here to save your sorry arse because I care about my *boss's* sorry arse, and she's in the shit because of you, but right now I'm sorry I ever set eyes on either of you.'

I spin on my heel and stomp out of the gym, attempting to slam the door behind me, but it turns out to be one of those concertinaed folding ones that shuts with a soft sigh. So I give it a vicious kick instead and go up to my room.

Well, I think, I have followed Lulu's instructions to loosen up a bit and change my life. And where has it got me? Watching *EastEnders* alone in the spare bedroom of a famous comedian who barely speaks to me.

I don't expect Randy to come up and apologize.

He doesn't.

On my walk into work through Regent's Park, I replay last night's conversation over again, adding to it just a little here and there. By the time I march past the aviary at London Zoo, I have our conversation ending with Randy admitting the error of his ways, apologizing politely and suggesting dinner out, which I accept. As I approach the fountain in the middle of the park, I have him so distraught at his actions that he's weeping on the floor of the gym in a foetal position. Hmm, maybe a bit *too* pathetic. When I finally push open the doors to the office, I've arrived at a satisfying scenario which ends with Randy falling off the treadmill and landing at my feet, begging for forgiveness. 'I've used you appallingly, Lizzy. I've been rude and selfish and thoughtless, I see that now.' In this scenario I am suddenly terrifyingly glamorous, and also about six feet tall, and I push him away with the pointy Louboutin stiletto at the end of my long, long leg. (Well, if you're going to invent stuff, you might as well make it good stuff.)

'Things are going to change around here, Randy,' I say coolly as he pleads. 'Now get up off the floor. You disgust me.' Ha, yeah, Randy Jones, take that. I'm not your boring babysitter now, am I?

At least at work there's some respite from it all. Camilla's taken me off working on anything to do with Randy so there's no conflict of interest, and it's good to immerse myself in the lives of other people to escape my own. I'm trying to work out a calendar clash in Damien Elliott's diary – how can we have booked him for the Venice Film Festival when we know he'll be filming in Vancouver in September? – when Camilla comes in. No Bob the Builder rucksack, no obvious stains on her Diane von Furstenberg wrap dress; she's carrying two Starbucks cups and looks totally calm and together. If I were nit-picking I'd point out that it's nine-thirty, but that's not too bad for her these days.

'Morning, Lizzy, darling, double-shot cappuccino for you – that's right, isn't it?' she beams, placing one of the cups on my desk.

'Yes, lovely. Thanks, Camilla. What's this in aid of?'

I'm instantly suspicious. It's not that Camilla wouldn't normally buy me a coffee, but she's usually in such a frantic rush that it's me who has to go out and get her one when I see she's about to hit the wall halfway through the morning. After the Randy Jones relationship incident, I'm wary. Does this unexpected coffee have an agenda? I lift the lid and peer into the cup in case my latest challenge is written on the top in chocolate powder.

'It's not in aid of anything. Why would it be? I just thought you could do with one since you've got rather a lot on your plate at the moment.' Camilla perches on the corner of my desk and sips at her own coffee, while I try to clear a space for her amongst the Post-its I've been using to sort out Damien's calendar cock-up. 'How are things going with Randy, then? Is he behaving himself?'

I look at her over the top of my Starbucks cup. Her roots are done. I haven't even had to remind her. And come to think of it, I haven't had to order a bike to the nursery for over a week (a good job, as Dave the Comedy Courier's patter has been distinctly subdued since the Queen's Arms debacle). Does this mean the boss is back? I can't take the risk.

'He's absolutely fine, Camilla,' I say in a steady voice, not quite meeting her eye.

'Are you sure, darling?' she says, tilting her head to get me to look at her. 'I know he can be pretty demanding at the best of times, and, let's face it, the only person who's more self-obsessed than a celebrity is a celebrity who's just emerged from intensive rehab.'

'Ha, yes,' I answer, non-committal. 'He's, erm . . . He's clearly got a lot on his mind.'

'And so have you, Lizzy. I don't expect Randy is very good at understanding that, is he?'

'Oh, Randy's just Randy, Camilla. You know what he's like,' I say.

'Yes,' she says, thoughtfully. 'Yes, I do.' She rises from the corner of my desk and strides into her office with calm, competence and a luminous yellow Post-it stuck to her bottom. Her door closed, I hear her pick up the phone.

Two hours later and Damien's diary clash finally sorted, an enormous bunch of flowers arrives at the office. Because our office is mostly women, the arrival of flowers at reception always sends a frisson across the partitions – are they for Jemima from an appreciative client (brownie points to client, boring for the rest of us)? Are they from Mel's boyfriend (also quite boring – she's a demanding sort and if he doesn't send flowers once a month she engineers a fight just to force him into it)? Are they for single but dating account exec Lucy (cue 'ha-ha, check the bouquet for gold lamé thongs in case they're from Peter Stringfellow' gags)? The one thing I can be certain of, in my unglamorous role and with my absence of a love life, is that they are never for me. But this time, they are.

> *Babe, I'm sorry to have been such bad company lately. Will you let me make it up to you tonight? Pick you up at six? Randy xxx*

I can't help thinking this card should read, 'Camilla's forced me into this, and not only ordered these flowers but probably paid for them out of her own money,' but as I'm doing this all for her benefit anyway, I think, fine, I'll go along with it for a while longer. At least I won't have to watch sodding *EastEnders* again tonight.

Randy's as good as his word and in reception at exactly six, flirting outrageously with Jemima, who has clearly whizzed out of her office at top speed on his arrival, desperate for his attention – how else can she lure him away from Camilla? I keep him waiting for a few minutes, thinking that time spent with Jemima and her aggressively coquettish hair-flicking is a suitable penance for last night. He looks up gratefully as I approach.

'Lizzy!' he booms so the whole office can hear, and curious heads pop up from the partitions like meerkats, for, even in our celebrity-saturated office, Randy Jones is still quite the big deal. I steel myself for a grand gesture of apology designed for maximum audience satisfaction, and am surprised, therefore, when he grabs my hand, looks at me properly and says, in a quiet voice, just to me, 'I've been a bit of a cock, haven't I?'

'Yes, you have,' I say, just as quietly, but I can't help a smile as he looks so utterly contrite. He may not be sobbing at my feet as in my imaginings, but he's doing a very good job of looking genuinely sorry.

'Come with me,' he says.

He takes me in a taxi – and he doesn't even speak to the driver – to St James's Park, where he guides me past the duck ponds and into the centre of the park. The pace here is somehow more sedate than in other London parks, and the slowly strolling tourists seem perfectly appropriate instead of maddening, as they do when you're racing to get to work. Evening sunshine glints through the trees, dappling a pair of toddlers who are begging their mother for more bread to throw at the ducks. Randy laughs as one of the children retreats rapidly from an over-keen swan, and when he reaches for my hand (Randy, that is, not the swan), I let him take it. He pulls me towards a wooden building, surrounded by a balcony on which tables are set with wine glasses and crisp white napkins. A waitress smiles welcomingly from the door.

'Wait here,' says Randy and runs up the steps of the restaurant.

I wonder why we don't just go in together, but then Randy emerges with two waiters who are carrying between them a huge wicker basket.

'This way, this way,' he urges them, pressing on into the middle of the park. The three of us process behind

Randy to a secluded spot underneath a large plane tree, where the waiters open the basket and take out a thick tartan blanket, which they spread on the grass. Randy gestures to me to sit down, and then joins me on the rug and lies back as the waiters set up. From deeper inside the basket they take out a bottle of chilled prosecco and two delicate champagne flutes; underneath those I can see covered plates and bowls. One waiter opens the bottle with a restrained pop and pours two glasses, while the other sets up a line of winking tea lights in jam jars around the blanket, ready for when dusk fell.

'Madam. Sir,' says the first waiter, handing us a glass each. 'We'll leave you in peace to enjoy your picnic. Please just press this buzzer if you need anything else at all. Enjoy your evening.' And they bow courteously and fade away.

'We will,' says Randy, turning to touch his glass to mine. 'Won't we, my fake girlfriend?'

'Yes, we will, my fake boyfriend,' I say, laughing despite myself.

'I'm sorry I've been a crap fake boyfriend,' says Randy suddenly.

'Oh, you haven't,' I protest politely, thinking, *You have*.

'I have,' says Randy, 'and I'm sorry. I've been so preoccupied with sorting myself out that I haven't given any thought to how this whole thing might be for you. I know you disapprove of everything about me, so thanks for putting up with me over the last few weeks. I owe you.'

'What? Disapprove of everything about you? What gave you that idea?' I say, thinking this isn't at all how I was imagining Randy's apology. Where is my glamorous Amazonian self? Why is he still upright and not prostrate upon the floor? Why am I suddenly feeling like I should apologize?

'Well, you've never exactly been my greatest fan,' says Randy, petulantly picking at a piece of fluff on the rug.

'That's not true,' I protest. 'I've always been perfectly professional towards you, Randy. When have you ever thought I wasn't a fan of yours?'

'Oh yes, you've always been *professional*,' says Randy, looking up, 'but it doesn't mean you've liked me. And Jemima told Bryan that you had to be forced into this . . . this . . . well . . . *this*.' He gestures around at the rug, the candles, the wicker hamper, us. 'I thought you were so disapproving of me and everything about me that I . . . well, I kind of couldn't stand to be in the same room as you.'

'Fucking Jemima!' I say before I can stop myself, and Randy raises his eyebrows in interest. 'God! I mean to say she has totally misrepresented this. It wasn't *disapproval* of you, Randy, that made me not want to do this. It was that I didn't especially want to have some stupid fake relationship and have to lie to my friends and see myself in a photograph in *Hot Slebs* after army training with mud all over my face and have to snog a man in public who won't speak to me in private and . . . and – '

I have to stop to take a breath. Randy is looking at me kindly. He refills both of our glasses.

'It looks like we've both started out on the wrong foot, don't you think?' he says. 'Let's see if we can be a bit better at this from now on. I promise not to ignore you any more.'

'I promise not to disapprove of you any more. Not that I did . . .' I start, but Randy shushes me with a finger on my lips.

'So, my fake girlfriend, let's start again,' he says. 'Like we're properly dating. Tell me something about yourself.'

'Umm, like what?' I ask, suspecting a trick question. Everyone knows celebrities only really want to talk about themselves; surely this is just the lead up to an 'enough about me, what do you think about me?' conversation.

'Like, if you're not a star-fucker – and I do believe you, you're not the type – why would a smart girl like you agree to enter into a fake relationship with me?' He settles himself on the blanket and looks at me with interest. See, I told you it would be all about him.

'Well, it's what Camilla said you needed, and I didn't

want to let her down,' I say, trying not to drop my boss in it. It's not going to help her cause for her top client to know she's losing the plot.

'You said that before,' says Randy thoughtfully, 'but I don't quite buy it. Oh, I can see you're loyal to Camilla, that's obvious. But there has to be something in this for you – something else.'

'I'm not getting paid, if that's what you mean,' I say tartly.

'I know that much, babe,' says Randy. 'Bryan's as tight as a gnat's chuff when it comes to finances. That's why I can't help thinking there must be something else going on. What's your story?'

'Look, I don't come with a press pack, Randy,' I say, exasperated. I have almost convinced myself I'm acting out of entirely selfless motives – Lizzy Harrison to the rescue! – and it's making me uncomfortable to have that challenged. 'I don't have a neat little story like yours to be summarized in one press-friendly paragraph.'

Randy looks at me sceptically.

'I just . . .' I pause. 'Well, there's nothing going on in my love life right now, so it's no big deal for me to pretend to be your girlfriend for a few weeks.'

'Aha,' he says, leaning back on his elbows with a triumphant smile. 'So that's the story then.'

'What is?' I ask, sipping at my fizzy wine.

'I've been getting a bit too much action, and clearly

you're not getting enough. Camilla obviously reckons that between the two of us we might balance each other out – am I right?'

I laugh. 'You reckon? Aren't you worried my lack of a love life might be catching? Think of the damage to your reputation, Randy.'

'Babe,' says Randy, sliding closer to me on the rug and taking off his sunglasses to look at me intently. I'm sitting bolt upright like a Victorian chaperone on a gabardine square, not giving an inch. 'I have absolutely no worries on that score. If anything, you're the one that should be scared.'

'Oh, really?' I say, beginning to flush under his intense stare. 'Am I suddenly going to turn into a raging nympho just from spending time with you?'

'You wouldn't be the first, Lizzy Harrison,' says Randy, lying back on the rug with a heavy sigh. 'My powerfully contagious sexuality is a cross to bear, believe me. I only hope it won't be too much for you.'

I start to laugh, but he throws me a look that suggests he's not entirely joking. He stretches one arm across the rug and clasps my hand.

'Thanks, babe,' he says. 'I should have said it before – thanks for agreeing to all of this. Thanks for putting up with me. We're still cool?'

'We're still cool, Randy,' I say, smiling. 'It's all going to be fine.'

'In that case,' he says, suddenly pushing himself up on to one knee in front of me, 'we must formalize our agreement.'

I'm wondering if he's going to whip out some official non-disclosure agreement for me to sign, despite Camilla's firm insistence that nothing about our arrangement should be written down at any time, her dictum being 'no paper trail, no problems', but instead he takes my right hand in both of his.

'Lizzy Harrison,' he says, 'will you do me the honour of continuing to act as my fake girlfriend for as long as, er – ' he pauses to think – 'for as long as this story shall live in the world of *Hot Slebs* and other quality publications in print and in any such electronic forms as may exist now or in the future?'

I rise up on to my knees and look him in the eye. 'Randy Jones, I, Lizzy Harrison, promise to do you that honour for as long as this fake story shall live.'

'Then let's drink to that!'

And we do. It's only much later that I remember Randy's not meant to be drinking at all.

10

Should it ever happen to you, it might be worth noting that when you start dating a celebrity there are a few things you should be aware of.

If you eat a large lunch and subsequently forget to maintain perfect posture, you're 'showing off a baby bump'. If you try to conceal your sticky-out tummy because you're feeling a bit porky, you're naturally 'hiding a baby bump'.

If the two of you walk down the street together with anything less than delirious smiles on your faces, your relationship is in trouble. And woe betide you if, while constantly grinning, you dare to look anywhere other than directly at your partner, never mind pavement hazards such as lamp posts, other pedestrians and dogs. Failure to gaze at each other incessantly equals growing apart, according to *Hot Slebs*.

If you cross your arms because you are cold in your thin summer dress and worried that your nipples might be visible to the photographer who's been following you around for half an hour, and you then glare at said photographer, the resulting photographs will be used to suggest that you are defensive and angry and also possibly unstable.

And if you are seen drinking fizzy wine in a park with your celebrity boyfriend, who positions himself on one knee in front of you, then of course you are getting married.

I should have seen it coming, but I thought we were safe in St James's Park. It's not like Primrose Hill, where you can hardly move for tripping over some boho actress and her photogenic brood, or Hampstead Heath, where everyone pretends to be too cool to notice anyone famous but frantically texts their friends the moment someone starry walks past. My private theory is that it's the too-cool-for-school brigade you have to watch out for. The straightforward fans will approach you and get their brief moment of glory, pop it on their Facebook page and everyone's happy. But the ones who seem not to notice, who carry on sipping their coffees and chatting to their friends, are often the ones who are surreptitiously texting the *Hot Slebs* website or trying to take a picture up your skirt with their camera phone. And I guess one of them couldn't believe his luck the other night, because somehow the *Sun* has got hold of an 'exclusive'.

Everyone at Carter Morgan thinks it's hilarious as

the Wild Man Randy Tamed At Last headlines are emailed round the office. They may not officially know our relationship is totally fake, but they're savvy enough to take anything like this with a giant pinch of salt. I find a large pile of bridal magazines on my desk first thing, liberally annotated with Post-its pointing to the most hideous ensembles possible (who gets married in a lacy crop-top and hot pants combo?), and Lucy calls round at my desk demanding to see my non-existent ring. In short, no one believes it except for Winston, the aged security guard, who gravely kisses my hand and wishes me every happiness.

Camilla beams as she bounds into the office at nine-fifteen. (Nine-fifteen! Practically on time!)

'The apology worked, then, Mrs Jones? Ha-ha! Good work, Lizzy. This one should keep everyone talking for a week or so.'

So I'm not taking any of this very seriously, and am bracing myself for yet another call from Dave the Comedy Courier (who has miraculously regained his comic confidence ringing me three times already this morning trying out variations along the lines of 'Is that Lizzy Harrison, cos we've got a wild man here who needs taming – fwwoooaooaar,' when I get a phone call from my brother, Ben.

I couldn't be more surprised if Ben's golden retriever had picked up the phone and tapped out my number with his claws. My big brother simply doesn't do the telephone. He does texts, and he does emails, too, but as they're mostly terrible jokes forwarded from his work colleagues at the garden centre he manages, they don't inspire long communications of a personal nature.

'Ben, wow! Good to hear from you. How are you?' I ask. 'How's Jenny? How's Graham?'

Graham is my nephew. (I know – who calls a baby Graham these days? Even my spiritual-journeying mother has admitted it took some intense meditation to reach acceptance for the chosen name of her first grandchild, but Jenny insisted that Graham was a reliable name that would stand him in good stead in later life.)

'Oh, Graham's fine, we're all fine. It's you I'm calling about,' says Ben, sounding a bit shifty. 'Er . . . I know this sounds a bit ridiculous, and I hope you're not going to think we're prying into your life, but Jenny says she's seen a picture of you in *Woman's Own* this week. With Randy Jones.'

'In *Woman's Own*?' I ask, my PR brain instantly computing the leap of demographics: so Randy and I have vaulted from *Hot Slebs* to *Woman's Own* in just two weeks? Whatever next? I have visions of Randy and me cavorting alongside the knitting patterns in *People's Friend* next week, and discussing household staff problems in *The Lady* the week after that – just how far will this story go?

'Yeah, *Woman's Own*. She saw it at the hairdresser's,'

says Ben, sounding embarrassed. 'I've told her it's probably just something to do with your job, but she says that the article says you're going out with him. With Randy Jones, I mean.'

'Ah, right, Randy Jones,' I say, playing for time. It never occurred to me that Ben and Jenny would have even heard of Randy Jones. The only television they ever watch is *CBeebies* or *Gardeners' World*. When I babysit, it's usually so they can go to dinner with someone from the garden centre to discuss horticultural fleeces and polytunnels. Randy seems so far removed from their world, and they from his, that hearing my brother speak his name is like hearing your granny tell you to chillax.

'Yes, Randy Jones. I know, it's ridiculous. So . . . obviously this is total rubbish, isn't it?' asks Ben.

'Ha! Yeah, God, Ben, you know what the media's like – you really shouldn't believe everything you read, not even in trusty old *Woman's Own*.'

'I *knew* there was nothing going on,' says Ben happily, and I hear him put his hand over the phone and hiss 'I *told* you', presumably to Jenny, who is probably poring through a copy of the *Guildford Advertiser* on the lookout for more scandalous revelations. 'I said to Jenny, Lizzy's far too sensible to get involved with someone like that.'

Instantly I bristle. My brother, married at twenty-three to the girl he's been going out with since he was eighteen, father of one, wearer of Crocs, for God's sake, thinks that *I* am the sensible one?

'Well, that's to say, it's not quite *nothing*,' I reply, stumbling over my words. 'I mean, I've been out on a few dates with Randy, but there's really nothing serious going on, despite what you might read. And, ha-ha, there's some crazy rumour going round that we're getting *married*, but I can promise you that one *is* total rubbish.'

'Hang on a minute – what did you say?' says Ben sharply. 'You *are* going out with Randy Jones?'

'It's not a *going-out* going-out. That's to say, we're just *seeing* each other, taking things slowly, going on a few dates, that sort of thing,' I bluster.

'Was there any reason you didn't tell us about this before?' says Ben, sounding cross. I can hear Jenny's voice in the background saying, 'I *told* you, whisper-whisper . . . *Woman's Own*.'

'God, let's not make a big deal of it,' I say, trying to sound nonchalant. 'I've only just started seeing him and I didn't want to make some huge family announcement.'

I don't know how I ever thought I was going to get away with this. I should have realized that Randy's rampant love life is of far broader appeal than I'd imagined from within my metropolitan media bubble.

'So you *are* going out with him then,' says Ben firmly.

'I am *seeing* him,' I admit, attempting to clarify the terms of my fake relationship. I don't know why I'm trying to make Ben understand the subtle difference between *going out with* someone (implying commitment, introduction to friends and family, future plans, calling each other boyfriend and girlfriend) and *seeing* someone (just hanging out and seeing where it takes you, no plans beyond next week, vehement denial of boyfriend/girlfriend status). He's been with Jenny for so long he has no clue how it works out there these days. It wouldn't surprise me if he asked how long Randy and I have been *courting*.

'Look, I'm not saying you needed to make any grand announcement, Lizzy, but don't you think you might have told us before we saw it somewhere else? Have you told Mum?'

'Of course I haven't told Mum, you lunatic, and don't you dare even think of telling her,' I snap.

It's probably the saving grace of my so-called relationship with Randy that it coincides with my mother's annual two-month stay at an ashram in the foothills of the Himalayas; however far Randy's star has risen, he is surely not yet a household name on the subcontinent, and certainly not in an isolated ashram where five hours a day are spent in silent contemplation.

'Well.' Ben has put on his Head of the Family voice. 'Lizzy, I'd never presume to tell you what you should be doing with your life.' Which obviously means he is just about to. 'But Mum has a right to know. I just hope you know what you're doing getting involved with someone like Randy Jones.'

I try to ignore the irony of a professional public relations PA being lectured on celebrity relationships by a garden-centre manager, because I know he feels his older brother responsibilities keenly ever since our dad died.

'I do know what I'm doing, Ben, and you're sweet to worry, but it's all very early days. I'm just having a bit of fun – you want me to have fun, don't you?'

I can hear Jenny's voice in the background again and I can just make out the words 'drug addict', and 'shagger'. Ben seems to be ignoring her.

'Of course I do, sis – sorry if I'm being too big-brotherly. Of course you should have your fun – just take care of yourself,' he says, though I'm sure I can hear Jenny protesting, 'What about Graham?' as if Randy's relationship with me is going to corrupt an innocent suburban two-year-old.

But Ben persists. 'And if it does turn more serious, you know you're always welcome to bring him down to Guildford any time for lunch or something.'

He sounds hesitant at his own suggestion, and I feel mean as I choke back a burst of laughter, swiftly turning it into a cough. The idea of Randy with his guy-liner and blond highwayman ponytail sitting on my brother's World of Leather sofa surrounded by Lego and gardening magazines is too ludicrous to contemplate. I don't think I could put poor Ben through it, even if Randy could be dragged beyond the M25 without violent protest.

'Aw, thanks, bro. You know you'll be the first to meet him if we start going out properly.'

We say our goodbyes and I promise to visit soon, with or without my celebrity boyfriend. I feel bad lying to my brother when he's being so sweet about everything, but I reassure myself that it's not for long, and anyway, it's good for him to realize I'm not always the sensible sister he imagines.

But I don't have time to dwell on it, as the phone barely stops ringing all morning. I get some weird messages, including a furtive voicemail from Jazmeen Marie, perma-tanned scourge of the Premiership footballer and Chinawhite attendee, asking if I'd like to meet up to 'compare notes' on Randy. As I don't think mine will match hers, I delete the message without answering. And I see right through Lulu's faked call from *Hello!* magazine wishing to cover my wedding ('We've room for a sumptuous feature right next to a photomontage of Prince Pavlos of Greece'). She redeems herself by inviting me over for supper on Saturday night, suggesting I bring along my *fiancé* (she doesn't believe a word of it). Although Randy and I are getting on much better since our big chat, I'm not ready to introduce him to anyone yet, and somehow I can't see him sitting round the battered Formica table in Lulu and Dan's Brixton kitchen, passing the wine back and forth and playing stupid parlour games for hours.

I say I'll check with him, though I have no intention of doing so. Saturday's my night off – Randy can amuse himself.

11

Dinners at Lulu and Dan's follow a standard pattern, and have done ever since they bought their flat in a terrace behind the Brixton Ritzy cinema five years ago. The first course is wine, and the second course is wine, and I have long ago learned that if I want to eat anything before nine-thirty I'd better bring it myself, so tonight I've arrived with a selection of toasted marcona almonds, olives and little balsamic-soaked pearl onions from the deli round the corner from Randy's house. Randy helped me to choose them, in fact, and sent the normally charming and accommodating owner into paroxysms of agony by sticking his fingers into everything. But as Randy, for whom the grand gesture is the only gesture, bought an entire leg of Parma ham to take home, all was well in the end. Randy was surprisingly annoyed not to be invited to Dan and Lulu's, especially as he'd not made any plans himself, but I've promised I'll come back to his afterwards so we can do something public and obvious all day on Sunday, such as look meaningfully into the windows of estate agents as if hunting for a 'love nest'.

Lulu is still perusing a cookbook when I arrive and hand over my deli haul.

'Wow, check this out – you *have* gone up in the world lately, Harrison. This is definitely an improvement on your usual bag of mini-poppadums.'

I tip the baby onions into a blue and white dish that's resting on the draining board and pass them to her.

'Well, you know my hot celebrity lifestyle these days, Lulu – just *everybody* is eating pickled onions at the moment in glamorous North London, didn't you know? Have you decided what we're eating yet?'

I pull a bottle of cava out of my bag and start picking at the foil wrapper. Lulu passes me two sturdy Ikea tumblers, the previous set of wine glasses having met a sorry end at their annual Halloween party last year.

'I was thinking maybe some sort of pie,' she replies. 'Dan said he'd go to the market after rugby practice and pick up whatever looked good, so we'll have to wait and see.' She shrugs contentedly and slams the cookbook shut, pushing it along the counter to join a stack of others that are jumbled up with magazines, tea towels and what appears to be the postcard I sent them from New York in March. I pass her a fizzing glass of cava and glance up at the kitchen clock.

I truly cannot comprehend how Lulu can bear not knowing what she's cooking for her guest by seven o'clock. When I invite people over for supper, I know within hours of their acceptance exactly what I'll be making (having looked through my special file of recipes cut out from magazines), and when I'll make time to get the ingredients (red asterisk on shopping list if they require a visit to any specialist shops like the Chinese supermarkets in Soho, or the Spanish suppliers in Borough Market), and what can be prepared in advance (pudding, always). I've even toyed with the idea of getting one of those grown-up lady's entertaining books where you write down what you served to people and when, so you don't give them the same dish twice in a row. But then I remember that I am not a 1950s housewife and I get a grip.

Lulu, on the other hand, is quite happy to freestyle it.

I'm a bit nervous about seeing Dan as we haven't been in touch since Randy turned up at Hyde Park, but when he bursts through the front door, weighed down with bags, he kisses me warmly on the cheek as usual. Lulu falls on the bags and pulls everything out on to the counter.

'Pasta, clams, tomatoes – spaghetti alle vongole? Parsley, garlic, French bread, butter – with garlic bread? Salad? Salad . . . ?' Dan passes her a brown paper bag that's fallen to the floor. 'Aha, rocket – thanks. And special-bought puddings for afters. Brilliant. Thanks, Danny.' She starts clattering in cupboards and drags out some saucepans, banging them heavily on to the gas hob.

'Yeah, well, I was thinking Thai chicken curry, but if that's what you think you can make with what I've bought, you do your best,' Dan teases, pulling off his jumper and hanging it on a hook behind the kitchen door. Lulu rolls her eyes at me as she energetically chops onions. I'm quietly surprised to see that there's not even a hint of the rugby shirt about Dan's person today. The removal of his jumper has revealed a plain white T-shirt which, though you wouldn't mistake it for high fashion, is mercifully free of the usual slogans declaring that the wearer ran the Reading Half Marathon 2004 or went On Tour for Johnno's Stag. He looks . . . well, as if he's made a bit of an effort. Though his hair is still as messy and sticking-up as ever. Some things never change.

'Any wine on the go?' he asks, grabbing a handful of olives from the table.

'Is there any wine?' scoffs Lulu. 'Of course there's wine. How else will we get Lizzy in a fit state to eat my cooking otherwise?' She sloshes some cava into another tumbler and slams it on to the table, where Dan and I have comfortably settled to watch her cook.

'Hey, I love your cooking, Lulu, you nutter,' I protest.

'Ah, you *think* you do, Harrison, because I always ensure my guests are pissed enough in advance to be grateful for whatever I put in front of them. Serve food late enough and people will eat anything and *love it*. Just a little tip you won't pick up from Nigella.' She takes a swig of cava.

'I never knew it was a conscious strategy,' I confess, reaching for a handful of almonds to keep me going until Lulu deems I'm drunk enough to eat. 'But it definitely works.'

The doorbell rings and I look at Dan quizzically as Lulu rushes down the hallway. I didn't know anyone else was joining us tonight. Dan elaborately mimes moustachetwirling, cigarette-smoking and other unidentifiable traits which leave me none the wiser until the non-smoking and entirely moustache-free Laurent, the *Le Monde*-reading Frenchman from Soho, enters the room with Lulu on his arm. She seems quite sweetly smitten, blushing as he whispers in her ear before he strides across the linoleum to kiss both me and a rather surprised Dan on both cheeks. He's clearly eaten chez Lulu before and produces a family-sized bag of Kettle Chips and a tub of taramasalata, which he dumps in the middle of the table.

I go over to Lulu by the sink, while Laurent and Dan tuck into the crisps. 'I meet Laurent properly at last!' I whisper. 'I'd begun to think he was a figment of your imagination.'

'You can talk!' says Lulu, laughing, 'with your celebrity fiancé that none of us has ever met!' She looks over my shoulder to smile indulgently at her new amour.

'Oh, shut up. You'll meet Randy when I'm ready. Tell me how it's all going with Laurent? This is coming up for three weeks, right? That's got to be a bit of a Lulu Miller record, hasn't it?'

Lulu tries to act casual, but she is positively radiant. 'He's lovely, Harrison, what more can I say? I don't want to talk about it too much right now in case I jinx it. But I'm really happy. And see?' She nudges me with her elbow. 'See how life can change? You scoffed at me that night, and here we both are, loved-up with new boys. And you thought nothing was going to change.' She looks at me intently, satisfied with her own predictive powers.

I long to own up, to tell her that there's nothing going on between me and Randy except in public, that I really need to talk about it with my best friend, that I haven't changed my life at all except on the surface, but instead I reach to open the oven door so she can pull the foil-wrapped garlic bread out and swing it in a reckless arc across the kitchen and on to the table.

'Ow, hot! Dig in!'

Having spent the last few weeks pretending to be something I'm not, it feels like coming home to sit around Dan and Lulu's battered old table on their ancient chairs that creak ominously with any sudden movement, teasing each other about the same old stories that we've laughed at for years. With Laurent as our audience, we battle to outdo each other with 'do you remembers'.

Dan is forced, yet again, to defend himself against the charge that he slept with their neighbour Mrs Whittaker, whose hedges he used to trim on summer Sundays in our youth, and who always insisted he share a jug of Pimm's with her afterwards. Of course he didn't sleep with her. She was about sixty, wore a cardigan that she'd knitted herself out of dog hair, and no more had carnal intentions towards Dan than she did towards the hedging shears, but it has always wound Dan up hugely to suggest that she got him drunk to take advantage of him. However, under Laurent's approving smirk, Dan merely shrugs his shoulders and returns Laurent's smile, implying a man-to-man understanding that Mrs Whittaker was in fact the foxy Mrs Robinson of the Guildford suburbs, and that Lulu and I are making up the dog-hair cardigan out of spite.

Lulu can't resist reminding me of the time I burned off my entire fringe at her and Dan's eighteenth birthday party, and how the charred ends sprinkled gently down into the lap of Will Banwell, the upper-sixth heart throb whose lighter I'd flirtatiously asked to use to light what was probably only my fourth or fifth cigarette ever. I certainly got his attention, but the smell of burned hair put paid to any romance, not only that night but for some time afterwards: I had to wear an extremely unfashionable hair band for four long months while it grew out, and there are people in my life who still unkindly refer to me as Bjorn Borg.

Which obviously means that I have to let Laurent know about the time that Lulu, after being bought numerous champagne cocktails by a rich banker she was dating at the time, fell off a bar stool in Claridge's in a micro-minidress, landing with her legs in the air and nothing but a tiny thong between her and the packed room. However, Laurent is far too interested in exactly what kind of thong it was (leopardskin) to see the funny side. It really must be love.

Once we've finished our tiramisu (Lulu's right – I can hardly remember what the spaghetti tasted like. I just was so glad to see it I scraped my plate clean), Lulu stacks the empty plates in a pile by the sink and produces a pad of paper and four pens.

'Oh God, no,' groans Dan, covering his face with his hands. 'Tell me we're not playing Person Most Likely.' He looks out from between his fingers, but of course he knows the answer.

'It's that or the Hat Game, Dan,' says Lulu. 'Come on, you know we *always* play Person Most Likely after supper when Lizzy comes round.'

'Personne Most Likely?' asks Laurent, looking apprehensive, as well he might. This is a game that has ruined relationships, spawned new ones, caused people to be 'off speakers' for months. And one of the best games I know.

'The rules,' announces Lulu officiously, though Dan and I know them by heart. 'Each player is given five pieces of paper. On each piece of paper they write down a sentence beginning "Person Most Likely to . . . " and then they complete that sentence.'

'With what? I don't understand,' says Laurent, looking baffled, as most novices do. Oh, the poor innocent. 'With whatever you like, darling,' says Lulu, reaching over to caress his cheek. 'If you were thinking of me, for example, you might write "Person Most Likely to make Laurent a very happy man tonight". But then, you see, you might regret that. Because when you have completed your five pieces of paper, they are all dropped into this hat.' She waves a red beret in his direction. 'Chose this one in your honour, darling.' She clears a space amongst the wine glasses and empty bottles and drops the beret in the middle of the table.

'They go . . . in the beret?' asks Laurent.

'Yup – in the beret they go, we mix them up, and then everyone takes out five,' explains Lulu. 'And then you read the five you've picked out, and here's where it gets interesting: you allocate them to the person you think is best described there.' Laurent looks confused.

'But what if I get the ones I write myself?' asks Laurent – a rookie question.

'You still have to hand them out,' says Lulu firmly.

'And what if they're ones that are about me?' he asks. Aha – a quick learner, I see.

'Then you can give them to yourself. And when all the pieces of paper have been allocated, we go round the table and read them out loud.'

'Hmm, sounds fine,' says Laurent confidently. Poor lamb. He has no idea.

This is the game in which Dan's horrible university girlfriend Pearl became so enraged on receiving 'Person Most Likely to lose their temper playing this game' that she dumped Dan that night (thereby proving Lulu's point, though obviously she never confessed to writing it). This is the game in which my cousin, on receiving 'Person Most Likely to have an affair', burst into tears in front of her husband and asked how we all knew. We didn't. Till then. So we try to tread a little more carefully these days, but that really depends on the company.

The first round is innocuous stuff: Person Most Likely to wear a string of onions around their neck (Laurent), Person Most Likely to have their wedding featured in *OK!* magazine (me), Person Most Likely to engage in french kissing (Lulu), Person Most Likely to get naked with fourteen men at once (Dan, in the showers after rugby, you understand, though it could easily have been Lulu at one time). It's all fun and games, and we stop for a moment as Dan reaches up to the cupboard behind him for a bottle of amaretto while Lulu brews up a pot of coffee to lull us into the belief that we're sobering up.

Laurent is leaning back in his chair with his arm slung around the back of Lulu's, his thumb slowly caressing the back of the seat as if she were still sitting there. His eyes follow her about the room. Lulu's pretending not to notice, but every movement is slightly exaggerated: the opening of the fridge door seems to require a seductive bend, even the picking up of the tea towel involves a flirtatious wiggle of the hips. Dan and I roll our eyes at each other as he pours the amber-coloured liqueur into shot glasses, but Lulu and Laurent are in their own world and don't notice.

Lulu dumps a dented silver coffee pot on the table and unsteadily pours out four coffees in between repeatedly pushing Laurent's hand off her knee. 'Really, Laurent! Down, boy – we haven't even got on to round two.'

'We have to play this again?' asks Laurent, looking mournfully into Lulu's eyes and manoeuvring his hand a little further up her leg.

'Of course we do, darling,' says Lulu briskly. 'This was just the warm-up.'

As the opener to the second round, Dan gets labelled Person Most Likely to die alone, and blames

Laurent for writing it – that loopy French writing is such a giveaway to anyone who's ever been on a French exchange trip. If you ask me, it's the person who gave it to him who deserves the blame, but that was me, so I'm not going to volunteer that one. I could hardly give it to either one of the happy couple, could I? And it's a little too close to the bone for me to give it to myself.

'Die alone? Right – so you all think I'm destined to end up in a dodgy bedsit eating baked beans that I've heated up on my one-bar electric heater. Thanks very much.' Dan looks properly upset, which is ironic because, of the three of us, he's the only one who's moved almost seamlessly from long-term relationship to long-term relationship. First there was elegant Eleanor from the year above Dan, who hung out on the side of the rugby pitch with Lulu and me when we were at school but was far too disdainful to actually speak to us. Then Pearl, his university girlfriend, beautiful and bossy, who treated him like a lapdog until her fate was sealed during this very game. We all adored Bella, who he broke up with just a year ago, but after two years without any sign of a commitment from him, she gave him an ultimatum and he chose singledom over matrimony. Lulu and I can't understand why he's still on his own. He certainly gets plenty of offers, but apart from a few short flings he seems determined to stay a bachelor.

'Oh, don't take it all to heart, Danny,' says Lulu.

'You know how these lovely Frenchmen get all existential when they've been drinking.'

Laurent nods solemnly at Dan from across the table. 'We all die alone. In the end, each of us dies alone. There is no together at the end.'

'Yeah, great – cheery stuff, Laurent,' says Dan, somewhat mollified.

'Now, time for Lizzy to read her next one out,' says Lulu, swiftly changing the subject before the evening turns horribly maudlin.

I obediently pick up the piece of paper in front of me to read, 'Person Most Likely to need to lose control. Oh, very funny, Laurent – thanks for that.' His swirly continental letters have given him away again. Although that doesn't mean he's the one who gave it to me.

'Ha! Well, we've established that you've already done that, thanks to a certain celebrity shagger,' laughs Lulu triumphantly, chucking Laurent under the chin. 'You're quite hopelessly out of date, my gorgeous darling – Lizzy is quite the reformed character.'

'Who says you need to lose control?' asks Dan, looking confused. 'Is this about Randy Jones?'

'Of course it is, Danny,' says Lulu, launching into a wildly exaggerated description of the night on which she met Laurent, who happily chips in with his thoughts.

'And then Lizzy agrees with Lulu that she needs to

lose control a bit more, to allow life to happen to her, you know? To take some risks. To not live by the rules all the time, to experience what is, rather than what should be,' Laurent finishes. I see what Lulu means about the drunken existentialism.

'Riiiight,' says Dan, looking dubious. 'And you agreed with this, Lizzy?'

'*Mais oui*, she signed a promise and I witnessed it,' says Laurent with a shrug.

'Well, that explains a lot,' says Dan, pouring out another round of shots. 'I might have known that Lizzy wouldn't even think of going out with Randy Jones unless my sister put her up to it.' He grins at me across the table as if we're sharing a tremendous joke.

'Er, what exactly do you mean?' I demand. 'My relationship with Randy has nothing to do with Lulu's ridiculous challenge. It's a complete coincidence, despite what Lulu might say.'

'Sorry, darling,' says Lulu, blowing me a kiss across the table. 'I was just excited for you. I didn't mean to take the credit for your lovely new man.'

'Oh, come off it,' says Dan, laughing. 'He's not exactly your type, is he? I mean, Lizzy Harrison and the Shagger of the Millennium? There's no way you'd get involved with him if it weren't to prove a point.'

'Are you saying you think I'm too boring for someone like Randy?' I say crossly. 'Well, cheers, Dan – that's really good to know.'

I'm not about to defend my fake boyfriend, but it seems my relationship with him is bringing to the surface the way people really see me. And I'm not sure I like it. First my brother thinks I'm too sensible to date Randy Jones, and now rugby-shirted style-vacuum Dan is getting on board the Lizzy-Harrison-Is-A-Bore bandwagon.

'I mean it as a compliment!' protests Dan. 'You're just . . . I mean, you're just really *together*, aren't you? Like, everything about you is all calm and ordered and . . . clean, and – well, that's not Randy at all, is it?'

'Clean?! You think it's a compliment to say I'm clean and ordered? You make me sound like a nurse or something,' I storm, feeling unaccountably furious. 'Let me tell you that Randy is just the man for me, and do you know why? Because despite what you all seem to think, I am perfectly capable of being a bit wild and crazy. Because despite what you think, I am not boring or sensible or . . . or . . . *clean*.'

My voice has risen far too high and loud, and when I stop speaking there is a long silence during which Dan won't look at me and Laurent looks imploringly at Lulu.

'Well, let's not take this too far. After all, you *are* clean, darling,' says Lulu, sounding practical. 'Don't go denying good hygiene for the sake of making a point. And you know Danny doesn't mean you're boring. As if he could possibly think that. Do you, Dan?'

Dan shifts his chair back to look me full in the face, and I stare back, challengingly. Laurent and Lulu shift uncomfortably in their seats, and I see Laurent reach for her hand under the table.

'I don't think you're boring, Lizzy,' says Dan at last, speaking slowly as if he is carefully choosing each word. 'I think . . . I think you're great. I think you're too good to be the latest notch on Randy Jones's bedpost, and I think he's going to end up treating you badly. That's what I think.'

I know there's a kernel of truth in what Dan is saying, and I know that, like my brother, he is only saying it because he cares. But I am filled with an amaretto-fuelled fury.

'Well *I* think you should mind your own business, Dan Miller, because I am old enough, and smart enough and – and – *sensible* enough to make up my own mind about my relationships without your advice.'

I cross my arms across my chest. I know it's childish, but I don't care.

'That's not what I—' Dan starts. And then suddenly, as if I had willed it from above, the doorbell rings.

Dan turns towards it, frowning. 'Who the fuck is ringing our doorbell at half past midnight?'

'That will be my taxi,' I say, stumbling to my feet and grappling for my handbag under the table. 'I booked it earlier.'

'Oh, did you?' says Dan with a harsh laugh. 'Wow, booking a taxi in advance is a pretty out-of-control thing to do. I can see I have totally misjudged your crazy, freewheeling ways. Yeah, I definitely owe you an apology for suggesting you were organized in any way.'

'Jesus, what is your problem, Dan?' I snap, grabbing my handbag to my chest like a shield. Ignoring him, although I can feel his eyes boring into my skull, I turn to the others with exaggerated politeness. 'Thanks, Lulu, for a great night. Laurent, it was good to meet you properly at last. I hope I'll see you again soon.'

'At Lulu's birthday, if not sooner,' says Laurent, making a half-hearted attempt at standing up to kiss my cheek. Lulu pushes him back down in his chair with a hand on his chest and restrains Dan, who is about to stand up, with no more than a glare in his direction. She comes out into the corridor with me as we hear the minicab driver sound his horn.

'Lizzy, I'm sorry – I don't know what's got into Dan. He'll feel dreadful about all of this in the morning.' She reaches over to hug me and then pulls back to hold me by the tops of my arms. 'Just ignore him and have a laugh with Randy. It's about time you had a bit of fun, and who knows where it might end up? It's all about the journey, Harrison.'

'Thanks for that, Mystic Miller. Your Frenchman's ways must be catching,' I say, kissing her cheek as I open the front door. 'Quite frankly, the only journey I'm interested in right now is the one that's going to deposit me in my bed.'

'In Randy's bed, you mean,' Lulu shouts, laughing as I race down the path.

If only she knew.

The cab journey home is one of those where, instead of sobering up, you realize you're drunker than you thought. So I'm feeling a bit worse for wear as I let myself into Randy's house at half past one and creep upstairs with the elaborate care of the inebriate, trying to make as little noise as possible. I tiptoe past Randy's room and am about to go into mine when I hear his voice calling my name.

'Lizzy? Is that you? Hey, come in here.'

There's a blueish sort of light in Randy's room as I push the door open; he's watching television in the dark, alone. He's unshaven and bare-chested, leaning back against the pillows, and he pats the bed, inviting me to sit down.

'Hi, Randy – did you have a good night?' I say, perching on the edge of the bed a little unsteadily.

'Yeah, just hung out here, really. On my best behaviour, of course. Fairly dull. How were your friends?'

'They were fine,' I say flatly. 'it was all just fine.' I think of Dan's angry face as I left the house and, to my horror, my eyes suddenly fill with tears. Luckily the room is dark enough for Randy not to notice, and I quickly wipe my eyes with the back of my hand.

'Fine?' says Randy, raising his eyebrows. 'That doesn't sound like a night I should be sorry I missed, my fake girlfriend.'

'Oh, you know,' I say, keeping my head low so he can't see my watery eyes. 'I was just catching up with old friends – nothing special.'

'Old friends, eh? Well, why don't you come and lie here next to your new friend for a little bit?' says Randy, patting a space on the quilt next to him.

''Kay,' I say, muffling a hiccup. The quilt is satin; cool and slippery. It takes me a few attempts to settle myself alongside him.

'Are you a little bit pissed there, my fake girlfriend?' asks Randy, turning to me with gentle amusement.

'Maybe a bit. Sorry. Just mostly really, really tired,' I sigh, leaning back. And I am tired. I'm exhausted.

'Wait,' says Randy, reaching over to place a pillow behind my head. I'm surprised to notice that his usual odour of fags and unwashed denim has been replaced with the sharp citrus scent of soap and shampoo.

'I don't know,' he says, chuckling. 'I thought you were meant to be keeping me on the straight and narrow, not being a dirty stop-out drunken influence, Lizzy Harrison.'

'Shurrup,' I murmur from my cocoon within the pillows. My hair has fallen into my face, but it feels like too much effort to move it. I can feel the ends of my fringe tickling my nose as I breathe in and out. 'Not a bad influence. *Sensible* influence, apparently. Sensible, straight Lizzy Harrison, that's me.'

'You're not looking especially sensible right now,' laughs Randy, lying down next to me and picking up the remote control. He nudges my leg with his own, teasing. 'See, I knew I'd get you into my bed in the end.'

'Oh yeah,' I yawn, feeling my eyelids begin to droop. 'I can't keep my hands off you, Randy. You're irresistible.'

'I know,' he says, and even though I can't find the energy to turn my head in his direction, I can hear the smile in his voice.

I listen to the steady rise and fall of his breath as we lie there, still, together. I'd forgotten how quietly comforting it is to feel another body so close by. To feel somehow watched over. Protected. Even if Randy, flicking between channels, is far more interested in the television than he is in me.

Randy turns the volume up a notch. I can hear gunfire and shouting.

'What're you watching?' I ask sleepily.

'*Magnificent Seven*,' says Randy. 'You know, Yul Brynner, cowboys and all that.'

'Yeah, Yul Brynner,' I say. '*M'nificent Seven*. Nice.'

I close my eyes. Just for a moment. I think, I'll just rest my eyes for a moment and then I'll go to my own room.

I wake to feel a slow, gentle, lovely stroking of my hair that makes me stretch myself out like a cat, eyes still closed. How long have I been asleep? I feel the hand move from my hair down to my face and begin to delicately trace the line of my eyebrows, the plane of my cheekbones, the curve of my jawline. Am I dreaming this? A finger draws itself along my nose and then down to my lips, where it stops. I open my eyes. Randy's face is very close to mine. The television is off. It is still dark outside and very quiet. He slowly takes his finger away from my lips and then he kisses me softly.

I think, *This isn't part of the deal.* I think, *I don't even fancy you.* I think, *When he speaks, I'll tell him to stop.*

But there's something hypnotic in his steady gaze, and he doesn't say a word. His hand moves away from my face and I feel his fingers expertly open the top buttons of my blouse to expose the top of my bra. He bends his head to drop fluttery kisses along my collarbone and into the hollow at the base of my neck. His fingers run down my front and, one by one, the rest of the buttons are undone. He opens the shirt wide and drops a kiss first on my right breast, then on the left. Then he inches the shirt down my arms, looking up at me with eyebrows raised as if to say, 'I'll stop any time you say so.' But I don't. His fingers teasingly trace the twists and turns of the lace pattern on my bra, and I feel my back arch impatiently to push my breasts further into his hands. Now he moves a hand lower still and tugs on the waistband of my jeans to pull me closer towards him. He kisses me harder and more urgently, gently tugging at my lower lip with his teeth, and he pulls me on top of him, pushing my hips down on to him with his hands so I can feel him hard against me.

I think, *This is where I should stop him*, but instead I find that I'm shamelessly wriggling my hips to help him slide my jeans all the way off. I kick them to the floor. He unhooks my bra and pushes me back on to the bed, straddling me so I can't move. I'm lying on Randy Jones's bed in just my knickers, and his right hand is drawing tiny circles on my stomach, tiny circles that are moving slowly, carefully downwards. His hand slips underneath my knickers and I arch towards him again with a little gasp. He grins as he begins to pull the lacy fabric down my thighs.

I think, *A hundred girls have been here before me*. I think, *Oh God, I'm such a cliché*. I think, *I don't care*.

I'm tired of being sensible.

It feels amazing.

12

Back at work on Monday, I have the oddest feeling that I've gone back to being sixteen and have lost my virginity all over again. Not that sleeping with Randy, great though it was, was some kind of divine revelation, as it always seems to be when someone loses their virginity in the movies, with a celestial choir in the background and simultaneous orgasms. (Nor were we in the back of a clapped-out Ford Fiesta in a pub car park, which is how it happened for me first time round.) It's more that I spend the whole day thinking that everyone must be able to *tell*. When Camilla races into the office with her phone clamped between ear and shoulder, I think surely she will notice something is different, but she just dumps Cassius's lunchbox on my desk with an apologetic grimace and mouths 'sorry'. I have lunch with account executive Lucy and wait in vain for the moment that she mentions Randy, but instead we spend the whole hour looking at bathroom catalogues and debating the merits of different styles of bath taps for her new flat.

I've always known that other people pay far less attention to one's life than one thinks, but this shift in my relationship with Randy feels actually tangible to me, and I can't understand how it isn't visible to anyone else. Surely there's a huge flashing sign above my head or something? I'm not so naive as to think that sleeping with Randy turns us from fake boyfriend and girlfriend into the real thing – we're talking about the Shagger of the Millennium – but Saturday night has changed something between us, even if I'm not sure what. Of course we still made sure we were seen out in public on Sunday – looking in jewellers' windows while holding hands, sharing coffees at pavement cafés, buying a copy of the *Big Issue* with a ten-pound note and refusing the change – but Randy's constant and tactile attentiveness didn't stop once we were on our own. Back at his house, he was all thoughtfulness and charm, and even as I left this morning he didn't grab me for his usual ostentatious doorstep snog for the benefit of the photographers on the pavement. Instead he gave me a gentle kiss on the tip of my nose as we stood in the corridor.

'You'll come back here tonight?' he asked, even though it's not one of the nights I usually spend at his house.

'Well, I was going to go home and do a few housey

things this evening,' I said in surprise. 'Laundry and stuff – you know.'

'You'd really rather do your laundry than come back here to see me?' he said with a filthy smile on his face that suggested he was offering something a little more fun than sorting my smalls into darks and lights.

'I'm just running a bit low on, er, you know, underwear and stuff,' I said. After all, it's one thing to drop your knickers on someone's bedroom floor in gay abandon, but quite another when you have no knickers left to drop. And I'm not really the sort of girl who's ever going to go commando, especially now my every move is photographed.

'Don't you worry your head about that, Lizzy Harrison. I'm happy to sort you out with some underwear if that's what it takes to get you back here tonight.' Randy said, kissing me again, and I allowed myself a small frisson of shamefully mercenary excitement. He's not the kind of man to do things by halves. What exciting scanties from Agent Provocateur will await my return?

Camilla types away furiously in her office all afternoon and barely stops for breath, except to race past barefoot at one point, muttering 'loo'. Being taken off Randy's PR has left me feeling strangely separated from my boss. Normally I know exactly where she's meant to be and when, but lately she's so absorbed in setting up a charity gig for Randy – I hear more about it from him than from her – that I hardly know where she is from one minute to the next. She disappears to lunches that aren't in my diary. She has meetings for which I don't need to write up her scrawled notes. She has taken off the automatic cc which sends all her emails directly to my inbox. Not to mention that she is suddenly free of her usual array of sick and baby food stains; my emergency wet wipes haven't been needed for weeks. Her hair is not only freshly highlighted but blow-dried in a manner that suggests the regular hand of a professional. If I didn't know her better, I'd think she was having an affair.

Late that afternoon I look up to see Bryan Ross, Randy's manager, striding purposefully down the corridor before stopping at my desk. He has the kind of craggy face and stern demeanour that suggests many years spent as a penitent priest before deciding to move into celebrity management.

'Lizzy,' he says, which is the Bryan Ross version of 'Hello, Lizzy, and how are you today?' He is a man of few words.

'Hi, Bryan. What a nice surprise. I didn't know you were coming in today.' Which is the Lizzy Harrison version of 'What the fuck are you doing here?' I flick open the electronic diary on my desktop in case I've missed something – surely Camilla isn't expecting him?

'Just passing,' says Bryan.

Camilla leans out of her office. 'Bryan, gosh – lovely to see you. Thanks for stopping by at such short notice.

Come on in.' So there *was* a meeting arranged; honestly, it's impossible to keep track of her at the moment.

Bryan turns to follow Camilla, and then suddenly looks down at a small Marks & Spencer bag that he seems to have only just realized he is holding. He turns back and places it on my desk, not looking me in the eye.

'From Randy, pet.' He clears his throat uncomfortably, a dark purple flush creeping up his neck, and heads into Camilla's office, closing the door behind him. I hear the murmur of their voices through the door as they settle down to business.

So what's Randy sent me, I wonder? I reach inside the bag. And pull out a three-pack of white cotton tummy-hugging granny-pants. Two sizes too big.

If this is Randy's idea of a joke, I'm not laughing. I'm surprised how upset I am at the sight of these innocently pristine white knickers. Whatever it was that happened between Randy and me over the weekend, clearly this afternoon I'm back to being the kind of girl whose underthings come from Marks & Spencer rather than La Perla. Spending several hours in Randy's bedroom has not, after all, turned me into an irresistible temptress to be spoiled and adored. I guess I should be grateful he didn't buy me a girdle.

I realize that, despite insisting to myself that our sleeping together doesn't change anything, a tiny, hopeful part of me, long dormant, has flickered into life over the last two days, fanned into flame by Randy's flirtatious attentions. Get a grip, Lizzy, I tell myself. You know exactly what Randy is like. Flirtation comes as naturally to him as breathing. What happened at the weekend was a mistake, an aberration. Obviously Randy thinks so too. That must be the message he's attempting to convey with the granny-pants in a kind of knicker semaphore.

But another part of me, also waking from a long sleep, sticks two fingers up at my sensible self. The shag drought is over, and in some style; so what? I know it doesn't mean anything to him; nor does it to me. I'm just having a bit of fun, and about time too. My sensible self sighs, shaking her head. This is real life, Lizzy, remember? Sleeping with the Shagger of the Millennium cannot possibly end well. Pull yourself together.

So I do.

Shoving the pants into my desk drawer, I decide that I will go home tonight after all.

13

It feels like I haven't been home for weeks, not just days. Post is piled up in the hallway, and a spindly-legged spider has built its web across the bath. The peace lily in my bedroom is looking particularly forlorn, its usually glossy leaves dull and collapsed on to the window sill, and the air in the flat smells stale. I open the windows and begin to sort things out. I find it immensely restful and pleasing to put things in their proper place – I put a load of laundry on, change the sheets on my bed, water the plants, draw up a shopping list to fill my echoingly empty fridge. Put the granny-pants aside for donation to a charity that might pass them on to an actual granny.

There is a message on my home phone from my mother, who still believes mobile phones will fry your brain and refuses to call me on mine.

'Darling? Darling! Oh, it's your blasted machine again. It's me, darling, just wanting to let you know I've been chanting for you. Sorry to miss you, my gorgeous one, but you know I only get one phone call a week – it's like prison! But I love it really, you know I do. And I love *you*. Miss you, darling. Big kiss. Love from Mum.'

I have no idea why she always has to sign off an answerphone message as if it were a letter, but there you go. For the first time since I started seeing Randy, I wish that Mum wasn't so far away. I wish she was the sort of cosy, stay-at-home mother that I could run home to and confess everything to over a slice of home-made cake, a fat Labrador curled at my feet, my childhood bedroom untouched upstairs. But our family home was sold years ago, and the only cakes that Mum makes these days are incredibly heavy vegetable-based creations with a reliance on hemp flour. Even if we still had a dog, I don't think it would eat them.

After Dad died in a car crash when I was sixteen, a well-meaning friend gave Mum a copy of *The Tibetan Book of Living and Dying*. From there it was a short journey via trips to WOMAD, a penchant for colourful tunics woven by small Tibetan cooperatives and a house full of stinky joss sticks (excellent for disguising teenage smoking, I found) to silent retreats, a renunciation of all caffeine and alcohol, and a mysterious refusal to eat mushrooms 'because they grow in the dark'. Since she retired from teaching five years ago, she's got more and more out there, but Ben and I reassure ourselves that if it makes her happy, who are we to judge? For all her nuttiness, she is my mother and I miss her. Tears prick my eyes as I realize I've missed speaking to her for another week, and I listen to her message three times.

By the time I've finished the hoovering and dusting and taken a long shower, I'm feeling much better. I take my dressing-gowned self, clean and content, to the sofa with the pile of post and a cup of some herbal tea that Mum left here last time she visited. It feels like a little connection with her, even if it does taste like boiled lawn clippings.

The post is the usual not-very-exciting assortment of letters from estate agents assuring me that they are inundated with buyers wishing to buy a flat just like mine, flyers for the local curry house, my credit-card bill, and a free magazine, *Peckham Life*, which is comically aspirational – I wonder what the Eritrean family of six that lives in the downstairs flat will make of the suggestion that simply everyone in SE15 is decorating their homes with Cole and Son wallpaper at £50 per square metre. At the bottom of all of this is an envelope which seems to contain what Camilla and her posh friends would call 'a stiffy'. It's a proper engraved invitation with swirly writing, and initially I'm confused – surely I would know if any of my friends was getting married? And the rush of christenings seems to have abated lately; who can it be from?

Mr Daniel Miller and Miss Lulu Miller invite

Miss Lizzy Harrison and guest

to celebrate their thirty-five years on this planet
at a dinner and dance to be held at

The Old Brewery, Spitalfields, London
at 8 p.m. on Saturday, August 22nd.

Dress: Black Tie
R.S.V.P.

'And guest' is underlined in gold pen and enhanced by three exclamation marks. I'm assuming this wasn't done by Dan, who I still haven't heard from since our argument at supper.

Oh good Lord, however did I forget that Dan and Lulu were having a proper, huge sit-down dinner and dance for their shared birthday? Their adoring parents had insisted on paying for a party with the proviso that Mr Miller could make a speech in honour of his children 'before I die of old age waiting for either of you two to get married'. Lulu, who has long declared her lack of interest in any kind of wedding, couldn't resist the idea of being the centre of attention without having to commit herself to a relationship. And Dan – well, Dan had decided it wasn't worth his while opposing the force of nature that is Lulu on a mission.

I fan myself with the invitation as I ponder 'and guest'. Would Randy come with me? So far our fake relationship has been entirely on his terms and on his territory. I don't think he even knows where I live. But maybe he'd actually like to spend time doing something as normal and non-starry as attending a totally civilian party? Maybe he'd like to go to a party full-stop; our social life, such as it is, has been spent mostly in his home or, on the rare occasions we have ventured out, by ourselves. I've barely met a friend of Randy's who isn't in some way paid to be in his presence. Maybe he'd like to meet my friends. And I know it would be the best birthday present ever for devoted celebrity-magazine-reader Lulu if I could bring along my so-called A-list boyfriend. If I could somehow get her photograph into *Hot Slebs*, she might just spontaneously combust with happiness. I'm contemplating my strategy when my mobile rings on the sofa beside me.

'Babe? Where are you? It's gone nine – I've been waiting ages.' Randy sounds perplexed. I can't imagine he gets stood up often.

'I'm at home, Randy. Like I said, I had some things to do,' I say coolly, back in professional mode.

'But I thought you said you'd come back here if you had some clean underwear. Bryan said he'd delivered some to you this afternoon. What's going on? Are you playing games with me, babe?' I wasn't expecting him to be so annoyed.

'Did Bryan tell you what kind of underwear he delivered to me this afternoon, Randy?' I ask, still cool, but slightly reassured that it wasn't Randy who'd purchased the granny-pants.

'Jesus, I don't know – knickers are knickers, aren't they? I don't care what kind you're wearing, babe. Frankly I just want to get them off you as fast as possible.'

The little flame in my heart flares for a moment, but I put it out before it can get any bigger.

'Well, next time you want to seduce me with underwear, perhaps you'd better not send your manager to buy it, Randy. Giant cotton pants two sizes too big did not do it for me, I'm afraid.'

'He bought *what*?' says Randy. 'Oh, fucking hell, babe. Is that what this is about? Look, I'll buy you the entire contents of Agent Provocateur if you will just get your gorgeous body over here right now. Please.'

'No,' I say, feeling oddly powerful and in control of this weird relationship for once. 'I want a night at home and it's too far and too late to come over to yours now. But I'll see you tomorrow night, okay?'

'Jesus, Lizzy – seriously? You won't come over at all?'

'I will tomorrow. Night, Randy.'

I hang up and take a sip of tea before tidying away the post.

Two hours later I get a text.

'I want you, I miss you, I need you. What do I need to do to get you back here, babe?'

Well, I think I've made my point. I've shown Randy

I'm not at his beck and call. That he's not the only one who calls the shots in this so-called relationship. I can handle this. Lizzy Harrison is back in control, oh yes.

So I let him call me a taxi.

14

In the end, it doesn't take much to persuade Randy to be my 'plus one'. I don't even have to resort to mentioning the dodgy pants. He's surprisingly excited at the opportunity to actually go out to a proper event; over the few weeks of our fake relationship, Randy's been far too focused on therapy and workouts and writing and his newly clean life to want to throw himself in the path of temptation. Invitations have piled up on the kitchen table, but Randy has instructed Bryan's assistant to turn them all down. Even though I'm not one for the limelight, it has pained my heart to see that he has declined all manner of film premieres, gallery openings and, in one devastating instance, an intimate dinner for six that included Johnny Depp. Johnny Depp! I wailed into my pillow over that one. But Camilla's strategy has been to keep everything low-key: dinners for two, daytime outings, trips to the local cinema, cosy nights in. She wants to save up the fireworks for Randy's comeback charity gig. I'd thought Randy was happy with it all, but the alacrity with which he accepted the invitation to Lulu and Dan's suggests he's straining to get off Camilla's tight leash.

In fact, he's so overexcited by the idea of a proper party that he decides we'll go out to dinner in Primrose Hill to discuss it properly, instead of staying in to eat the cordon bleu speciality that Nina the Cleaner has left for us in the fridge. Randy takes half an hour to get ready while I flick through a copy of *Hot Slebs* downstairs, having spent ten minutes touching up my mascara and lipgloss. I don't think I've ever been out with a man who wears more make-up than me. I don't think I've ever been out with a man who wears make-up full stop, and there's something slightly disconcerting about the fact that, when he comes downstairs, Randy has managed to achieve a smoky-eyed look that I couldn't pull off if my life depended on it.

'Ready to go, babe?' he asks, holding out his arm.

Despite the smoky eyes, he's pretty dressed down tonight – just his usual tight jeans, a pair of battered boots and a ripped white T-shirt that has 'Helmut Lang' written across it in what appears to be magic marker. His blond hair is messily pulled back, unbrushed. Standing next to him in my sleeveless gingham shirt, cropped jeans and ballet flats, I feel like Doris Day heading out for an evening with a member of Motley

Crue. I reassure myself that this is precisely the point of our pairing and that my pristine appearance is nothing to be ashamed of. But I can't help surreptitiously mussing my hair up as we walk down the street towards the gastropub on the corner.

For once, Randy requests a quiet table in the corner and, in any case, the locals in this pub are so used to celebrities they hardly bat an eyelid. The only person who has ever melted the notoriously cool bar staff is Madonna, who famously called in for a pint of ale during her flat cap Ye Olde English phase. Although everyone studiously ignored her for the hour that she perched her yoga-honed self on a bar stool, once she left it was total carnage – the girl behind the bar even fainted, said Mel, who claimed to have been there. But there are no megastars here tonight – just a few faintly recognizable faces, with whom Randy exchanges a little mutual celebrity nod: 'You're famous, I'm famous, we're just acknowledging that.' Randy adds a slight uplift to the chin, a subtle refinement which translates as, 'Even so, I think we both know I'm more famous than you, and my acknowledgement of you is therefore all the more gracious.'

'So, a party – cool!' he says once we've ordered the kind of hand-reared, organically grown, heartily rustic peasant food that no peasant could possibly afford.

'You're really good to come with me, Randy,' I say, picking at a chunk of herby focaccia. 'Thanks.'

'S'not good,' he says, refusing the bread. 'You're my girlfriend aren't you? Course I'd come to a party with you.'

'Well, it *is* good of you, because I'm only your fake girlfriend,' I whisper, with a quick glance around the room to make sure no one's listening.

'Are you saying you've been faking it?' teases Randy, pushing a denim clad knee firmly between mine.

'Ha! I think you know I haven't been faking anything, Mr Shagger of the Millennium,' I say, flustered. I busy myself with more bread to hide it.

'Thought not,' he says, leaning back in his chair with a satisfied grin, one leather boot rubbing against my leg. 'There's nothing fake about you, Lizzy. That's why I like you.'

'Really?' I ask, looking up shyly.

'Yeah,' he says, a small smile lurking at the corners of his mouth. 'You're different from the girls I usually go out with.'

'Randy,' I say, quietly, 'we aren't actually going out, remember?'

He frowns.

'Babe, you spend just about every night at my house. We're shagging like Duracell bunnies. I want to see you all the time. What's fake about that?'

There is a part of me that wants to believe him, to let myself swoon into his arms, to fall for him instead of holding myself back. But the hard shell around my heart won't let me do it. Not yet. I can't deny, though, that Randy's constant attention has caused a few cracks to appear. I'm not saying I've suddenly become some Sandra Bullock character, weakening as I realize I need to let love into my life, or anything that cheesy and ridiculous. In any case, unlike Miss Congeniality, I am perfectly capable of walking in high heels without comic pratfalls. But I will admit that there is a hint of something real in this formerly fake relationship, and I'm not going to entirely refuse to allow its existence.

'Seriously, babe,' Randy continues, smiling at me across the table. 'Why would I have to fake it? You're smart. And funny. You're all good and pretty and, I don't know, you're all . . . clean.'

Why is it that when *he* says I'm clean it makes me feel unspeakably dirty? It felt like such an insult from Dan, such a condemnation of sensible Lizzy Harrison, but in Randy's mouth it seems flirtatious, exciting, challenging.

'Clean?' I say, laughing.

'It kind of makes me want to mess you up, babe,' he says, leaning over to cup my face in his hand. 'Know what I mean?'

I know exactly what he means, and it's making me blush like a schoolgirl, so I'm a bit relieved when the waitress comes over with knives and forks and glasses and our conversation is temporarily interrupted. By the time she's finished, Randy's attention has already moved on to what the two of us should be wearing for our first official event as a couple, though it becomes obvious as he speaks that my role in this sartorial partnership is going to be as accessory to Randy rather than equal partner. He's talking about using a stylist, about bringing in a hairdresser, about borrowing jewellery and shoes. I'm too grateful to him for agreeing to come to say that all of this sounds like my worst nightmare.

'I'm thinking a sort of denim and leather theme,' says Randy thoughtfully, as if this is a completely dramatic and unexpected departure for someone who is rarely seen in anything else.

'I thought you might be,' I say, waving a forkful of lamb shank at him, 'but you can think again if you think you're going to get me dressed up like Suzi Quatro.'

'Hey, that's an idea, babe,' Randy coos. 'Matching leather jumpsuits. I like it.'

'Er, look – I've promised Lulu that I'll go shopping with her, so I don't know yet what I'm going to wear,' I protest, rejecting the visions of myself forced into hideously unflattering, not to mention unbearably sweaty, skintight pleather. This is not the sophisticated ensemble I've been imagining for Lulu and Dan's party.

'Don't worry, babe,' says Randy, leaning forwards. 'Leave it to me. Let me treat my girlfriend. I'd like to.'

His girlfriend. He's said it twice now. Without the 'fake'. It can't be an accident.

When the waitress offers us the pudding menu, Randy declines it with scandalized horror as if she's presented him with a syringe on a tray with a row of pills to follow, and instead suggests that we go back home for coffee. As I know that Randy's as anti-caffeine right now as he is anti-sugar, I have a pretty good idea what he's got in store. The sun is just starting to set as we start to walk home, and suddenly Randy pulls me down a different road, heading away from Belsize Park, lined with tall houses painted in ice-cream pastels.

'Where are we going?' I ask.

'You'll see,' he says, entwining his fingers with mine as he leads the way.

As we pass the cafés and bars of Regent's Park Road, where crowds have gathered outside on the pavement, a few people call out to Randy. People he knows, beautiful girls in summer dresses, two tall men wearing sunglasses, a statuesque girl dressed entirely in leopardskin. He just raises a hand in greeting and keeps on walking. As we get to the gates of the park, he wraps his arm around my shoulder and pulls me in closer.

'Are you cold?' he asks.

'No,' I say, leaning in towards him.

It's a beautiful night. The sky is a pale pink streaked with delicately rippling grey clouds, which darken to red close to the horizon. The park is dotted with clusters of people stretching out the summer evening for as long as they can. As we climb up the path to the top of the hill, we pass a group of teenagers. Four girls watch adoringly as a tall, angular boy with long dark hair picks at a guitar. A chubby boy sits on his own a little distance from them, chewing his lower lip and glancing in their direction. Randy waves at him, and he turns, open-mouthed, to watch us.

'That's sweet of you,' I say. 'Especially as I bet you were the guitar-playing boy when you were his age.'

Randy turns to look at me in surprise. 'No way, babe. I was the lonely kid all the way. I wasn't a chubster, mind you, but being four feet high at the age of fifteen and lumbered with a pair of inch-thick plastic NHS specs does not a ladykiller make. Surely you've heard all this before? It's all in my bio – Speccy Geek Turns Celebrity Swordsman? Funnyman Randy Jones Gets His Revenge on Childhood Bullies?'

'Seriously? Weird, I can't imagine you with glasses.'

'Yeah,' he laughs, but sharply, like he doesn't find it funny at all. 'The kids in the playground used to throw my glasses into the bushes and leave me trying to find them. Mrs Hopkin used to have to help me search for them at the end of every morning break. It doesn't do a lot for your popularity to end up spending most of your free time with a fifty-something head of maths.'

'So, what happened?' I ask.

'Contact lenses, babe. Contact lenses and the miraculous powers of puberty,' says Randy, waving a hand over his face like a street-corner magician. 'Grew two feet in a year, lost the glasses, changed my life. You'd think Bryan could get me some kind of endorsement deal out of it, wouldn't you?'

'Mmmm,' I say, still trying to imagine the famous man beside me as a bespectacled weed set on by bullies. 'But I don't know that puberty actually needs a spokesperson, Randy.'

'Oh, very funny,' says Randy, squeezing my fingers with his own. 'I'll make the jokes around here, babe.'

We walk on towards the top of the hill. At the highest point, with London stretched out in front of us, Randy leads me off the path and pulls me down to lie on the grass next to him, hidden away from anyone else. He doesn't say anything and nor do I. We just lie there side by side, holding hands and looking at the sky as the first winking stars emerge.

'So, were you one of the adoring girls, then?' he asks. 'When you were younger, I mean.'

'Oh I didn't really go out much when I was a teenager,' I say, suddenly feeling a panicky flutter in my chest. I don't want to talk about this.

'Why's that, babe?' says Randy, rolling on to his stomach to look at me. 'Were you hideously ugly? Did no one never ask you out?'

'No,' I say, laughing nervously and pulling at a piece of grass next to Randy's arm.

'What then? Were you brought up Amish or something?' he asks.

'Yes, that's it,' I say. 'I wasn't permitted to mix with the English and all their new-fangled gadgets and temptations. However did you guess?'

'Ah, it's your lack of proficiency with the DVD player that gave it away,' Randy teases, pushing a strand of hair away from my forehead. 'That and your love of a horse-drawn carriage. No, really – were you a speccy nerd, too?'

'Um . . .' I say, not really sure how much of my life I want to share with this almost-stranger. 'My dad died when I was sixteen. I didn't really feel like going out much for a while after that. And when I did, it kind of took some time before anyone would treat me normally.'

'Oh, babe, I'm sorry,' says Randy, gently kissing the top of my head.

We lie in silence for a while before Randy asks, 'What was he like, your dad?'

It's hard to know where to start.

'He . . . was just my dad, you know? He was a biology teacher, but his real love was botany. If he was here with us now, he'd probably be giving us a lecture on all the different kinds of grasses we're sitting on.'

'Grasses?' says Randy dubiously. I realize that I probably should have tried for a more interesting fact about Dad, especially for Randy, Mr Zero Attention Span, but that's all that came to mind in the moment.

'I know,' I say. 'My brother and I thought it was

about the most boring thing in the world to listen to him going on and on about plants and grasses. But I've forgotten it all now. I'd give just about anything to have him tell me about it one more time.'

'Oh, Lizzy,' says Randy, his face pressed close to mine. 'That's too sad.'

I curl into him as it gets darker, and he gently strokes my hair. It's all very innocent and chaste, and yet somehow it feels more intimate than any of the time we've spent in his bedroom.

Though of course we do go back there afterwards.

15

Lulu is practically beside herself when I tell her that Randy and I will be attending her party as a couple. It almost distracts her from the question of what she will wear.

Dan and Lulu's shared birthday parties are legendary amongst our friends, and when we were younger it often felt as if the rest of the summer's parties were just a series of rehearsals for theirs, the main event. For years they insisted on fancy-dress themes, from 'Hello, Sailor' to 'Footballers and their Wives', and discussion about appropriate outfits would dominate for weeks. But since Lulu got banned from a bar last year for surfing down the stairs on an inflatable alligator (theme: 'In The Jungle'), Dan had declared that their next party would be a more civilized affair. Lulu and I have been bitterly lamenting the lack of opportunity to dress up in stupid outfits, as we are both firmly of the Fancy Dress Should Be Funny school, and are always slightly contemptuous of girls who use fancy dress as an opportunity to dress as sexily as possible. It's just too easy to dress yourself up as a gold-bikini'd Princess Leia for an Outer Space party. How much more inspired to come along as Miss Piggy from the Muppets' *Pigs in Space*. Then again, that may well be why I haven't been chatted up at one of their parties for years. (Lulu, of course, didn't let a plastic snout and ears stop her from going home with the bouncer on that occasion.)

Once their parents decided to fund a posh do instead of the usual gathering in a pub garden, the lack of fancy dress was a condition Lulu was happy to agree to. Not least, she said, because the idea of her sixty-five-year-old mother dressed as a showgirl (Lulu's preferred theme for this year being 'What Happens in Vegas Stays in Vegas') was too disturbing to contemplate. So, on reflection, Lulu and I are glad of the opportunity to look attractive instead of mental, and have spent several happy hours flicking through magazines and discussing what to wear.

Lulu's realization, however, that Randy's presence also means the presence of the press, has stepped her sartorial considerations up a gear. After two fruitless hours in Selfridges, we retire to the champagne bar to restore ourselves with a quick drink and a shopping post-mortem.

'I mean, Harrison, we've got to think about this much more carefully now, don't you realize? Like that black dress I tried on in Liberty's this morning – out of the running entirely.' She shakes her head ruefully. (The copper curls are gone as of last week, replaced by a ruler-straight sheet of ash blonde.)

'Why? You looked gorgeous in that one, Lu – don't rule it out.'

'But I'd have to go bra-less, Harrison, and with those super-strong flashbulbs from all the cameras, you'd totally be able to see my boobs through the fabric.'

'Look, I'm sure Randy and I can manage to throw off the paps on our way to the party. You don't need to worry about this, honestly. I don't want it to spoil your night.'

'Are you kidding? Don't you bloody *dare* throw off the paps! I'm not about to spend five hundred quid on a dress for it to be seen only by my *friends*,' says Lulu, appalled. 'I won't be happy unless I'm totally blinded by flashbulbs when I arrive, okay?'

'Okay, okay – we'll be sure to bring along the full contingent if that's what you want. What does Dan think about it all?' I ask. While Lulu has kept me up to date on every single development of the party over the last two weeks, from canapé selections to wine choices and whether or not her dad would pay for a fleet of semi-naked butlers (he would not), I haven't heard anything from Dan at all.

'Oh, it's easy for boys, isn't it?' says Lulu. 'He's just going to wear bog-standard black tie and I've told him that under no circumstances is he to join any of those rugby boys in wearing cummerbunds or waistcoats with wacky cartoon characters on, and especially not –' she shudders – 'braces. But he's far more interested in sorting out the DJ, so I've left that entirely to him. Prepare yourself for an evening dominated by the sounds of Eighties soft rock.'

'And is he . . . bringing anyone?' It feels weird having to ask Lulu about Dan; normally I see him often enough to know exactly what's going on his life. But lately the only person I've seen often is Randy.

'Well, funny you should mention it, but I think he is, yes,' says Lulu. 'God knows who – he's gone all mysterious and secretive about it, but we were sorting the table plans last night and he put in a place next to him for a guest.'

'Well I never. He's a dark horse, isn't he?'

'You know, he *is* a bit of a dark horse lately,' Lulu says. 'I mean, I usually find Danny so easy to read it's like he's transparent, and I don't mean any of that nonsense about twins being all telepathic and stuff. You know what I mean – Dan's just so straightforward he's practically binary. But lately he's changed.'

'Changed how?'

'I don't know. I can't put my finger on it. But there's something going on. Maybe it's this new girl? I guess we'll have to wait and see.' She drains her champagne glass. 'One more for the road?'

Of course one more turns into two more and then, fired up by champagne, Lulu decides we should head off to a posh sex shop in Covent Garden to buy underwear on an account Randy has set up for me. I thought five hundred pounds was a quite ridiculous sum to spend on underwear, but he insisted that it was the least he could do after the granny-pants debacle, and anyway, wouldn't he get the benefit of it? Once Lulu and I have stopped giggling at the leather spanking paddles and the crotchless knickers, we realize that five hundred pounds won't actually go very far in here. The sales assistant hovers at my shoulder in a too-tight shirtdress, her bra clearly visible under the straining buttons, snapping prices at me with barely concealed hostility as if she's unsure that I can afford them. And if I was spending my own money, she'd be right. The matching toile-de-jouy bra and French knickers set is one hundred and twenty-five pounds, madam. The black broderie anglaise set with foamy lace trim is one hundred and ten pounds, madam. If madam's friend has stopped laughing at it, the rose quartz dildo with fox-brush attachment is one hundred and eighty-five pounds, but if this is to go on Mr Jones's account, I should advise you that Mr Jones has already purchased this item.

'*Has* he now?' says Lulu, waving the fox-brush attachment at me.

'I have never, never seen one,' I insist, flushing

scarlet – and I'm telling the truth. If Randy keeps a suitcase of sex toys under his bed, then I have yet to see them, thank God. Who knows where they've been?

'Oh, he *definitely* has one, madam,' says the sales assistant, her painted eyebrows raised challengingly at me. My blush deepens. Is she implying . . . ? She holds my gaze, smirking, and twirls a strand of long black hair slowly between her fingers. She is definitely implying . . .

'Well,' says Lulu briskly, dropping the underwear on to the counter and staring the sales assistant in the eye. 'I guess some girls need all the help they can get their hands on. Thank goodness you're not one of them, Harrison. Shall we just get these and get out of here?'

'Certainly, madam,' says the sales assistant. She rings up the total in utter silence (four hundred and twenty eight pounds!), painstakingly wrapping each item in tissue paper before dropping them into a paper bag decorated in a jaunty paisley that, on closer inspection, is entirely composed of risqué anatomical illustrations. I feel like I've been standing there, face flaming, for hours.

'I'll add this to Mr Jones's account, madam,' she says finally, holding the bag out towards me by the tips of her fingers. As I reach for it, she lets go of the handles so I'm forced to crouch down and pick it up from the floor. She leans over the counter, teetering on her patent leather stilettos, giving me an eyeful of her bountiful cleavage.

'Do tell him to drop in and settle up with me any time.'

'Oh, I'm sure he settled his account with you a long time ago,' says Lulu fiercely, shepherding me out of the shop before I can hurl a multicoloured vibrator at the shop girl's retreating back.

'Can you believe that woman?' I gibber as we stand in the cobblestoned street. 'Can you *believe* her?'

'I can believe her, darling, and so should you,' says Lulu, steering me towards a small metal table outside the hotel across the road. 'Sit down. We need a drink.'

'Can't we go somewhere else, Lu?' I protest as she places us firmly in the eyeline of the evil sales assistant, who is now gossiping with her colleague at the back of the shop.

'No, darling, don't let her intimidate you. We're going to sit here and let her see us have a lovely drink and a chat in the sunshine while she folds underwear for a living, okay?' Lulu gestures over to a waiter. 'Now. Harrison. Clearly that woman is a spiteful little witch, but if you're going to date the Shagger of the Millennium, I think you've got to accept that you're not exactly part of an exclusive club.'

'Well, I know that, Lu, of course I do. I mean, even Jazmeen Marie has been in touch to say she's had carnal dealings with him – Jazmeen Marie!'

'Yeah, well – her and lots of others, I expect. You're sharing a shag tree with a lot of other women, and you're not going to like all of them. Or any of them, for that matter.'

'Ouch, Lulu – don't try to protect my feelings or anything, will you?'

'Two ginger Martinis, please,' Lulu says, smiling up at the waiter. 'We need the hard stuff, Harrison. It's not up to me to protect your feelings, it's up to you, okay? I know this is all exciting and fun, but you've got to keep your eyes open.'

'Look, I know Randy's got a bit of a reputation,' I say. Lulu snorts into her Martini. 'My eyes are wide open, honestly, Lu. But really – he's different when it's just the two of us.'

'I do understand, darling, I do – after all, I saw his potential while you were still complaining about his hygiene issues. And God knows you needed to get back in the saddle. But something's changed since I last saw you.' She leans across the table to look me hard in the face. 'I can see it. I don't know what it is, but I just want you to be a bit careful. Don't fall too hard.'

'I am being careful, Lu. I don't know where this is going, but, like you said, I'm just trying to enjoy the journey. And I really am enjoying it.'

'Well, I'm sure you're right, darling. Just remember that Randy might be good for you in the short term, but don't go getting too caught up with a guy who's . . . well, who's more of a transitional shag than a long-term prospect.'

I'm suddenly overwhelmed with a desire to own up to it all. To the fake relationship, to the staged encounters, the photographer-friendly embraces, the spontaneous moments that have been carefully choreographed by Camilla. To the subtle shift in our relationship recently, to my confusion about everything. But I can't. Randy and I have only a few weeks left of our fake relationship to run. His US promoters are flying over especially to see his charity gig, and if they think he's back on form (and if his drug tests come back clean), his thirty-city US tour will start in September. And then I'll see whether Randy really is a transitional shag or something more. Until then we're both still play-acting; and I'm not sure if we're still reading from the original script.

'I promise I know how to take care of myself, Lu,' I say. 'Trust me.'

'I do, darling,' says Lulu. 'Now, quick – laugh hysterically, because that silly bitch is looking this way and she needs to see you couldn't care less about her.'

And, actually, with a ginger Martini in my hand, several hundred pounds' worth of posh underwear under the table, my best friend by my side and my hot boyfriend awaiting my return at home, I really couldn't. Everything is so utterly bizarre and ridiculous that it's easy to laugh my head off.

16

When Randy gets home from seeing his personal trainer that evening, I'm ready for him in the kitchen. The toile-de-jouy bra and knickers are not quite covered by a transparent matching chiffon robe, and I am wearing the most ridiculous marabou mules, which are crippling but leg-lengthening in a gratifying way, and just about bearable when I'm sitting down. With my hair artfully pinned up in a manner that looks effortless but took nearly an hour, I'm quite pleased with the overall effect – a sort of sophisticated and pampered housewife who's saucily entertaining a gentleman on the side. With sufficiently dim lighting I convince myself I can pass, if not for Catherine Deneuve in her *Belle de jour* heyday, then perhaps a distant relation. Nina the not-cleaner-but-cordon-bleu-chef has helped me to make a chicken casserole, which is warming in the oven. I plan to thank Randy properly for my shopping spree.

I hear his key in the door and swiftly turn off the kitchen light, leaving just a few candles burning on the kitchen table. I arrange myself as seductively as possible in the agonizing mules on one of Randy's cold plastic chairs. But his tread in the hall is accompanied by another, and I can hear two male voices instead of Randy's usual shout of greeting. Oh, surely not? He's brought someone back? Suddenly my seductive housewife look seems hugely trashy and embarrassing. I glance around the room in a panic – where can I go? As the voices come closer, I have to rule out a desperate rush up the stairs; there's no way I could make it unseen. I lurch towards the larder door and quickly shut myself in, realizing as I do that there doesn't appear to be a handle on the inside. And that, despite the evening sunshine, it's like being shut inside a dark, cold fridge. Great.

'Lizzy?' calls Randy. 'Liz? God knows why it's so dark in here.' The glimmer of light I can see under the larder door becomes brighter as he flicks on the kitchen light. 'Guess she's not home yet.' As if I'd leave candles burning if I'd gone out – is he blind?

'Something smells good, mate,' says Randy's companion in a strong New Zealand accent, confirming his identity as Wade, the personal trainer.

I can hear the sound of the oven door being opened. 'Yeah, it's a stew or something. A Nina the Cleaner special, looks like. Fancy a bowl?'

What? He's not even going to wait for me? He

knew we were meant to be having dinner together this evening. I've been priming him with flirtatious texts since five.

'Yeah, go on, why not?' says Wade, and the legs of a chair scrape on the kitchen floor as he sits down. 'Just a little bit – got dinner with the missus later.'

'Yeah, me too,' says Randy. 'But she'll never know if we make a little dent in it, will she?'

Thanks a bundle, Randy, you old romantic, you. I shiver in the larder and rub my arms to keep warm. I'm absolutely starving, and the smell of the casserole as they take it out of the oven is far too much for me. I fumble along the shelves in the dark in search of Nina's secret biscuit supply, rip open a packet and shove two into my mouth, chewing viciously. They turn out to be Garibaldis, full of evil raisins and possibly my worst biscuit of all time. I eat them anyway.

'Delicious, mate,' says Wade, tucking into my supper. 'Speaking of making a dent in things, got anything to help this stew slide down easier?'

'Are you thinking what I'm thinking?' says Randy.

'Well, it might not be part of your training regime, but it is Saturday night, isn't it?' says Wade with a matey chuckle.

'You're absolutely right, Wade, absolutely right. A beer on a Saturday night is not just a privilege, it's a man's fundamental bloody right. Just wait here a minute.'

Randy's footsteps head at great speed downstairs towards the basement and make a sprinting return, then I hear the hiss of two cans of beer being opened. I am appalled – Randy's house has been a booze-free zone ever since my first visit (well, okay, since my second visit – Randy was so inebriated on my first that he counted as a booze zone on his own). Many's the time I've wished for a glass of wine after a long day at work only to have to make do with a cranberry juice to show solidarity with Randy's sobriety. And all along he's been hiding booze downstairs?

'I keep a secret stash in the gym fridge,' says Randy in a near-whisper, as if he knows I'm hiding only feet away. 'The bloody babysitters would have it off me in a flash if they knew, but as long as I'm not doing any of the naughty stuff, I think I'm allowed to indulge in a bit of the legal stuff, don't you?'

'Whatever floats your boat, mate,' says Wade, and there's a metallic clunk of tin cans colliding as they toast each other.

By the time they've finished, I'm half asleep with cold and boredom at their earnest discussion of sets and reps and carb-loading, whatever that means (though I wonder if it has any bearing on the ten unsatisfying Garibaldi biscuits I've eaten in the past half-hour). The Tupperware box I'm perching on gets more uncomfortable with every minute that passes. I hear Randy take Wade to the door and then return to the kitchen.

There's a click and then a faint beep – his mobile phone?

My mobile suddenly trills in my handbag, which I'd flung on the kitchen window seat when I came in. Not that Randy had noticed it while boozing with his trainer.

'What?' says Randy to the empty kitchen, obviously clocking at last that my phone is in the house, and therefore I must be too. 'Lizzy?' He shouts up the stairs. 'Lizzy, where are you?'

I bang feebly on the larder door, half wanting to be found and half wishing I could just stay hidden in the dark for ever. I feel so ridiculous.

The door is flung open and I flinch in the sudden glare, throwing a hand across my eyes.

'Lizzy?' says Randy, clearly torn between concern and amusement. But not that torn. He starts to laugh as he wraps his arms around me and pulls me towards him. 'Babe, what the frigging Nora are you doing in there? And what are you wearing? You're freezing!'

'I know,' I say crossly. My whole seduction routine is ruined. The Tupperware box has left red lines on the backs of my thighs and I've gone an unattractive corned-beef colour from the cold. Not to mention the Garibaldi crumbs in my cleavage.

'Oh, babe, let me warm you up – you're a block of ice,' says Randy, pulling me on to his lap on the kitchen window seat. I'm too embarrassed to look at him properly, especially as I can feel his shoulders still shaking with laughter. I face primly towards the kitchen door while he rubs his hands up and down my arms until some sensation returns to them at last. He places a finger underneath my chin and turns my face towards his. I keep my eyes downcast.

'Now, my gorgeous girlfriend, can you please tell me just how it is that you feel so cold, but look so unbelievably hot?'

'Really?' I ask, looking down at my finery. 'You like it?'

'Like it? Babe, you look like a million dollars.' He runs a hand over the toile-de-jouy cups of my new bra and pulls me further up on his lap.

'One hundred and twenty-five pounds, actually,' I sniff, daring to glance up at last. 'Four hundred and twenty-eight in total.'

'A total bargain,' murmurs Randy, nuzzling into my neck. 'Are you feeling warmer?'

'A bit,' I say, giggling as he moves his hands lower.

'Warm enough to think about . . . taking this off?' he asks, sliding the chiffon robe off my shoulders and on to the floor. I shiver a little and he looks at me questioningly.

'Oh, I'm definitely warming up,' I say, turning to straddle him.

Suddenly he stands, lifting me as if I weigh nothing; I wrap my legs around his waist and my arms around his neck. His eyes are very dark in this light.

He swings me over to sit on the edge of the kitchen table, kicking the chairs out of the way. 'Warmer or colder?' he asks with a filthy grin and kisses me, hard, before I have time to answer.

'Warmer,' I murmur, reaching for the waistband of his football shorts. 'Warmer; moving towards hot.'

'I should say you are, babe,' says Randy, leaning over me on the table.

The rest of the casserole dries out in the oven, but we're not hungry any more.

17

Camilla's charity gig for Randy has begun to hurtle towards us at great speed, and I'm quite relieved when she finally ropes me in to work on it with her once it's just two weeks away. Her idea of a small underground gig for an invited audience of generous friends and fans has been eclipsed by Jemima's grander ambitions. Jemima has insisted that Declan Costelloe and Jim 'Mandy' Manders, two of her up-and-coming comedy clients, could benefit from the exposure of a gig with Randy Jones, and since she has pointed out that more people in the audience mean more money to charity, Camilla has found it hard to protest (despite the fact that both she and I know Jemima's interest in charity pretty much starts and ends with popping into the Kensington branch of Oxfam once a month in the hope that some old lady might have donated a vintage Hermès Birkin). Now we find ourselves preparing for a major event in the Royal Festival Hall on the South

Bank, an incongruous venue but the only one available at short notice thanks to the unfortunate demise of a Hungarian conductor which has freed it up unexpectedly. The audience will be well over two thousand people, and even at that capacity tickets sold out in just three hours.

As the gig has grown, so has the administration attached to it, which means Camilla and I are in the office until past nine each night making sure that the press tickets are allocated to the right journalists, that the US promoters have the best seats, that the exclusive after-party in a basement bar across the river is hyped enough to be eagerly anticipated by those who are invited, but not so much that we're pestered for invitations by those who aren't, that the two less-famous comedians stop fighting over who gets the better dressing room. A tedious dispute over the precise contents of fruit baskets in the hospitality suite takes me over two hours to resolve, but there is a certain list-ticking satisfaction in sorting out such problems before they can escalate into proper dramas. While Camilla is often absent during the day on her mysterious errands, she always returns to work after hours, ordering in sushi for us both each night until, like one of Pavlov's dogs, the very sight of a maki roll instantly makes me feel exhausted and overworked.

Camilla works furiously in her office; she spends hours on the phone absent-mindedly twirling pens and pencils in her pinned-up hair and then leaving them there until it fairly bristles with them. I think she forgets they're there after a while. At nine-thirty on Friday night I've done all I can for one week, and pick up my handbag and jacket ready to head back to Randy's.

'I'm off now, Cam,' I say, leaning into her office. 'Hope you don't have to work for much longer. It looks like it's all shaping up amazingly.' And it does – for all that it's frantic, we're inundated with requests for comps and special dispensations and plus-ones and press passes. If nothing else, this will be the most anticipated gig Randy has done for years.

'Do you know, I think it is,' she says, brightly. 'I didn't agree with her at first, but Jemima was right – the bigger the better for this gig. I've been speaking to Jamie from African Vision about how much they can do with the money we're raising, and it's really quite extraordinary. Randy's little act of redemption might actually save some lives.'

'It certainly puts the fruit baskets in perspective, doesn't it?' I say, and Camilla laughs.

'Oh gosh, darling, I know. All that fuss over a sodding kiwi fruit. Frankly I'd like to ram one down Declan's throat right now. I mean, what kind of a weirdo is allergic to a kiwi?'

'Oh, you mustn't trivialize it, Cam,' I say, rolling my eyes. 'Declan has a very specific and life-threatening allergy to the killer combination of furry skin and black seeds. In fact, I'm thinking Randy's next gig should be in aid of his terrible affliction.'

'The next gig Randy does after this one, Lizzy,' says Camilla, suddenly serious, 'is going to be the first in his thirty-city US tour. Don't forget what we're doing all this for. How is he at the moment, anyway? Behaving himself?'

'Oh yes, he's taking it all hugely seriously, Cam – he's working mad,' I say, and it's the truth. Randy has supplemented his daily workouts with hour after dedicated hour developing new material with a couple of writer friends. 'And he's absolutely as clean as clean. The drugs tests won't be a problem, I can promise you. He's on really good form. Really good.'

Camilla looks at me with interest. 'And he's still behaving properly where you're concerned?'

I'm not quite sure how to reply to this one. Randy is behaving to me extremely improperly; and with my full and enthusiastic encouragement. But that doesn't feel like a conversation I can have with my boss. And it certainly wasn't part of the deal of being Randy's fake girlfriend.

'Oh yes,' I say. 'He's absolutely fine these days. I don't know what you said to him, but it definitely did the trick.'

'I told him if he messed you around, I'd fire him as a client,' says Camilla matter-of-factly.

I open my eyes wide in surprise.

'You did?'

'I did. Now go off and have a good evening – what's left of it, anyway. I'll see you on Monday.' Camilla smiles and turns back towards her computer.

I walk out through the dark office; a few pools of light show that Camilla and I are not the only ones ending the week with a late one. I wave over at Francoise, Lucy's workaholic assistant, and manage a polite good night to Mel, but I note there's no sign of Jemima. Once she'd manoeuvred her clients on to the bill, she 'allowed' Camilla to make the project exclusively hers. I don't think it's any kind of an accident that Jemima's brainwave has effectively doubled Camilla's workload.

In reception, Winston the security guard puts down his copy of the *New Yorker*, unlocks the front door and wishes me a good evening with a formal little bow.

I decide to take the bus. Camilla always insists on paying for a taxi if I've worked late, but I feel I need a bit more time to think before I get back to Randy's. Camilla has confused me by telling me about her ultimatum. I know she values me as her PA, and that Randy's been a difficult client for her, but why would she be so insistent about keeping him out of Jemima's clutches one minute only to threaten to drop him the next? It doesn't add up. Randy might be demanding – I know that better than anyone these days – but he's also the star client, not just on Camilla's books, but on the whole of Carter Morgan's. His existence allows us to get the rest of our clients the best possible press coverage: without him, we'd lose one of the golden carrots we dangle in front of the media.

Although I can't help but be flattered by Camilla's loyalty to me, I've got to question her judgement in even considering getting rid of Randy. Clearly her renewed efficiency and drive over the last few weeks are only surface-deep. I can see that I'm going to have to keep Randy in line even more than ever. Camilla would be committing career suicide to lose her superstar client. How can she not see that?

18

When I finally make it home, that is to say, to Randy's, Camilla's superstar client is not looking especially super. He has dark lines under his eyes that look as if they've been drawn on with his much-abused eyeliner pencil, and his hair clearly hasn't been washed since his morning workout. When I poke my head round the door of his study, he grabs me into a bear hug until I think I'll snap in half.

'Babe,' he says, 'I missed you. Have you been at work all this time?'

'Yup,' I say into his chest. 'Working like a loon, and all for your benefit, my fake boyfriend.'

'Hey,' he says, pulling away to look at me with a wry smile. 'I thought we'd talked about faking it?'

I know this way of looking deep into my eyes is a trademark Randy-Jones move – God knows I've seen him do it to enough girls in the past – but tell that to the flutter in the pit of my stomach. No matter how much my head says that this is not a real relationship, that for Randy this kind of flirtation is nothing more than a reflex action, my pounding heart begs to differ.

He drops a kiss on the top of my head and reaches over to the desk behind me to pick up a small package wrapped in tissue paper.

'Little something for you, babe,' he says.

I half expect to find it's yet more underwear as Randy's gifts to me over the last few weeks have been exclusively lingerie-based, but the parcel is too small and too heavy.

I open the layers of tissue to discover a small, green book that has definitely seen better days. The corners are battered, the pages yellow. The title reads: *The Observer's Book of British Grasses, Sedges and Rushes.*

I flick through the pages, not trusting myself to speak.

'Do you like it?' asks Randy, looking at me as if he's worried I might burst into tears. And for a moment I think I might. 'I just thought – because of your dad . . . Babe, say something.'

'It's really, really lovely of you, Randy,' I say, unable to stop staring at the book in my hands in case I cry. 'I think it's the nicest thing anyone's done for me in years.'

'We could . . . we could go and, er, check out some grasses on the Heath this weekend if you like,' says Randy hesitantly.

This offer touches me almost more than the present itself. The idea of Randy Jones, international megastar, spending an afternoon painstakingly identifying assorted British grasses is as adorable as it is ridiculous.

'You don't have to do that, Randy,' I say, looking up at him at last.

'Oh, thank God for that, babe,' he says, rubbing his unshaven chin with his palm. 'I mean, not that it wasn't a genuine offer, but really – grass is grass, isn't it?'

He pulls me back into his arms, where I'm happy to stay until, it has to be admitted, the pathos of the moment is overcome, as am I, by a whiff of armpit.

'Urgh, Randy. I say this with a lot of love, but when did you last have a shower?'

'Are you saying you don't love my natural manly scent, my grass-loving girlfriend?' he asks, elaborately sniffing one armpit.

'No, I don't – your natural manly scent is revolting. I hope you're going to scrub up better than this for Lulu and Dan's party tomorrow night,' I tease, poking him in the stomach.

'Now, I was just going to talk to you about that,' says Randy.

I frown. 'You'd better not be saying you're not going to come, Randy – you promised.'

'Of course I'm going to come, babe. Have I ever let you down?' Randy drops a kiss on the top of my head and then sits me down on his chair while he paces about the room. 'But I was just thinking that maybe Lulu and David would like me to say a few words at their party – you know, try out some of my new material, kind of a birthday present for them? What do you think?'

'It's Lulu and Dan, Randy, not David. And, blimey, er . . . I don't know about your saying anything at the party.' In fact I can't think of anything worse than Randy upstaging not only the birthday twins but their aged father, whose speech will have been lovingly crafted for weeks.

'Don't you think they'd like an exclusive gig from Randy Jones? Totally free? And it would be great for me to get some audience feedback before the big gig next week.' Randy is all puppy-dog enthusiasm at his brilliance.

'I think it's an amazingly generous offer, Randy, I really do. But I think they're just thrilled to have you there as a guest. I'm not sure they'd want to make you actually work the party; they'd just like you to enjoy it. Maybe you should save yourself for the Royal Festival Hall.'

Doesn't he see how inappropriate this is?

'I don't mind, though!' says Randy. 'Really, I'd be happy to do it. For them, I mean.' And I do think that, even though Randy has never met Lulu and Dan, he has genuinely persuaded himself that performing at their birthday would be an act of selfless generosity instead of one of naked self-interest.

'I know you would, my lovely one; you're so thoughtful,' I soothe. 'But imagine if one of their guests filmed you on their phone? There are going to be a hundred and fifty people there. It'd be all over YouTube before you know it, and wouldn't that spoil the surprise of the gig next week?' I reach out my hand to Randy reassuringly to let him see that I'm on his side even as I crush his plans.

'Yeah,' he says, taking my hand and sitting down on the edge of the desk, shoulders slumped. 'Yeah, I suppose. I hadn't thought of it like that.'

'Just think how much fresher it will be next Saturday if it's the first time you've performed it in front of an audience,' I say. 'That extra adrenaline will really fire you up, won't it?'

'Yeah. Yeah, you're right.' Randy looks resigned. 'I hope Lulu and David won't mind, though.'

'I'm sure Lulu and David, I mean Dan, won't mind in the slightest.'

I feel I've dodged a bullet for all of us.

19

Having spent the whole week locked away in his study, Randy is ridiculously fired up this morning about attending tonight's party for two people he's never met. He has insisted on buying inappropriately expensive presents for the twins (a diamond tennis bracelet for Lulu and an Omega watch for Dan) and has signed their birthday card with his full autograph, just in case anyone at the party might be in doubt about his identity. I sealed the envelope myself to ensure he didn't have a chance to slip in the glossy 6x4 loitering suspiciously on his desk.

And he's brought in his stylist to spend the afternoon with us, to coordinate our outfits in a way that I'm strongly resisting. Rochelle is convinced that nothing says 'happy couple' like fully matching ensembles, while I'm still haunted by the spectre of Britney Spears and Justin Timberlake dressed in his-and-hers denim at the MTV Awards some years ago. But then Rochelle is a terrifying six-foot diva in a leopardskin minidress with wet-look leggings and towering platform shoe-boots. Her afro hair is teased into a huge quiff that casts an intimidating shadow over me; it is clear we may not share a fashion sensibility. We strike a compromise. I will be allowed to wear my favourite black dress if I submit to wearing jewellery and shoes of Rochelle's choosing; these will colour-coordinate with Randy's ensemble. I veto anything in red (red and black being a bit too Ann Summers for my liking), and Rochelle busies herself in the three suitcases of accessories she's brought with her.

At six, Randy's hairdresser arrives. I would have thought it would take no time at all to tie Randy's thick blond hair back into a ponytail, but Guido insists he must attend to my hair first so that he can devote the rest of his time to Randy's. He sits me in a chair in the makeshift salon he's established in the kitchen, and holds a strand of my hair between finger and thumb. His spotty teenage assistant leans against the sink, watching us sulkily from beneath a directional fringe of an unseen-in-nature aubergine colour with hot pink tips.

'When did you last have your hair cut?' snaps Guido, pursing his lips.

'Er, gosh, not since I've been seeing Randy, probably. So that's at least six weeks, maybe a bit more?' I wriggle uncomfortably in my chair. My hair hasn't exactly been a priority during this chaotic time, but I thought I was getting away with it with my low-maintenance look.

'And your highlights?' He smoothes my parting to show a horribly dark half-inch of roots.

'Umm, probably the same, I'm afraid.' I shrink a little lower in my seat at his patent disapproval. He picks up his scissors and twists my head from right to left, assessing my profile.

'Well, you expect me to work a miracle,' he huffs, hands on his skinny hips.

'No, no, of course you can't work a miracle, Guido, I quite understand,' I say, with an attempt at an ingratiating smile.

'Humpf – you think so, Randy's girlfriend? You think I, Guido, can*not* work a miracle?'

Oh dear. I've obviously said very much the wrong thing.

'I meant . . . I meant that, if anyone could work a miracle, Guido, it would be you. You're . . . well, clearly you're a complete legend. But my hair is a disaster and you don't have all day and, umm . . .' I run out of steam under Guido's withering stare.

'Stop talking, Randy's girlfriend. I need to concentrate if I am to make something of . . . *this*.' He fluffs my hair up with both hands so that it's completely covering my face. There is no mirror in the kitchen, so I stare fixedly into the ends of my fringe while he stands two feet away, sighing in exasperation. For five long minutes

I sit and he stands. Then suddenly he launches himself at me with the scissors. I manage not to flinch as they whirr and snap near my ears, the sounds punctuated only by Guido's exasperated sighs.

Once he's finished snipping at my dry hair, he pronounces himself satisfied but refuses to let me get up to have a look. 'It is not finished,' he pronounces, and his assistant slouches moodily across the floor to take over.

After a heavenly head massage and a blow-dry, Guido reappears and begins backcombing my hair. I begin to recall, with horrible clarity, the huge crimped bird's-nest coiffures that are Guido's high-fashion trademark and have to slide my hands underneath my legs to stop myself from snatching the comb out of his hand. I'm anticipating a vast Marge Simpson-style bouffant, but when he finally allows me to look in a mirror I gasp in delight.

Guido cracks a satisfied smile. 'So I cannot work a miracle, Randy's girlfriend? What do you call this?'

'It *is* a miracle, Guido, a total miracle.' He's turned my fine blonde hair into a fabulous Bardot-inspired sweep high up on the back of my head, with soft, fat curls falling down to my shoulders. A long fringe half-covers one eye. My roots, instead of looking unkempt, suddenly look rock-chick intentional. I've never seen myself like this, and can't stop turning my head from one side to another to admire Guido's work. Somehow it doesn't feel vain; it's not like admiring myself, it's like appreciating an artist's creation that is nothing whatsoever to do with me.

'Now shoo-shoo,' says Guido, ushering me out of the kitchen. 'Out of here now. I need to think about my creation for Randy.' He places his hands on his temples, closes his eyes and takes a deep breath.

'All I ask is that you don't reproduce this,' I say, pointing to my amazing coiffure. 'I'm not sure it's a look that's going to work for Randy.'

'Out!' he shouts, slamming the door behind me.

I head off to my bedroom with the spring in my step that you only get from a ridiculously good hair day, and see that Rochelle has already laid out my black dress on the bed. Despite her attempts to wrestle me into something more fashion-forward, she had to admit that my much-loved softly draped jersey dress, cut low in the front and with a matching V in the back, was the most flattering of all the outfits we tried. She's accompanied it with a pair of gold strappy high-heeled sandals which tie in a bow at the ankle. An armful of delicate gold bangles lies on top of the dress, and sparkling beside them sits a pair of long earrings, whose strands of tiny golden chains are studded with rose-coloured stones.

Remember when I said this wasn't like *Pretty Woman*? Well, I take it all back. I feel like I'm living someone else's life. Someone rich, someone glamorous, someone wonderful. Someone spoiled and adored. I've lost control and gained . . . well, everything.

When I tiptoe down the stairs at a quarter to eight, I am shyly confident that I've never looked better. It's not just my borrowed accessories, or my fabulous hair, or the make-up that Rochelle spent half an hour on. It's a sense that I'm desirable and wanted and cherished in a way I haven't been for years. I'm going to a party with a gorgeous, famous man who can't keep his hands off me. Sensible Lizzy Harrison, with her lists and her routines, and her tiny one-bedroomed Peckham flat, seems a million miles away.

Downstairs is empty. The kitchen is spotless and there's no sign of Guido or his assistant. One of Rochelle's many bags is still in the hallway, so I assume she's helping Randy with the finishing touches to his outfit. I pour myself a glass of cranberry juice and again curse Randy's refusal to have any alcohol in the house. I could do with something to calm my fluttering nerves on my first official outing as Randy's girlfriend. I know I could grab one of the secret tinnies hidden in the gym fridge, but it would mean confronting Randy about his stash, and this doesn't seem to be the time or the place for that conversation. Maybe he's right anyway; as long as he's not touching anything illegal, how much harm can a beer or two do? Best not to rock the boat.

I'm still alone by the time the taxi driver rings on the doorbell just after eight, so I ask him to wait for a few minutes.

'Randy?' I call up the stairs. 'Randy, are you nearly ready?'

I can hear laughter from his bedroom.

'Coming!' calls a voice.

Ten minutes later Randy announces from the top of the stairs, 'Here I am!'

I come out into the hallway to see him posed resplendently on the landing, arms outstretched. 'So? What do you think?'

He looks spectacular and ridiculous at the same time. Like Louis Quatorze in his Sun King pomp, he dazzles in gold, but without the long, curly seventeenth-century wig, thank goodness – his hair looks surprisingly like normal after Guido's efforts. I should have guessed about the golden theme from my own accessories, but I suppose I was lulled into a false sense of security by the delicate and subtle jewellery Rochelle laid out for me. Randy has forgone his usual double-denim in favour of a shiny shoulder-padded gold lamé jacket that is cut in waspishly at his waist and then flares out over his snake hips. Ropes of heavy gold chains loop and jangle around the waistband of his leather trousers; the trousers, thankfully, are not in gold but an unusually restrained black. Gold buckles sparkle on his patent-leather boots. The bauble on the top of his cane – yes, I did say his *cane* – shines in the hall light.

'Wow, Randy,' I say when I finally stop staring, open-mouthed. 'You look . . . astonishing.'

'Thank you, babe,' says Randy, sauntering down the stairs with a careful tread – with heels nearly as high as my own, I'm not surprised he's being cautious. As he gets closer I can see that his black eyeliner has been supplemented by a suggestion of golden glitter up to his eyebrows. I am partly impressed by his effort, and partly dreading what Dan and his rugby mates are going to make of this peacock. Lulu, of course, will love it.

'We really should go,' I say. 'The taxi's been outside for ages.'

'All in good time, my gorgeous girlfriend,' says Randy, adjusting the cuffs of his white shirt while checking his reflection in the mirror. 'All in good time.' He dabs at his mouth (is that . . . lipgloss?) with a finger.

Rochelle struggles with one of her suitcases on the landing. She looks flushed and harried; even her hair is a mess. I'm not surprised – Randy's appearance bespeaks hours of effort. I take a step up the stairs to help her with the bags, but Randy grabs my arm.

'Leave it, babe. Rochelle can manage. You're all right letting yourself out, Chelle?'

'Yeah, you two head off. Have a great night,' she huffs, dragging another bag out of Randy's room.

'Oh, we will,' says Randy, marching ahead of me towards the front door. 'We most definitely will.'

20

Bryan has struck a classic celebrity compromise with the paparazzi tonight. The photographers have agreed not to crash Lulu and Dan's party, or otherwise hassle the guests, in exchange for five minutes of posed snaps at the beginning of the evening. The fact that they wouldn't have known the party was happening at all if it weren't for Bryan's intervention goes unmentioned. And Lulu, of course, is thrilled that the photographs will be posed ones instead of candid snaps, as that way she can make sure she's present in every shot. I've primed her with a text from the taxi, not least because it looks like we're going to be pretty late, but Randy doesn't seem to be bothered.

'It's not being late, it's making an entrance, babe; don't they teach you anything at that PR office of yours?' He crosses a leather-clad leg over mine.

'I know, Randy, I know – but you will remember that

tonight is Dan and Lulu's night, won't you?' I twist the gold bangles on my arm nervously.

'Course I will, babe. I'll just fade into the background, don't you worry,' says Randy, shimmering resplendently next to me in a distinctly foregroundish manner.

The reception we get as we step out of the taxi suggests there will be no fading tonight.

'Randy! Randy!'

'Over here!'

'Randy! Lizzy!'

Never again will I judge celebrities for wearing sunglasses at night. Randy strides confidently towards the pack of paparazzi, but the combined flashes from a crowd of jostling cameras is so overwhelming that I take a step back towards the open door of the Old Brewery, and my heel catches in a paving stone. As I begin to stumble my elbow is caught by an unseen hand.

'Careful, Lizzy,' says Dan, appearing from nowhere in a black tuxedo. I lean gratefully on his arm to regain my balance.

'Dan! How did you know . . .'

Dan smiles and gestures at the paps. 'The noise was just a bit of a giveaway. Not to mention that Lulu's had us standing by the door for five minutes waiting for you. She says we have to have some photographs taken with your boyfriend before we're allowed do anything else – is that right?'

'Sorry, Dan,' I say. 'I know this isn't your thing at all. I didn't mean for Randy to take over.'

We look over to where Randy is now affecting a series of nonchalant poses with his cane, rearranging the chains around his waist as he moves from position to position.

'It's okay. But I'd have thought Randy would at least have made a bit of an effort with his outfit,' he says, unable to suppress a smile.

'Ha, you know Randy – never knowingly under-dressed. At least Lulu looks like she's enjoying it,' I say; she must have passed by in a blur of speed for I haven't even seen her, and yet suddenly there she is, gorgeous in a shimmering green fitted dress, posing at Randy's side.

If you've never seen someone famous have their photograph taken, it's quite the education. There is an extraordinary amount of footwork involved in posing for a casual paparazzi snap: one foot always has to be in front, but with very little weight put on it so that it can be slightly bent. Then the same shoulder as the front leg should be turned towards the press pack for the most flattering angle. Naturally one knows from experience and media training whether to offer one's right or left profile (just you try to see if you can find a single photograph of Mariah Carey's left side). Head tilted, chin slightly dipped, mouth open just a touch, but not enough to look gormless. Minimize a double chin by pressing your tongue firmly on to the roof of your mouth. Keep smiling while you remember all of this, unless you are intentionally going for a moody smoulder, aka sexy face. But be careful if attempting a combination of sexy face and open mouth – the possibility of looking witless increases exponentially. If the photographers can be placed at a slightly higher level than you, then all the better – never, never let them take a photograph from below unless you fancy being foreshortened to Hobbit-like proportions. Tonight they're all massed on the pavement and we'll just have to take our chances.

Lulu has taken to posing as if she's been practising her whole life. As a girl who, aged fifteen, rehearsed smoking while looking in the mirror to ensure she looked cool, I wouldn't put it past her.

'Lulu Miller!' I hear her shout in answer to a call from the crowd. 'M-I-L-L-E-R. It's my birthday party! Well, how old do you *think* I am? It's my brother's birthday, too.' She suddenly appears to realize that Dan and I aren't actually next to her.

'Dan! Lizzy! Get yourselves over here!' She waves at us, beaming.

'Come on then,' says Dan. 'Let's get this over with.'

'Urgh. I do hate having my photograph taken,' I grumble as Dan guides me towards the mob.

He turns to me in surprise. 'Lizzy, you've got nothing to worry about. You look beautiful. You really do.'

He takes up position next to Lulu and squares himself to the cameras, with nary a bended knee nor a flattering angle to be seen. Randy, seeing my approach, grabs my hand, pulling me in tight towards him.

'Where did you get to, babe?' He manoeuvres me into a tight groin-to-groin hold, and I try not to blink as the flashbulbs start up all over again.

By the time we get through the doors of the Old Brewery, every possible combination of Randy plus the three of us has been photographically exhausted: Randy and Lizzy! Randy and Lulu! Randy and Lizzy and Lulu! Randy and Dan and Lulu! Randy and Dan! Randy and Dan and Lulu and Lizzy! The photographers disperse happily, wishing us a good evening. At last we can get on with just enjoying the party.

As we enter the vast brick hall, Randy stops in the doorway and the chattering voices of Lulu and Dan's guests fall silent. He's perfectly still, both hands on the top of his cane, gazing off into the middle distance like a catalogue model; I half expect him to point at a non-existent object, or bring a hand broodingly to his chin. It's the first time since the comedy night in Balham that I've seen him in full superstar mode in front of a crowd, and I can't deny he's brilliant at it. He hasn't said a word, he hasn't made a noise; he's just standing there. But every eye in the room is drawn to him. And a whisper begins to spread around the room. Oh my God. Is it . . . ? Did you . . . ? Isn't that . . . ? What the *hell* is he wearing?

I nudge Randy hard in the ribs.

'Come *on*, you're fading into the background tonight, remember?' I hiss through my teeth.

'I'm not doing anything, babe, just taking in the room,' says Randy, offering his left profile to the guests for a moment. When he's sure he's been fully appreciated from both sides, he reaches for my arm. 'Right, my gorgeous girlfriend, let's show them how it's done.'

We process through the tables, Randy waving beneficently like some sort of potentate accepting the good wishes of his subjects.

Lulu, just ahead of us, waves us over to a table at which her parents are already seated, her mother gently fussing over the table decorations, her father engaging Laurent in stilted conversation. It must have been years since Lulu last introduced them to one of her short-lived amours, and I can see the glint in her father's eye that betrays a hope this might actually be the relationship that brings Lulu one step closer to matrimony.

'Oh, Lizzy!' exclaims Sue Miller, seeing us arrive. 'You look just gorgeous, my love, and this young man must be . . .'

'Randy Jones,' says Randy, grabbing Sue's hand to kiss it with practised charm. 'I thought Lizzy said we'd be sitting with Lulu and David's mother but – you can't be. I mean, surely you're their sister?'

'Oh, goodness, you flatterer!' shrieks Sue delightedly, fanning herself with a name card from the table.

'Their sister! Oooh, I can't tell if I'm burning up from your silliness or from a hot flush.'

'Hot flush,' says Dennis Miller, standing up to introduce himself. 'It's like sleeping next to a furnace. Lizzy, my dear, you look wonderful. And this must be the famous Randy Jones.' He looks Randy up and down with a completely unreadable expression on his face.

'Mr Miller, I'm delighted to make your acquaintance.' Randy bows low with a sweep of his arm. I get the feeling he's channelling the courtly dandy a bit too strongly. What next? Will he drag me on to the dance floor for a series of gavottes?

'Well, I'm delighted you've made it at last.' Dennis looks pointedly at his watch. 'Take your seats. I'm going to say a few words, and then we can get on with the party.'

Dennis points us towards the other side of the round table, where Dan is sitting with a girl I've never seen before. She's a petite brunette whose ample bosom is spilling out of the top of her dull-gold strapless dress. Her dark curls are loose around her heart-shaped face and her big doe eyes are staring up at Dan in simple adoration, even though all he's doing is offering her some water.

'Sparkling, please,' she says in a breathy whisper, and then reverently watches him pour it as if he's enacting a deeply meaningful religious rite.

'Ah, here you are,' says Dan, looking up. 'Can I

introduce you to Emma? Emma, this is Lulu's best friend, Lizzy Harrison.' Her eyes flick over me dismissively. I hate her on sight.

'And this,' Dan continues, 'is—'

'Randy Jones!' she says, so breathlessly that I wonder if she's expelled all the air in her diaphragm with that far-too-tight bodice. She stands up to offer Randy her hand and I see his eyes irresistibly drawn towards her cleavage. To be honest, I can't stop staring myself, just trying to work out how that dress is staying up when so much of her bosom is effectively on top of it instead of underneath it.

'Ravishing, ravishing,' says Randy, kissing her hand. Ravishing? Who does he think he is? The Prince Regent?

'Oh, look,' says Emma, looking up at Randy from under her long eyelashes. False, I bet. 'We match!' And it's true – her dress is a far better match for Randy's golden flamboyance than my understated accessories would ever be. Rochelle would be delighted with the picture they make.

'So we do,' says Randy, slowly looking her up and down. 'So we do.'

'Perhaps you could sit down?' says Dan, pulling out a chair for me next to Laurent. Randy places himself on my other side, next to the supposedly ravishing Emma, who looks thrilled at her placement. Dan stands alongside his seat in between Lulu and Emma and, with a nod at his father, taps a knife on an empty wine glass to silence the room.

'Hi, everyone,' says Dan, and a cheer goes up. 'You go, Windy!' The rugby boys are here in force tonight.

'Before my father says a few words, Lulu and I just wanted to thank you all for coming tonight. We've both been fortunate enough to be guests at many of your weddings,' (another cheer) 'your children's christenings,' (a collective aww) 'and other family celebrations. So we thought, in the absence of anything like a wedding from Lulu or me, we should repay the debt and entertain you all for a change.' Everyone applauds politely, and Randy takes advantage of the break in the speech to quickly pour out some wine for us.

'Should you?' I mouth silently. Randy places a finger on my lips and, with my disapproval held safely at arm's length, empties half his glass in one swallow.

'And in addition,' says Dan, 'my father has been working on his father-of-the-bride speech for nearly fifteen years and has asked to be allowed to deliver a version of it before it's too late. So may I ask you to raise your glasses to my father, Dennis Miller.'

'Dennis Miller,' the crowd murmurs, and after a brief shuffling and shifting of seats, all is silent as Lulu and Dan's father stands up to speak.

Dennis's speech is charming and witty and full of ridiculous stories about Lulu and Dan's youth (even

I hadn't heard about the time when, aged eight, the twins set fire to the living room while attempting to cremate their dead hamster on a homemade funeral pyre), but having Randy twitching and fussing next to me throughout makes me realize it's of limited interest to those who don't know the birthday twins. Or, at least, it's of limited interest to Randy. I can feel his agitation as Dennis fails to build adequate suspense for a punchline, or allows a burst of laughter to drown out an aside. Randy, full of nerves and preparation for his gig next week, can't help himself silently judging my friends' father by the rigorous standards of the comedy circuit, and, naturally, finds him wanting. But Dennis has an appreciative audience in the rest of us, and Randy joins in the applause as he finishes, mostly, I think, from relief that it is over.

'Great speech, Mr Miller,' he says, leaning over the table. 'I can see I've got some competition.'

Dennis smiles back politely; I can tell that, although he might be aware of Randy's fame as an abstract concept, he has no real idea who he is or what sort of competition he is referring to. But I'm grateful to Randy for making the effort.

'That's sweet of you,' I say, leaning over to kiss him on the cheek. He places a hand on my knee and, in one swift movement, pushes my dress up towards the top of my thigh, knuckles grazing my knicker elastic.

'Randy!' I hiss, pushing it back down as I see Sue's eyebrows fly up in surprise. She reddens and looks away.

'Sorry, babe – you know I find it hard to keep my hands off you,' he grins, thoroughly enjoying causing a little scene.

I whisper into his ear: 'Just behave yourself tonight, Randy, and I promise you can misbehave as much as you like afterwards.'

'As much as I like?' he asks, leaning in towards me. 'Now there's an offer I can't refuse.'

Once the meal is over and toasts have been drunk to Millers past and present, we're released from sitting at the tables. There is a sudden rush of guests towards Randy, emboldened by alcohol into grabbing their moment with him. Several giggling girls have their photographs taken with him by their unsmiling boyfriends, but Randy charms even these disgruntled swains with self-deprecating jokes about just being here as a plus-one tonight.

The rugby boys bundle over as one, and Randy, to his credit, pretends to remember them all from the night at the Queen's Arms, even though he and I have long established that he recalls nothing at all from that first encounter. Johnno, Bodders and Bangers delight in reminding him that they were the ones who carried him to the minicab, while Dusty and Paddy are careful to make sure their own contribution (picking up Randy's jacket and keys from the floor) doesn't go unremarked. Randy greets them all as dear friends, and the boys return to wives and girlfriends with a certain swagger, and with autographed place cards clutched in their beefy fists. I give Randy a little wave over the heads of his fans and decide to leave him to it for the moment.

It doesn't take more than a few brief conversations with other guests to realize that all anyone really wants to talk to me about is Randy. I can hardly recall some of the people from my youth who come up to remind me of our close friendship and to express a desire to catch up soon, perhaps with my new boyfriend? Even Sue Miller can't resist dragging me over to meet her friends from the Jacob's Well Amateur Dramatics Society, who whisper and giggle amongst themselves before admitting they hope I might bring Randy to the first night of their September production of *Calendar Girls*. I murmur politely to Linda (Miss April) about Randy's existing commitment to his US tour before excusing myself.

I've seen a kind of bunting hung around the walls of the vast hall, and, as I wander over to inspect it, I discover that it's entirely composed of photographs of Lulu and Dan throughout their childhood. Two tiny babies nestle in a brown tartan blanket; it's impossible to tell which is which. Dennis Miller's resplendent sideburns bristle in the upper left corner of the picture as he gazes at them adoringly, though it must have been hard for him to see anything over those vast wing collars. Here's the infant Lulu, desperately earnest in a leotard and ballet shoes, one chubby leg extended in front of her, toes pointed. Here's Dan, carrying a football in what must have been a momentary flirtation with the game. Ah, here he is looking far more comfortable with a rugby ball tucked under his arm, his stripy socks falling down and two front teeth missing. As I move along the lines of photographs, the years pass. School uniforms change. Dan is suddenly a foot taller than his sister. Oh God, here I am, lips liberally frosted with Rimmel's Heather Shimmer lipstick while Lulu, already firmly on her career path, secures my hair in a side ponytail. Her own hair is, of course, far more adventurous – she must have hit hairdressing college by this time: the top of her Louise Brooks bob is peroxide blonde, while the bottom is raven black. It looks like a large bird has pooed on her head.

'Weird how you can tell the year just by what Lulu's hair was like,' says a voice behind me. 'It's more accurate than carbon-dating.'

'Jeez,' I say, turning around to see Dan. 'It's completely terrifying to see all of these pictures – where did you dig them up from? And what did we think we looked like?'

'Yeah, it was fun going through them all,' says Dan as we walk slowly along the row of pictures. 'Brought back lots of memories.'

'Most of them hideous,' I say, grimacing at a picture from the late Eighties. 'Check out my turquoise and pink paisley dungarees in this one.'

'I think you looked cute,' laughs Dan.

'Cute?' I ask doubtfully. 'Do you mean cute as in "looking like a colour-blind lesbian"?'

'Nah,' he says. 'More cute like a *blind* colour-blind lesbian.'

'Thanks, Dan,' I say. 'You sure know how to flatter a girl.'

It feels good to be back to normal with Dan – to shared jokes and teasing instead of that strange tension that's come between us ever since I started seeing Randy. I realize I've missed him over the last few weeks.

I stop at a picture of Dan and me in the early Nineties. I'm giving it full grunge in a long black cardigan, shredded at the sleeves, worn over a floaty floral dress with ripped tights and eighteen-hole Doc Martens. My dark-lipsticked mouth grins uncertainly from between limp curtains of long, mousy-blonde hair – so far from the glorious curly mane of Pearl Jam's Eddie Vedder to which I aspired (I still maintain that hair was wasted on a man). Dan looks tall and hearty and timeless in – what else? – a rugby shirt and jeans.

There is a clear two feet of space between us, as if someone invisible were standing there and pushing us apart.

'Dan, you know –' I say, nudging his arm with my shoulder – 'all those years of taking the piss out of you for always looking the same, and now I see your rationale.'

'You do?' he asks, eyes crinkling into a smile.

'You look exactly the same in every single one of these pictures, you total bastard!' I laugh. 'Lulu and I go from ridiculous outfit to ridiculous outfit, but you – you haven't changed one bit since you were sixteen. You're unembarrassable. It's so unfair.'

'Oh, I don't know,' says Dan, shoving both hands in his pockets and hunching his shoulders. 'I remember being pretty embarrassed in that picture.' He nods his dark curls in the direction of my grunge-era shame.

'Were you?' I ask, peering at it. 'Why? You don't look any different now.'

'Don't you remember it being taken?' He turns to look at me, raising a questioning eyebrow.

I look more closely at the photograph. 'Well, I know where it is – your back garden. The blue shed gives it away. And I know from the clothes and hair that it's before I went to university, so – early Nineties? But I don't remember the actual picture being taken.'

'I do,' says Dan. 'You and Lulu were going to a gig—'

'We were? Who were we going to see?' I ask, not

getting any clues from my clothes. I never was the band T-shirt type.

'Probably one of your bands with the stupid names – Carter the Unstoppable Dustbin or something.'

'Sex Machine,' I say automatically. 'Carter the Unstoppable Sex Machine.'

'Whatever,' says Dan, laughing. 'I'd found you on your own in our kitchen . . .'

Now I do remember.

I'd been crying over some stupid bass player in a band who'd just dumped me after a hot and heavy three-week relationship, and once the tears had started, I'd found I couldn't stop. I was crying about everything and nothing, about Dad and hormones and how life was just generally unfair and dreadful. I hadn't wanted Lulu to see, so I'd snuck off downstairs to weep alone.

'I remember,' I say quietly, still looking at the photograph.

Dan had come into the kitchen and, without saying a word, had wrapped me in his arms. I hadn't even known he was there until that moment. I'd cried into his shoulder for a full five minutes before I could get a hold of myself. Dan had kissed the top of my head and, as I'd turned my tear-streaked face up towards his, he'd very gently pressed his lips on to mine. Almost immediately we'd both heard the sound of Lulu thundering down the stairs.

Dan and I had leapt apart as if our bodies burned.

Two seconds later, Lulu had burst into the kitchen demanding that Dan take a series of pictures of us in our best clothes before we headed off to the Windsor Old Trout. The final picture, of Dan and me, she'd taken herself. No wonder we both look so uncomfortable. That night, at the gig, I'd met a floppy-haired indie kid called Matt, with whom I enjoyed a ridiculously tempestuous on-off relationship until I went to university at the end of the summer. I'd forgotten all about that moment in the kitchen until now.

'Do you?' says Dan. 'Do you remember?'

Even though my eyes are fixed on the photograph, I am intensely aware of his every movement, and I can tell he is turning to look at me.

Suddenly I'm grabbed from behind in a huge bear hug and swept off my feet.

'Wa-hey!' says Johnno, swinging me round. I didn't actually think people said 'wa-hey' for real – I thought it was one of those words like 'kapow' or 'oof' that you only see in cartoons. But Johnno has just shouted it unmistakably in my ear while performing what feels like the Heimlich manoeuvre on my abdomen. My feet scrabble for the ground.

'All right, Johnno,' says Dan, only slightly betraying his weariness as we are suddenly surrounded by the full complement of his rugby friends. Bodders, Bangers, Dusty and Paddy all look a little embarrassed as they mumble their hellos.

'Great party, mate, great party,' says Johnno, finally putting me down and straightening his Homer Simpson cummerbund. 'Just came over to say that while you're chatting up the lovely Lizzy over here, it looks like someone else is chatting up your bird.'

I think I realize before Dan does that this almost certainly has something to do with Randy. We turn as one to see that the crowd around Randy has now dispersed. He has sat back down at the table, where he's deep in conversation with Emma. If I thought Emma was staring at Dan with divine adoration, that was as nothing to how she's staring at Randy. Dan was merely a minor saint, the sort whose desiccated finger might be sealed in a reliquary; Randy is the full Messiah. Her eyes flick upwards to his mouth every few seconds before dropping down to the table in front of her as if she is terribly shy. But the way her hand is placed on his leg has nothing shy about it. Randy's head is bowed low as if to catch her every word, but I suspect it's more to get a better look down the front of her dress. One golden arm is snaked around Emma's hips. For one moment I am struck by the image of the two of them, shiny and beautiful together.

And then my stomach lurches. What does Randy think he's doing? Don't I mean anything to him at all? I leave his side for ten minutes and he's instantly putting the moves on someone else. On Dan's girlfriend!

I feel Dan start next to me. 'What the fuck?' He turns to face me. 'Lizzy, are you okay?'

'I'm fine,' I say in a small voice. 'Are you?'

'I'm fine,' he says, teeth clenched. 'But Randy fucking Jones . . .'

I know I mustn't let Dan see how angry and upset I am. I can see that he'd happily punch Randy given half the chance, and that can't be allowed to happen. Not only will it ruin the party for everyone, but Randy's gig is next Saturday and I've promised everyone that I'll keep him under control until then. Getting into a fight is not a part of the deal.

'Look. Leave this to me,' I say, getting a grip of myself. I put my practical work-head back on. Randy is my so-called boyfriend second; above everything else he is a client who's about to get himself into trouble. It's my job to stop him. 'Let's not cause a scene. Randy can't resist a bit of female attention – that's all this is.'

'That's all this is?' says Dan furiously, backed by the full Greek chorus of rugby boys who surround him, arms folded and faces florid with anger and alcohol.

'Bloody disgrace,' mutters Bangers in Randy's direction.

'What kind of a way is this for him to treat you?' says Dan, pulling at my arm as I try to move away. 'Or for him to treat Emma, for that matter, pawing her under your nose and mine?'

'Mumble-mumble . . . rip off his bollocks . . .' goes the rugby boys' chorus.

'Right, that's it,' says Dan, taking a step towards the golden couple. I clutch at the lapel of his dinner jacket in a manner that would, in other circumstances, make me want to laugh. Any minute now I'll be shrieking, 'Leave it, he's not worth it!' like someone from *East-Enders*.

But instead I turn to face the rugby boys, still holding Dan by his jacket so he can't make a run for it. 'Dan. Johnno,' I say. 'Paddy, er . . . boys. You are all so lovely and chivalrous to be looking out for me like this. But this is between me and Randy, and I'd really appreciate it if you'd just leave it to me. I can handle it.'

'It's between me and Randy, too, Lizzy,' growls Dan, still trying to move towards the table where Randy and Emma are utterly oblivious to the scene they are causing.

'No, it's not,' I say, holding on tightly until my knuckles are white. 'Dan, please – for me. Let it drop.'

'Let what drop?' says Lulu, appearing from behind the rugby boys with Laurent in tow. 'What *are* you boys all doing huddled together like this? Starting up a scrum?'

Oh, thank God – I could kiss her.

'You know what the boys are like, Lu,' I say, instantly relieved. 'They think that because Randy's talking to Emma, my honour is somehow at stake!'

'Oh, is that what it is?' says Lulu, peering over at the table and swiftly assessing the situation. 'Honestly, what is Randy like? He's so hung up on maintaining his lady-killer reputation, he can't let it rest for a moment, can he? You should've seen him pretending to try it on with me earlier!'

Laurent frowns and I see Lulu squeeze his hand, hard, to silence him.

'You know,' she says conspiratorially, and all the boys, even Dan, lean in closer to hear her, 'he'd absolutely run a mile if he thought Emma was serious. It's all show, isn't it, Lizzy?'

'Absolutely,' I say, far more confidently than I feel. 'He'll be quite relieved when I go over there to rescue him – just you watch.' I exchange glances with Lulu and she flicks her eyes over to the table quickly. Under her breath she whispers, 'Go!'

I approach the table on wobbly legs. For all my bravado, I have no idea how Randy is going to react when I spoil his little flirtation. In nearly all the time we've spent together it has been just the two of us; I've never had to compete with anyone else for his attention. As I get nearer, I see Emma look up. Her eyes widen and she nudges Randy, who lifts his face from where it has been hovering over her cleavage for the last five minutes.

'Hello, Randy,' I say calmly.

'Babe!' he exclaims, leaping up from his seat and

standing unsteadily next to me. 'Have you met the ravishing Emma?'

'Yes, of course – Dan's girlfriend,' I say pointedly.

'Oh, I'm not Dan's girlfriend,' she says, giggling. 'We've just been on a few dates, that's all. I'm not tied to anyone at all. Not unless they want me to be.' She giggles at Randy again, and he grins back.

'Isn't she lovely?' he says to me, nudging my side as if I'm going to join him in appreciating her finer points. And I think I know which of her finer points he's most interested in: the ones that are about to pop out of the top of her dress.

'Ravishing,' I say, smiling grimly. I can see I'm going to have to raise my game a bit here. I drape my arms around his neck so he's forced to look directly at me.

'Randy. I think it's time we went home, don't you? You've been good for long enough,' I say, sufficiently loudly that I might be overheard.

'But I'm really enjoying myself,' protests Randy unrepentantly, his wine-soaked breath on my face, 'and the dancing hasn't even started yet.'

'I'm just really, really ready for bed, Randy,' I say, staring pointedly into his eyes – or I would be if they weren't a little unfocused. Frankly, I would like to take my hands from behind his neck and use them to throttle him instead, but I know I have to get him out of here with the minimum of fuss, and this is the best way to do it.

'Well, why didn't you say so?' says Randy with a gentle hiccup. 'Come to think of it, I'm ready for bed myself now. And . . . Emma?'

'What about her?' I say.

'Well, babe . . .' Randy looks like a small child begging for sweets. 'You did say if I behaved properly then I could misbehave as much as I liked later.'

I keep my arms round his neck in a semblance of devotion – I can feel the eyes of the rugby boys' chorus upon us – but every part of me has tensed into stone. 'Let me get this straight, Randy Jones. Are you . . . are you actually asking for my permission to take another woman home with you tonight?'

'Not with *me*, babe,' says Randy, pawing at my side in what I assume is supposed to be a persuasive manner. 'With *us*. Don't you think it would be fun? You said she was ravishing.'

'Jesus, Randy!' I say, far too loudly, and then drop my voice to a whisper. 'What the *fuck*? No, I do not think it would be fun to take Emma home with us. I can't believe you even suggested it.'

'But you said . . .' says Randy sulkily. It's clear he doesn't think he's done anything wrong. In fact, he seems to believe that I am the one who's spoiling everything.

'Randy,' I say warningly.

'I'm just so bored of being good,' he says, eyes downcast. 'Can't we liven things up a little?'

'Randy.' There's nothing else for it. I reach into my arsenal for the one weapon that I know will silence him. 'What do you think Camilla would have to say about this?'

Five minutes later we've said our goodbyes and are in a taxi home.

That night we sleep in separate bedrooms.

21

Randy and I still haven't spoken by the time I leave for work on Monday morning.

His house is so vast, it's easy to avoid someone if you really want to, and he spent all of Sunday either downstairs in the gym or locked in his study. At one point I knocked on the door, but there was no answer. When Lulu called for a Sunday afternoon post-mortem, I had to conduct the entire conversation in a hissed whisper, so sure was I that my voice would carry in the mausoleum-like silence. But actually Lulu did most of the talking. Apparently she'd spent the rest of the evening dancing on a table, but this is hardly gossip, just standard behaviour. It seems Laurent, while Lulu was otherwise occupied, had danced so energetically with her mother that Sue's ankles had swollen so much that, even by Sunday afternoon, she still couldn't get her shoes on. Dennis had accepted a whisky-downing challenge from Bodders and Dusty at one a.m., and was the only one able to walk out of the Old Brewery without assistance afterwards. And finally, Dan and Emma had had an argument and she'd tried to storm out, but he, ever the gentleman, had insisted on seeing her home. He hadn't come back to the flat in Brixton until eight that morning.

When Lulu asked me how things were with Randy, I just said everything was fine. I didn't feel like going into the whole story, and Randy's pointed ignoring of me had made me start to doubt myself. *Am* I too uptight? I would never have gone along with his threesome idea, especially not with Dan's date as our third party, but what does it say about our relationship that Randy wants to liven it up so soon? I thought we'd moved beyond my being the sensible babysitter and him being the dangerous reprobate, but now I'm not so sure. Is he bored of me already? Either way, Lulu is the veteran of at least two threesomes in her past, though she swore off them after the last one ('Just a bit too much like hard work, Harrison – two lots of everything'), and I know she wouldn't share my instinctive horror at the very idea.

Wade calls for Randy at seven, and I'm out of the house by seven-thirty. There's no time for a morning run or a proper breakfast when everything's so hectic in the office. I pick up two coffees on the way, anticipating that Camilla will be at the office before me as she was all last week. But when I get into the office, the person sitting at Camilla's desk is Jemima.

'Lizzy,' she says flatly, looking up from the papers spread on the desk in front of her. There's not even a hint of embarrassment that she has been found sitting in her colleague's office at eight in the morning. In fact it's as if she's expecting me.

'Camilla had to go to a last-minute breakfast meeting – she called me earlier. So I'm sure she won't mind if I take her coffee.' She reaches out a hand, her painted nails grasping towards me.

'Okay,' I say slowly, putting the paper cup on the desk and pushing it towards her as I might to a homicidal maniac who is holding my entire family hostage. No sudden moves, no letting them see you're scared, just play along.

'Sit down,' says Jemima, snatching up the coffee and taking a sip. She makes a face. 'Full-fat cappuccino?'

'You're welcome,' I say sweetly.

She smiles a tight little smile. 'I just thought you and I hadn't had a chat for a while – you've been so busy, what with one thing and another.'

'Yes, well, one thing and another seems to be going just fine,' I say, holding my own coffee in both hands in case I need to use it. Maybe I'll have to throw it as a distraction if she lunges at me in a crazed rage. What does she want?

'And how does Camilla seem to you?' Jemima leans forward on the desk, her eyes glinting. Don't let the homicidal maniac see you're afraid, I think. Keep calm.

'Just amazing, Jemima,' I say. 'She's really on everything at the moment. This gig for Randy is going to be a triumph.'

'And has she . . . has she said anything about what happens afterwards?' asks Jemima, twisting the paper cup round and round in her hands as if it's the neck of a small bird she's trying to strangle. I half expect her to let out a hysterical cackle.

'Afterwards? When Randy goes on his US tour?' I don't understand. 'Well, I guess we hand him over to the US promoters and let them handle him for a change.'

I haven't really been thinking about afterwards. Everything to do with Randy and Camilla has been so of-the-moment that I haven't given any thought to what happens beyond the gig at the Royal Festival Hall. But Jemima has a point. What *will* happen afterwards? Will Randy want me to go with him to America? Or will he want me to wait for him in England? Suddenly I feel a bit sick. Maybe he'll just be glad to be rid of his fake girlfriend. Maybe he'll forget all about me the moment his plane leaves Heathrow. Maybe he'll be picking up golden, ravishing Emmas in every single city in America. Having threesomes with non-uptight girls each night. I'll have to go back to my flat in Peckham. To my meals for one. To Sunday nights alone on the sofa instead of wrapped in my boyfriend's arms. Suddenly my life before Randy seems hopelessly flat and lonely and dull.

'I meant with Camilla,' says Jemima, interrupting my thoughts.

'With Camilla?' I echo, my thoughts still with Randy. I still have no idea what she's on about. Remember, I tell myself: she is maniac, I am hostage negotiator. Must keep control of this conversation.

Jemima is clearly thinking exactly the same thing and enunciates every word of her sentence as if it is me who is the nutter: 'Has. Camilla. Said. Anything. To. You. About. Afterwards?'

Mimic their speech patterns to show empathy, make them think you're on their side: 'No. She. Hasn't.' I say carefully. 'I'm not sure I'm quite understanding the question, Jemima.'

'Oh, I'm sure you are,' says Jemima, smiling her thin-lipped smile and standing up. 'Camilla has a lot to thank you for. I used to wonder how she'd cope without you. But now I find myself wondering how you'd cope without her.'

She stalks to the door of the office leaving me sitting there, frowning in confusion.

'Thanks for the coffee,' she says and click-clacks off down the corridor on her pointy heels. Really, she gets madder and madder every day.

Camilla's in the office at ten. No deliveries to the nursery today; she glides in serenely with a huge smile on her face.

'Good breakfast meeting?' I ask.

'Oh, golly, I wasn't at breakfast, I was at Randy's final drugs test before the gig,' she beams, plonking herself down on the edge of my desk. 'Didn't he tell you? He insisted I should come to the clinic for the results to see for myself that he's clean as a whistle.'

'Oh yeah, yeah, he mentioned something about that,' I lie. 'Everything was okay?'

'Of course it was, my lovely Lizzy – everything is working out just beautifully.'

Camilla strides confidently into her office and closes the door. Immediately she picks up the phone. I'm beginning to wonder if there isn't something in what Jemima says. Camilla is up to something.

When I check my mobile at lunchtime, there's another message from Jazmeen Marie. I really don't know why she persists in calling me – there's absolutely no way I'm interested in a girly heart-to-heart with her. She's the kind of famous-for-being-famous starlet whose every holiday (inevitably in some resort in Dubai that has given her a room in exchange for publicity) ends up with her being snapped, totally unawares of course, adopting a series of calendar-girl poses while frolicking in the surf. Or with her bikini top falling off. She's been engaged four times. She's twenty-two. You know the sort of thing. I'm in no doubt that she's telling the truth when she says she's had a fling with Randy – she's absolutely his type. Or was before rehab. I'm only surprised that I haven't yet seen her side of the story all over a Sunday tabloid. Perhaps she thinks that speaking to me would give her a different angle for her exposé? Whatever her reasons, I'm not interested in speaking to her, and I delete the message from my voicemail.

The American tour promoters are flying in on Friday night, so I confirm their reservations at the Connaught and speak to the driver at the car service that will be driving them around over the weekend. I can practically hear him rubbing his hands with glee at landing this job; everyone knows that Barry Spiller and his business partner (and life partner) Nolan MacDonald are fabulously generous tippers. If you can just stop staring at the fact that, courtesy of multiple facelifts, Barry's eyebrows have migrated so far north of his eyes that he's had to have new ones tattooed on, and that his face never moves a millimetre, then you, too, could be in line for one of the bank notes he spreads liberally in his wake. Barry once dropped fifty pounds in my handbag when he thought I wasn't looking, and all I'd done was pick up two doubleshot decaf soy lattes from Starbucks. I want them to have the best of everything for their own sakes because they're both delightful, but I also want to be sure they have no excuse not to give Randy their full attention on Saturday night.

So I anticipate everything. I make sure the Connaught knows they have to have fresh flowers every day – but no lilies as Nolan is allergic to them – and inform the staff that they share a weakness for Terry's Chocolate Oranges (which they can't get in New York), so please could the suite's usual fresh fruit be replaced with several of the foil-wrapped chocolates in a bowl. Two Diptyque candles in Baies should be lit twenty minutes before their arrival. Nolan will have had to leave his beloved miniature schnauzer, Whitman, behind in New York, so (after enduring Dave the Comedy Courier's latest routine, 'Feeling Con-naughty today, are we, Lizzy?') I bike over a box of Fortnum & Mason dog biscuits wrapped in a MacDonald tartan ribbon for him to take back with him. I agree with the concierge at the hotel that, although I would never for one moment suggest that the coffee at the Connaught is anything less than first class, they will send someone out for Starbucks whenever required as Barry will drink nothing else. The minibar must be cleared of alcohol as Nolan is in recovery, and restocked with Lipton Ice Tea and Diet Coke. I book the River Café for six people on Friday night, and ask them to ensure there is no repeat of the Christopher Biggins incident during Barry and Nolan's April visit (which, as it is still in the hands of lawyers, I regret I cannot share). I make a reservation at the Wolseley for Saturday brunch. I ensure that

Randy's most recent DVD is prominently placed in their suite. I am sure I have forgotten something.

Sometimes I wonder how it would feel to be like Barry and Nolan, or, indeed, Randy. Your every wish anticipated, your every whim accommodated. It must be a bit like being the Queen, travelling in a bubble in which the world always smells slightly of fresh paint, nothing ugly or difficult is allowed to intrude, everyone genuflects in your direction and laughs at your jokes whether they're funny or not. At least no one calls Randy ma'am. All of a sudden it doesn't seem so weird that he has chosen to check out of this world every now and again. He probably thinks hanging out with his dubious druggie mates is somehow keeping it real. The grubbier the bedsit, the more authentic the experience, the further from the air-conditioned sterility of your average celebrity encounter. I'm almost beginning to feel a bit sorry for him when the phone rings again.

'Camilla Carter's office,' I say briskly.

'Is that Camilla Carter's wonderfully efficient not to mention gorgeous PA?' says a familiar voice.

'Why, yes, it is,' I reply in my best nineteen-fifties telephonist's voice. 'How may I be of assistance, caller?'

'Well, you could assist me by forgiving me for Saturday night,' says Randy. 'And for not speaking to you on Sunday. I think I let the stress of the gig get to me.'

'And the alcohol,' I say.

'And the alcohol,' he replies obediently. 'I shouldn't have drunk anything. I don't know what got into me.'

'About a bottle of red wine, I should say.'

'I'm sorry, babe. I'm sorry for getting pissed.'

'So you bloody should be, Randy – not just for my sake, but for yours. It's less than a week till your gig. Do you really want to risk everything?'

'I know, Lizzy, I know. I'm sorry. And I'm sorry about Emily, too.'

'Emma,' I say, stupidly pleased he can't remember her name.

'Emma, yeah. Look, I should have realized that threesomes weren't your thing.'

'Well,' I say, suddenly brisk and efficient as I see Mel passing down the corridor within earshot. 'That's not something I feel like discussing at work. But thanks for apologizing. It means a lot.'

'So am I forgiven?' asks Randy hopefully. He really does think it's this easy. He says sorry and that's it.

And yet being cross with Randy for being Randy feels like being angry with the sky for being blue. At least, I tell myself, Randy wasn't going behind my back here. He might have made an error of judgement, a drunken one, in trying to recruit Dan's date for bedroom antics, but it was just to make things fun for us. He's got different expectations of a relationship from me, but that doesn't mean we can't work it out. It's not like he was trying to play away, more that he wanted to add someone else to the game. Lulu's right. If I'm going to have a relationship with him, then I'm going to have to accept him just the way he is.

'Of course you're forgiven, Randy,' I say, and really try to mean it. I want this to work. I don't want to go back to my old life. To being single, sensible Lizzy Harrison.

'I'll make it up to you when you get home,' says Randy. 'I promise.'

'Okay, Randy,' I say. 'See you later.'

I'm pretty sure I know what his idea of making it up to me involves, and for once the idea doesn't give me a thrill of anticipation. It just makes me feel a bit tired. In Randy's world, it seems, sex is both the problem and the solution. It's the apology and the cause of the apology. It's the alpha and omega of Randy's existence. But this is what being with Randy means, and aren't relationships all about compromise? I have to remember this. I've been single for too long. I've become inflexible. My expectations are unrealistic; for all that I've scorned the cliché of the happy ending, I was beginning to believe that I might get one. I need to remember that this isn't some candyfloss fairytale confection of a relationship; it's real. At least I think it is. And I'm going to make it work.

Camilla interrupts my thoughts by appearing at my desk looking anxious. 'Lizzy, darling, has someone been in my office today?'

'Er, yes – Jemima was at your desk when I came in this morning, but she seemed to suggest . . . well, the way she spoke to me, I – I thought you knew all about it,' I say, wrong-footed. I should have told Camilla about Jemima as soon as she came in.

'Was she now?' says Camilla. Her eyes sweep over the office from corner to corner as if it might be bugged. 'Good to know.' She shuts her door and picks up the phone again. Quite honestly I wish that her office *was* bugged – by me. At least then I'd have a chance of knowing what's going on with her right now.

Out of the corner of my eye I watch her swivelling on her chair between laptop, office phone and Black-Berry. Her forehead is furrowed with concentration as she reaches into her bag and grabs a silver strip of pills. She pops out a couple, knocking them back with a swig of water and a shake of her head. She looks like the before picture in one of those adverts for indigestion or headaches or unspecified female 'bloating', whatever that is. I wish I could tell her what's been going on with Randy – she'd know exactly how to handle it. But what would be the point? She's busy enough already, and everything else is going so well. Why risk her firing Randy just days before everything's sorted for good? I can take care of it. There's no need to worry her.

Lizzy Harrison has it all under control.

22

As I descend the office steps that evening, scanning the road for the glowing yellow light of an available taxi, I hear someone calling my name from across the street. Standing outside the darkened windows of Pret a Manger with his hands in the pockets of his tan-coloured trench coat is Dan. He moves shiftily from foot to foot, looking anxiously up and down the street as if he were a secret agent instead of a desk-bound lawyer. What can he be up to? Why didn't he just call my phone like a normal person?

'Greetings, Agent Dan, the swans fly low over the Volga tonight,' I say as I approach him.

'What?' says Dan, hesitating halfway towards kissing my cheek.

'Well, what do you look like, hanging out on a street corner like someone from a dodgy spy thriller? Aren't we meant to be talking in code?' I tease, but he's not smiling. In fact he looks distinctly grim.

'Look, Lizzy, I need to talk to you,' he says. 'I thought if I met you from work I might actually be able to speak to you on our own for once. No interruptions.' He pushes his fingers through his tangled curls, looking down at me with a serious expression.

'Okay, Dan. Goodness, it must be something important,' I laugh, not used to this unsmiling, intense version of Dan Miller.

'It is,' he says. He takes my elbow and leads me towards the ropy pub on the corner of the street. Even though it's merely steps from our office, I've set foot in here precisely once before. No self-respecting Carter Morgan staffer would pass through the doors of the Dog and Daffodil unless an emergency dictated the need for a medicinal drink. It's not the sort of place you'd choose to spend time in unless you had no alternative. The menus are laminated, the tables are sticky and the bar staff greet each new customer as a trying interruption to their demanding schedule of taking it in turns to smoke outside and play on the quiz machine in the corner. The pub dog, a Staffordshire bull terrier with the short, squat dimensions of a footstool, is notoriously aggressive in its pursuit of crisps, pinning unsuspecting customers into corners to get its jaws on their cheese and onion Walkers. After my one visit two years ago, a desperate lunchtime drink with Lucy while Camilla was on maternity leave, I returned to the office to discover my purse had been stolen from my bag.

'Yeah?' says the girl behind the bar, without looking up from her copy of the *Evening Standard*.

'I'd like a bottle of San Miguel, please,' says Dan. 'Lizzy?'

I ask for the same, less out of a desire for beer than the feeling that I'm less likely to get a second-hand smear of lipstick on a bottle than on a wine glass. Dan leads us over to a table by the window, where a blue-jellied air conditioner on the window sill engages in an unsuccessful battle with the odour of ancient cigarettes that clings to the brocade curtains. I put my bag on my lap, clamped between my knees in case anyone comes near me with devious intentions. I'll admit I've felt more relaxed.

'Dan, I just need to tell you that I can't stay long – it really will have to be just the one,' I say.

'I know all about you and Lulu and Just The One,' says Dan, cracking a smile at last. 'Just The One usually ends with Lulu scrabbling at the door at two in the morning having lost her keys.'

'Ha, I know, but I really do have to get back to Randy's. He's expecting me,' I say.

It's like shutters have come down on Dan's face. All trace of his smile disappears.

'Randy. That's what I wanted to talk to you about,' he says.

'Is this about Saturday night?' I ask, fidgeting in my seat. Do we really need to go over this again? 'He's really sorry about it all. So am I. But there's no harm done, is there?'

'Maybe not to Randy,' says Dan.

'Is this about Emma?' I feel a disturbing pang of jealousy at the memory of Randy's head bowing low over her golden cleavage. And of Dan's angry defence of her.

'Look, Emma and I . . . ' Dan looks uncomfortable. 'The thing is, there isn't any Emma and me – we had a long talk on Saturday night, and we agreed to be just friends.'

'Dan, I'm sorry if Randy messed things up between you. He'd be mortified if he knew,' I say.

'It's not that, Lizzy,' says Dan crossly, slamming his beer bottle down on the table. 'Look, it's just that Emma said some things about Randy—'

'I'll bet she did,' I snap, leaning back in my seat and crossing my arms, ready to hear the worst.

'What's that supposed to mean?' says Dan, his eyes narrowing.

'I'm just saying that he's only human. He was pissed and she was throwing herself at him.'

'Are you blind?' asks Dan in disbelief. 'He was all over her.'

'She certainly didn't seem to object.'

Dan's eyebrows are drawn together in a deep frown and his eyes have gone dark with anger. I can see that he's struggling to keep his temper.

'What I'm trying to say, Lizzy, is that Randy said

some things to Emma that I thought you should know about.'

'Is this about the threesome?' I ask, and Dan looks horrified.

'Threesome? Is that what he . . . ? Jesus, that wanker.' He glares out of the window as if Randy might be standing there on the pavement to be scorched by his furious stare. 'No, it's not about a threesome. Look, I know this isn't what you want to hear about Wonder Boy. In fact Lulu says I shouldn't be having this conversation with you at all.'

My stomach clenches with dread.

'Maybe you shouldn't,' I say.

'Lizzy,' says Dan sternly. 'I couldn't forgive myself if I didn't tell you what Randy is saying behind your back.'

Oh God, Randy thinks I'm boring. He hates me. He thinks I'm hideously unattractive. He can't stand spending time with me. He thinks I'm rubbish in bed. Whatever it is, now Dan knows it too. I can't bear it.

'Lizzy.' Dan's voice has become much more gentle and I flinch – if he's trying to be kind then he must be about to tell me something truly awful.

'Yes?' I whisper, hardly able to look at him.

'Lizzy, I don't want to upset you, but he told Emma that his relationship with you was fake. That you weren't his real girlfriend.'

'He said what?' I almost want to laugh with relief.

'He said,' says Dan very carefully, as if each word might wound me, 'that your relationship was set up by your boss to help rehabilitate him in the eyes of the public, and that you didn't mean anything to him.'

'I can't believe it,' I say with all honesty. I truly can't believe that Randy has been idiotic enough to reveal the truth, especially to a stranger, but I'm not sure I can bring myself to lie to Dan's face. And yet the idea that Randy is telling people I mean nothing to him has hit me with unexpected force. There's nothing pretend about how upset I am.

I look down at the table so that Dan can't see my confusion.

'Thing is, I know it's total bollocks,' says Dan.

'You do?' I ask wonderingly. Is Dan about to unwittingly defend me against the truth?

'Of course it is. I know you'd never get involved in something like that,' he says firmly, and I feel a wave of guilt wash over me. 'I'm just worried that this is what Randy's telling other people. Girls, I mean. It's obvious he's saying this to go behind your back with other girls.'

'Dan,' I say, peeling a beer mat off the table and tapping it nervously on the edge, still not looking at him. 'I know it's hard for you to believe – it's probably hard for lots of people to believe – but I do trust Randy.'

Dan snorts in disbelief and takes a violent swig from his bottle of beer.

'I do,' I persist, intently folding the beer mat into squares. 'You don't know what he's like when it's just us. I don't think he'd do anything to hurt me. I think he was just leading Emma on, saying what he thought she wanted to hear. You know, letting her have her "the time Randy Jones put the moves on me" moment.'

'You really think that?' says Dan, pushing his chair away from the table in exasperation. 'You really think that if you hadn't been there to stop him he'd have just gone home by himself for a cup of Horlicks and a night on his own?'

'He doesn't need to be on his own, Dan,' I say, the beer mat now shredded beyond recognition by my nervous fingers. 'He's got me.'

I'm not just trying to convince Dan. I'm trying to convince myself.

'Right,' says Dan, looking angrily across the room to where the pub dog is noisily rearranging the furniture in search of abandoned crisps. 'Right. Well, good luck, Lizzy. Good luck with that.'

'Thanks for looking out for me, Dan,' I say, trying to get him to meet my eyes, but he's fixated on the stupid dog. 'I know you're only trying to help.'

'Yeah,' he says, pulling his coat off the back of his chair and looking at his watch. 'I guess I shouldn't take up any more of your time. You'll be wanting to get back to your boyfriend, won't you? Probably best not to let him out of your sight. You've no idea what he'll be up to when you're not there.'

I raise my eyes to his.

'That's unworthy of you, Dan,' I say quietly.

'Is it?' he says, standing up. 'I guess I'm unworthy of you too, now that you're involved with your famous boyfriend.' He stands over me accusingly. I'm about to answer when the barmaid appears between us, slapping down a wet grey cloth on the table.

'Finished?' she says, holding my beer two inches from my face as if she's about to hit me round the head with it. Dirty water from the cloth drips from her hands on to the table.

'Finished,' I say, finally releasing my bag from between my knees to stand up. The barmaid takes both bottles in one hand and pushes the shredded beer mat to the floor with the cloth. I squeeze past her as the pub dog comes over to investigate.

Dan stands by the door.

'Bye then,' he says stiffly.

'Dan, don't be like this,' I say, tugging at his sleeve, but he pulls away from me and pushes out of the door.

When I pass him in a taxi five minutes later, he's storming down the pavement, hands deep in his pockets, his dark head bent so low I can't see his face at all.

I don't understand why I can't have a conversation with Dan these days without arguing with him. My reliable rugby-shirted friend, the quiet backstage presence to Lulu's dramatics, has somehow pushed himself forward to front of stage, and I'm not sure I like it. This angry person, so disapproving, so critical, is not the person I thought I knew. If it wasn't Dan and me we're talking about, I'd think there might be something behind this sudden change of personality. I mean, if this were a movie, this would be the point at which I'd realize in a lightbulb moment – fountains springing into life behind me, fireworks above my head – that Dan's dislike of Randy stems from his passionate love for me. I'd be all, 'Woe is me, for I am torn between two lovers. On whom shall I bestow my hand?' But this is me: sensible Lizzy Harrison, who, far from being torn between two lovers, has only a possibly fake boyfriend to her name. And this is Dan: Lulu's brother, who has known me for more than half my life. Aside from that long-ago kiss in the kitchen, Dan has never so much as held my hand. If he's secretly in love with me, he's managed to keep a lid on it for over twenty years, which hardly suggests he's overcome with unstoppable passion, does it?

I'm not entirely discounting the fact that Dan might have developed a little crush on me lately – that would explain a few things – but if there was anything more to it, wouldn't I have heard all about it from Lulu? She's incapable of having a thought without broadcasting it to the entire world, and if she had the smallest suspicion that Dan had feelings for me, I'd never hear the end of it.

Anyway, I tell myself, it's not worth overthinking this. Even if it turned out that Dan was madly in love with me, I have a boyfriend already. Haven't I?

23

Watching from the wings as the Royal Festival Hall fills up, I can't believe we've actually made it to this point.

There has been a minor scrap between the merchandise sellers in the foyer (but Mandy Manders' mother was persuaded to sell her home-made T-shirts elsewhere), and I had to personally remove the kiwi fruits from the hospitality suite before allergic Irishman Declan could see them (even now I have six of them rolling about in the bottom of my handbag), but everything else is running better than we could ever have imagined.

I wave to Barry and Nolan, sitting in a box to the left of the stage and impossible to miss, thanks to Barry's towering candy-floss bouffant (the box has the best seats in the house, but is also the only location in which Barry's hair won't obscure the view for someone else, as it rises into a Mr Whippy-style point several inches above his forehead). They blow me kisses and indicate something small and orange in Nolan's hand, which I can only guess is one of the Terry's Chocolate Oranges I had placed in their suite. A light behind them causes them to turn round, and there, silhouetted in the doorway, is the unmistakable Lego snap-on hair of Jemima Morgan, no doubt there to bore them about Declan and Mandy's chances of a US tour. Honestly, can't she appreciate that tonight is meant to be about Randy?

There's a tap on my shoulder and one of the riggers suggests I should shift my arse out of there unless I fancy being brained by a large piece of set dressing. With one final glance at the box, where Barry and Nolan appear to be paying attentive court to Jemima, I head back towards the hospitality suite. All three comedians are already in their dressing rooms – Randy has banned any visitors until after his performance, and the others have followed suit, even though they aren't exactly besieged by fans, being practically unknown. Camilla is firmly shooing our special guests away from the warm white wine and Twiglets and towards their seats. It is part of her strategy never to provide anything too enticing in the hospitality suite (artists' dressing rooms are a different matter), as she says that tantalizing canapés only make people linger when they should be watching the show. To my surprise, as the room clears, I see Nina the Cleaner refilling her glass in a corner of the room.

I almost didn't recognize her, wrapped in a patchy grey fur stole, her cheeks rouged to match a floor-length red dress whose gigantic shoulder pads and satin-effect material suggest it first saw active service in the mid nineteen-eighties. Nina will be totally unaware of it, but her look accidentally catapults her into the realms of contemporary high fashion.

'Wow, Nina – you look like a movie star,' I say, and I mean it.

'Huh, like movie star's mother, maybe,' she says, draining every last drop of wine from her glass with one tilt of her head. 'Randy gives me a ticket for a present, isn't it? He's good boy, really. Except,' she whispers, primly folding her hands under her substantial bosom, 'he leaves the ticket at the box office in name of Nina the Cleaner, not Nina Naydenova.'

'Oh, he is awful,' I say, trying not to laugh. 'I expect it's because he can't spell your last name – you know what he's like. I'm sure he'll be thrilled that you came. Shall I take you to your seat?' I offer, not that she isn't perfectly capable of making it there herself, but there is something rather queenly about her this evening which makes me think she might like to be escorted.

She holds out an imperious arm. 'Yes, Lizzy. Take me to my seat.'

The house lights are already dimming as I lead her to the second row from the front. She bows her head graciously to everyone as they stand up to let her pass to her seat in the middle, and people crane their necks to see who she might be. I overhear someone suggesting she might be Randy's mother, and think I must remember to tell him this afterwards, as he banned his own mother from coming because there would be 'language'. I guess he assumes Nina is made of tougher stuff. I see her settle into her seat and pull out a large packet of biscuits, offering them generously to the rather surprised people next to her. I leave her to it.

Camilla is lying on a sofa in the hospitality suite, eyes closed, her hair splayed out behind her and her shoes kicked off on to the floor.

'Cam, are you okay?' I ask as I come in.

'Urgh. Put a bowl of Twiglets on the floor within range and I'll be as right as rain,' says Camilla without getting up.

'And a glass of wine?' I offer.

'Hmm, I wasn't going to drink until we get to Savoy Street later. But go on, just the one. You won't want to drink more than one once you've tasted this bloody awful plonk.'

I pour us each a glass and put Camilla's on the floor next to the Twiglets. I lie on the other sofa and close my eyes. From the stage I can hear the faint sounds of Jamie from African Vision introducing Declan, the first act. It's all going according to plan. I breathe a huge sigh of relief.

'Cheers, Camilla,' I say. 'Here's to you and to the rehabilitation of Randy Jones.'

Camilla swings her legs down on to the floor and sits up. She grabs her glass and raises it towards me. 'Here's to *us*, Lizzy. This is your success every bit as much as it's mine. I couldn't have done any of this without you.'

'Oh, pssht,' I say, embarrassed but happy. I have worked like a dog. Like a dog who has been having a passionate fling in the name of work. But Camilla doesn't need to know that bit.

'I mean it,' she says. 'You've been amazing. Especially when I . . . well, when things were a bit chaotic earlier this summer. I hope I never forgot to thank you for everything you did.'

'Cam, you're always thanking me – don't be crazy. I'm your PA – I'm just doing what I'm meant to be doing.'

'Well, when all of this is over, we should have a talk about what happens afterwards.'

'Afterwards,' I say.

There it is again. Afterwards. Everything I've been trying to avoid thinking about is contained in that one word.

'Afterwards?' demands a shrill voice from the doorway, and Camilla leaps in her seat, spilling wine all over her wrap-dress. Thank God I chose the nasty Italian white for her instead of the nasty Hungarian red. I grab a handful of paper napkins from the table and pass them to her.

Jemima strides into the room in a structured metallic dress that might be incredibly fashionable but which, combined with her fiercely blunt bob, makes her seem even more like an emotionless automaton. 'What's this about afterwards?' she barks.

'Lizzy and I were just discussing the after-party at Savoy Street,' lies Camilla, so smoothly that I almost forget that's not what we were talking about at all. 'Lizzy thinks that mini Yorkshire puddings with roast beef are hopelessly passé these days, but I don't agree. What do you think?'

'Canapés?' snaps Jemima, swivelling her head between Camilla and me. 'You were talking about canapés? Hmph.'

She turns on her heel, strides to the table and pours herself a glass of red wine.

'Jesus, what is this stuff?' she says, grimacing.

'Horrible, isn't it?' I say, swigging from my own glass. 'We're saving the good stuff for Savoy Street, of course.'

'Of course,' says Jemima. 'How many people are we expecting there?'

'A hundred and fifty seven on the guest list,' I say as she picks viciously at a plate of cold meats like an expensively dressed vulture.

'Right,' she says. 'Make that a hundred and sixty seven. I invited a few extra.'

I glance over at Camilla behind Jemima's back. This is the first we've heard of any other guests.

'Did you put their names down with the club secretary, Jemima?' asks Camilla calmly. 'You know it's a private club so it's named guests only.'

'Why would I have done that?' says Jemima, turning to face us. A piece of ham dangles threateningly from her talons as if she's about to throw it at us. Can a flung slice of ham do much harm, I wonder? 'That's a job for a PA. Lizzy can sort it out, can't you?'

She stares at me challengingly.

'Er, I'll do my best,' I say, looking at Camilla for confirmation.

'I hope you do,' says Jemima. 'We'll call it a little test, shall we? Of how things will go . . . afterwards.' She stalks out of the hospitality suite and into the corridor where the artists' dressing rooms are. I hear a door slam.

'She's probably gone in to speak to Mandy before he goes on,' says Camilla as a burst of applause suggests that Declan's set is over. 'Look, I know Jemima can be difficult, but it's not in your interests right now to get on the wrong side of her.'

'But Camilla, it's totally unreasonable! How am I going to get them on the guest list when I don't even know who they are?' I protest.

'You'll get there early, before Randy's set is over, and speak to Rebecca Iveson,' says Camilla, whose soothing tones are belied by an unmistakable clenching of her jaw. 'In fact, call her first. She's very reasonable and I'm sure you can think of some way to persuade her. Look, I need to make a phone call, so why don't put your feet up for a bit and then go and watch Randy from the wings later? I'm sure he'd appreciate your support.' She gets up and disappears off down the corridor herself, and I hear another door slam.

I have absolutely no idea what's going on between Camilla and Jemima now. What was once just an uncomfortable undercurrent in the office has progressed to open skirmishes. It can't be long before we're into a full offensive, and I'm still not sure what the stakes are. Or whether Camilla has any kind of battle plan. The fact that she's letting Jemima walk all over me suggests not. God, I'm tired of this. I close my eyes on the sofa for a moment and take some deep breaths as taught by Mum. In through the nose, out through the nose.

'Heavy breathing, are we, babe?' says a voice. Randy is looming above me, blocking out the light with what appears to be a tricorne hat trimmed with ropes of gold braid. The frayed ends of a leopard-print scarf tickle my nose as it hangs from his neck over a loose white shirt. I can hardly see his skinny legs, covered up as they are by a pair of thigh-high black patent-leather boots. Underneath the boots he appears to be wearing . . .

are they? Yes, they do appear to be horizontally striped leggings.

'Well, shiver me timbers, Randy,' I say, sitting up and rubbing at my eyes in case this is just an illusion. 'You look fantastic.'

'Rochelle calls it urban pirate,' he says, shifting from foot to foot, eyes rapidly scanning the room despite the fact that we're the only two people in here. He wipes the back of his hand under his nose and pulls it away with a disgusted expression. 'God, I'm sweating already.'

'Are you nervous?' I ask, because this jumpy, edgy Randy is a new one to me. I guess it must be stage fright.

'Nervous?' he laughs, grabbing me into a hug. 'Of course I'm nervous, my gorgeous girlfriend. Tell me I'm fabulous.'

'You're going to be wonderful, Randy, I know it,' I say, flinging my arms around his neck. 'The new material is amazing. You'll blow them away. Don't forget Barry and Nolan are to the right of the stage from where you're standing. Give them a wave or something, won't you? Just let them see you acknowledge them.'

'All right, babe,' says Randy with an annoyed little shrug. 'Don't forget I was doing this for quite a few years before I met you.'

'God, sorry – I didn't mean . . . I just so want this to

go well for you, Randy,' I say, putting my hands either side of his face. 'You've worked so hard.'

He leans down and kisses me.

'So come with me to the wings, my lucky charm, and watch me work a bit harder,' he says, pulling me by the hand towards the stage. I feel like my stomach has taken up residence halfway up my throat. If this is stage fright by proxy, how is Randy not hurling into a bucket by now?

'You again,' says the exasperated rigger when he sees me. 'I told you—' but then he spots Randy. 'Oh right. Sorry, mate. Didn't see you there. Manders is due off any minute. All good to go?'

When Randy finally steps out on stage, there is no doubt that his public is ready to forgive him. There is a roar and the crowd leaps to its feet. I can see Barry and Nolan applauding from their box, and then looking approvingly at each other as the applause goes on and on and on. Randy stands in the centre of the stage, arms outstretched, eyes closed, absorbing it all.

'So,' says Randy, when the cheering and whooping stop. 'A few things have changed in my life lately.'

'You're still gorgeous,' shouts a voice from the audience.

'Why thank you, darling – aren't you delightful? And yes –' he flexes an arm, which is hidden under his billowing shirt – 'I have been working out, madam. Thank you for noticing. Yes, my lovely audience, you see before you the new, improved Randy Jones. Leaner and cleaner and meaner than ever.'

The audience cheers and applauds. Barry and Nolan nod happily to each other: they've seen the drug tests to prove it.

'I've even got a new girlfriend. Oi, Lizzy, give everyone a wave.' He motions to me to come on stage, and I protest, shaking my head. This wasn't part of the new material he showed me at home. Suddenly I'm shoved, hard, from behind, to stand like a lemon on the side of the stage. I give a small wave to the faceless mass and race back into the wings, where Rochelle, resplendent in leopardskin, is standing with an intent look of such innocence on her face that I know she must be the culprit.

'Ahh, she's lovely, isn't she?' says Randy from the stage. 'I'm not used to dating a girl with a brain. Take my last girlfriend before rehab. We were talking about deductive reasoning, as you do when you're in bed with a nineteen-year-old model from Estonia. Yeah, deductive reasoning. Well, you've got to pass the time somehow, haven't you? So anyway, I asked her if she knew what a syllogism was. And do you know what she said? She said, "I know what jism is, Randy."'

The crowd screams its approval and I decide to retreat backstage for the rest of the gig. Rochelle raises a questioning eyebrow as I beat my retreat. It's not that I don't think Randy is brilliant – I do; but it's clear his set is going according to plan, and I need to get that phone call in to Rebecca Iveson at Savoy Street. Now that I've thought about it, I can see a way forward. She's wanted Randy as a member for years; their reputation is just a touch stuffy (a few too many purple-nosed over-fifties snoozing in chairs after lunch) and needs the oxygen that someone like Randy would bring. But so far he's turned down all her offers of free membership. If I can get him to say yes tonight, and I'm sure I can, then surely she'll turn a blind eye to a few extra guests at the party.

In the hospitality suite, Camilla is deep in conversation with Jamie Welles, the director of African Vision. I decide it's best to make my phone call elsewhere. The door to Declan Costelloe's dressing room is open and it seems he's holding an impromptu party: people are spilling out into the corridor and it's altogether too noisy for any kind of serious phone call with Rebecca. Randy's dressing-room door is firmly shut but when I try the handle it opens, thank God. I let myself in and close the door behind me, leaning against it. It's perfect. Quiet, soundproof and empty. I flick my mobile open and dial Rebecca's number.

It rings and rings. Savoy Street has the dubious distinction of being the only members' club in London that's entirely underground. This is great if you want to get away from insistent mobiles and buzzing BlackBerrys as they simply don't work there. But when you're actually trying to get in touch with someone, it's infuriating. While it rings, I wander around Randy's dressing room which, if I didn't know him better, I'd think had been ransacked while he was on stage.

A suitcase lies abandoned on the floor, clothes piling out of it as if trying to escape in one tangled mass towards the bathroom; crushed under a pair of silver-buckled ankle boots I can see the gold lamé jacket Randy wore to the party last week. The preponderance of leopardskin – scarves, belts, hats, gloves, even tights – betrays Rochelle's influence, and I assume hers, too, are the alligator platforms left abandoned by the armchair. That woman is not satisfied unless some part of her form is disguised as an exotic animal. I stuff the clothes and shoes back into the suitcase and close the lid; tempted as I am to fold everything up properly, I have to satisfy myself with getting them out of sight for now. I pick up an assortment of magazines and newspapers from the armchair in a corner of the room and rearrange them on the table so there will be somewhere to sit when Randy gets back. A sweep of my arm shunts a grubby collection of apple cores, peanut shells and cereal bar wrappers into the bin. I put the half-empty water bottles back in the mini-fridge.

I give up on Rebecca's mobile and dial the reception desk at Savoy Street instead. It rings and rings again as they try to transfer me.

The dressing room already looks vastly improved by

my little tidy-up, so I head into the bathroom to see what can be done there. As I expected, every surface is covered with some sort of beauty product. Randy is as obsessed with skincare as any one of my female friends, and can happily debate the merits of all the major brands with absolute authority. There's Clarins Beauty Flash Balm, MAC Strobe Cream and Yves Saint Laurent Touche Éclat; there's Laura Mercier Mineral Powder dusted all over the sink, into which a fat black brush has been dropped and is being dripped on by the tap. I move it on to the counter to dry out. Eye-shadows of every colour jostle up against six different kinds of black eyeliner and two eyelash curlers. A mascara wand is drying out underneath the glowing bulbs that surround the mirror. The open container must be somewhere around here, I think, grabbing a make-up bag to make a start on clearing this up. As I move it, something behind it catches my eye. It's not make-up.

'Rebecca Iveson,' says a voice on the other end of the phone.

For a moment I can't answer.

'Rebecca, it's Lizzy Harrison. Sorry, I'm going to have to call you back.' I snap the phone shut and look again at the counter.

The distinctive remnants of two fat lines of coke are visible next to a rolled-up tenner. Randy's credit card lies incriminatingly next to them.

I start to scrabble around – where's the rest of it?

There's got to be a wrap here somewhere – he wouldn't have done a whole gram at once. No wonder Randy was all sweaty and jumpy, the absolute little fucker. All I can do now is make sure he doesn't do the rest of it tonight or he's going to ruin everything.

But I can't find it anywhere.

24

'Oh, Lizzy, my dear, I *love* what you've done with him,' says Barry, descending the stairs at Savoy Street in a cloud of Chanel Égoïste with a purple quilted man bag tucked under his arm.

'Er, sorry?' I say, greeting him with a kiss on both cheeks. My head is so full of the party and the guest list and how to get between Randy and his coke at the soonest opportunity that I have no idea what Barry's on about. Not to mention I think I'm getting a contact high from his aftershave.

'With Randy, my dear. He was wonderful, just wonderful, and we hear it's all your doing. Quite the vision of good health, and clearly he owes all that new material to your influence. You're wasted as a PA, my dear. Nolan and I are quite agreed that you have found your new role as artist's muse. Aren't we, Nolan?'

'Quite agreed, my dear,' says Nolan. 'And I hear we have you to thank for the divine doggie cookies for

Whitman. You are marvellous.' He leans over to bestow a paper-dry kiss on my cheek.

'Now we need to celebrate Randy's upcoming US tour, my dear, so let's enjoy the party.' Barry offers me his arm.

'Really?' I say, grabbing his arm with both hands. I have to hear him say that again. 'You're definitely going ahead with the tour?'

'After tonight we'd be fools not to,' says Nolan. 'The boy is back on form.'

'Oh, Barry, Nolan – that is so fantastic! Have you told Randy yet?'

'Of course, my dear,' says Barry. 'He's just on his way here with Camilla. He was busy signing autographs for his slavering fans when we left. Now come on, I need a drink.'

'I'll have to join you both later,' I say with a shrug, indicating my door-Nazi clipboard. 'I'm on duty for a bit. Just a few guest-list issues to sort out.'

'But they can't have Mrs Randy Jones on the door, my dear,' says Barry, scandalized, hand flying to his throat. If he could have raised his eyebrows any higher, he would have. 'You need to be at his side to share the triumph. Leave this with me.' He pats my hand reassuringly.

He and Nolan process down a further flight of stairs towards the main room and I can hear, floating up the stairwell, cries of greeting. It's only just gone ten and the room is already nearly full. Rebecca has kindly turned a blind eye to the extra guests, who are hoovering up canapés as if the party was being held entirely for their benefit. I guess I shouldn't have expected anything else from Jemima's friends. Jemima herself stalked in just ten minutes ago with Mel dutifully in tow like a pilot fish on the fin of a shark.

I scan the guest list. There are only nineteen names left to be ticked off, two of them Randy and Camilla's. Normally I'd expect at least a third of the guest list to be no-shows, but Randy's after-party has been the hot ticket all week. Jazmeen Marie's voicemail messages to me have become ever more plaintive over the last few days – I guess she had her heart set on an invitation. But then so did everyone else. The photographers outside are gearing up for a bumper evening. I can hear them now, shouting as the door upstairs is opened.

'Randy! Randy!' The flashes illuminate the stairs as Randy trips down them in his thigh-high boots, tricorne hat in hand and Camilla following in his wake.

'Lizzy Harrison!' He grabs me and swings me off my feet. 'I'm going to America!'

'Randy, you superstar. I'm so proud of you!'

While I'm outwardly congratulating him, I'm also wriggling a little out of his grasp, trying to look properly into his eyes. Has he done more coke?

'Jesus, Lizzy-Liz, that was amazing – did you hear the crowd at the end? Three times I had to go back for more applause – three times! Then the door was mobbed coming out – we had to get security to take us to the car, and even then they wouldn't let us leave. Oh my God, they loved me. Randy Jones is back! Is everyone here? Enough people for me to make an entrance?' He pushes his hair off his face three times before replacing the tricorne hat, eyes flicking from my face to the stairwell and back again, and again and again.

Er, yeah – I think I would say he has done more coke. But maybe he's just high from coming off stage. It's hard to tell. Hopefully everyone else will think it's just exuberance, too. I feel like an undercover narcotics cop as I mentally scan his outfit for his hidden coke, but it's not like he's attempting to smuggle a kilo through customs. It's probably just one tiny flat wrap and it could be anywhere. The band of his hat? The pocket of his shirt? Down his boots? Surely not secreted inside the skin-tight leggings, but I can't discount it.

'Definitely ready for your entrance,' I say, continuing my surreptitious surveillance (hidden in the purple ring?) and waving the clipboard under Camilla's nose so she can be primed as to who's there already. She scans it swiftly and hands it back with a nod.

'The room's jammed, Randy – they're all waiting for you. Barry and Nolan can't stop going on about how wonderful you were.'

'That lovely pair of old fruits – let me at them,' says Randy, turning as we hear a thudding tread rising up from the stairs that lead down to the party.

The heavy footsteps slowly reveal themselves as belonging to Mel, who is ascending the stairwell at glacial speed. Her mouth is screwed up into a sulky little twist, her eyes narrowed as she glares in my direction. And then she spots Randy.

'Hey, wow – congratulations, Randy,' she beams, skipping up the last few steps towards him. 'You were amazing!' She attempts to flick her hair in a flirtatious manner, but as she is unwisely attempting to make homage to Jemima's trademark lacquered and sprayed bob, everything stays resolutely and unflirtatiously rock-hard and unmoving. Instead she looks like she has an unfortunate tic of the neck.

'Thanks, babe,' he says mechanically, looking beyond her as if she wasn't there. 'They all ready for me downstairs?'

'Oh yes, they're all waiting – the party hasn't started until you get there, Randy. Jemima says—'

'Great,' says Randy, hurtling head first down the stairwell without a backwards glance at the three of us left on the landing. There is a roar from the room as he opens the door, and Camilla smiles with satisfaction.

'Barry says you're to go downstairs and I'm to look after the door,' intones Mel flatly to me, her flirtatious ways instantly abandoned.

'Thanks, Mel, that's really good of you,' I say, schooled by Camilla Carter to be nice no matter what.

'Just go,' she says, rolling her eyes and grabbing the clipboard from my hands. School of Jemima Morgan.

'Right then,' says Camilla briskly. 'Ready for battle?'

And she's not kidding. It's carnage down there. The noise and heat of the crowded room hits us like a wet towel as Camilla opens the door. I spot Rebecca standing behind the bar, her usually elegant composure slightly dampened by a cloud of steam from the bar dishwasher. One sweating barman hauls a crate of empty champagne bottles towards the kitchen; another is opening new bottles as fast as he can and handing them to the ridiculously beautiful waitresses who squeeze their way through the crowd. No one even gives these women a second glance: so intent are they on having their glasses refilled that they could be being served by Quasimodo for all that they notice. The champagne's been flowing a little too freely and I can't see a single tray of canapés in circulation to sober people up. All is explained when I spot a pack of hungry guests hovering expectantly by the swing doors to the kitchen. No sooner does a tray emerge than it is picked clean in seconds. The waiter has to retreat for new supplies before he's taken two steps into the room. Because we're deep underground there's no air conditioning, and the combination of all these people and all that booze has turned the place into a furnace. Coiffures wilt, foreheads glisten, mascaras run; even Barry's Mr Whippy bouffant is drooping. Suspicious drips fall intermittently from the low, arched, painted-brick ceiling. Jemima gives a fierce look upwards as one lands on her snap-on hair, as if the ceiling can be compelled into dryness by the sheer force of her withering stare.

Camilla glides off into the throng towards Jamie from African Vision, who greets her with an exuberant kiss before introducing her to his companions. Nina the Cleaner is offering an enchanted Nolan MacDonald one of her biscuits – I hope it's a shortbread; he's obsessed with his Scottish roots. Randy's tricorne hat bobs above the crowd, though how he can bear to wear it in this heat, I don't know. Next to the hat is Barry's diminished bouffant, and next to that Rochelle's quiff, not even slightly affected by the atmosphere. I think her hair is probably too afraid of her to misbehave. As long as I can keep my eyes on Randy, I don't think I need to be glued to his side all night, so instead of going straight to him I head over towards the bar to check on Rebecca.

'Everything okay?' I ask, leaning across the concrete surface.

She grimaces cheerfully. 'Jesus, they can drink! Are you okay for me to open more champagne or do you want to move on to wine yet?'

'Stick to champagne,' I say. 'It's a celebration.'

'Jim – I'm afraid you're going to have to head to the cellar for more,' Rebecca says to the barman, who's only just straightening up, a hand on his back, from shunting the empties aside. His white shirt clings to his retreating shoulders as he wearily leaves the bar. She turns back to me. 'And the canapés are nearly finished,' she says, nodding in the direction of the kitchen, where the waiter is being mobbed once again.

'Thanks to that pack of vultures,' I groan, looking over at Jemima's cronies. 'Is there any way the kitchen could rock up some bread and cheese? And chips? Anything to stop this lot getting any more pissed.'

'I'll see what I can do,' she says, and pushes her way through the crowd to the kitchen.

I owe her. I make a mental note to courier her a present first thing on Monday. Camilla's account at Liberty's will have to take a hit for this.

Squeezing past a young couple who are energetically getting to know each other in a corner that is not as discreet as they think it is, I make my way over to a cluster of reviewers and newspaper diarists who are all noisily comparing notes on Randy's performance, the party in general and the behaviour of the other guests. If I want to know what's going to be in the papers in the next week, this is the place to be. Caspian Latimer, the *Telegraph*'s young and gangly arts reviewer, turns to greet me, nervously pushing his glasses up his nose, only to have them slide down again.

'Ah, hello. So very nice to see you.' He wipes his hand on his tweed jacket before proffering it to me, which is a thoughtful gesture but one I rather wish I hadn't seen. 'Very nice indeed. Randy was very good. Ah, very good indeed.'

Poor Caspian, a Classics graduate from St Andrews with a passion for antique furniture of the Edwardian period, is far more at home at the Royal Academy than in Savoy Street, and it's not just his tweed jacket that's making him uncomfortable here. But he's scrupulously honest and I know he'd have politely avoided saying anything about Randy's show if he hadn't liked it. We have one in the bag.

'Indeed?' I say. His manner is contagious. 'I'm so glad you enjoyed it, Caspian. So, what did the rest of you think?' Caspian shuffles backwards so that I can get a clearer view of his companions.

Rikk Dyer (don't forget the two Ks) sneers in my direction, but this is not an immediate worry as it's a habitual facial expression formed in his punk-rock youth. I do actually believe the wind changed one day and now, pushing fifty, he's stuck like that.

'Rocking, Lizzy, rocking,' he says solemnly, his faded black T-shirt straining across the gentle paunch that betrays his age. 'Loved the new material. Four stars – wicked. You can quote me.' He nods decisively. Two broadsheets down.

The dumpy blonde diarist from *The Times* bustles her way forward to thrust a tiny tape recorder under my nose. 'What did you think about his material on *you*, Lizzy Harrison?'

'I thought it was very, very funny, Tilly Abbott,' I say clearly into the machine, in the firm tones I have learned at Camilla's knee. 'Randy's a genius.'

'Do you think he's really a changed man?' she says with a dreamy stare in Randy's direction. 'Can you actually trust him?' I know she's one of the few women here that he hasn't tried it on with and clearly she hopes he hasn't mended his ways before she gets her chance.

'I think Randy is Randy,' I say diplomatically, 'and we wouldn't want him any other way.'

'Really?' she says, bustling closer in a confiding way as if we are just two chums having a cosy chat. The Dictaphone between us rather spoils the effect. 'So you don't object to – ow!'

She turns to glare at Roy Matthews, charming arts correspondent for the *News of the World* (I know – you didn't think they had one, did you?). This jovial forty-something devoted father of three little girls is as far from the clichéd tabloid hack as you can get. He runs pieces when he says he will, he answers his phone, he doesn't stitch people up for no reason, he apologizes for mistakes. Camilla and I adore him.

'Lizzy, he was brilliant,' he begins, grasping my hand effusively and squeezing himself between me and Tilly, until he is shunted aside himself. By Daz 'Dazzler' Davies, showbiz chief for the *Sunday Reporter*.

'Liz, yeah, hi, good to see you again,' he says, though

we have never actually met because I have always been palmed off on one of his many minions. His affected nonchalance is betrayed by the vicious elbow in the ribs with which he despatched Roy, who is wincing beside him. Daz's highlighted hair is flicked low over his face, Flock of Seagulls-style, making him instantly recognizable and also, say his rivals, covering up a Botox-related cratering on the left side of his face. The fact that it obscures his eyes makes him rather accident-prone, and a large red wine stain is already visible down the front of his purple shirt.

'So, cool – how are things with Randy? You're in love, yeah?' He cocks his head to one side expectantly, one beady eye visible through his hair.

'Er, well – it's early days, Daz,' I say. Like I'm going to admit it first to a tabloid journalist. Even my best friends haven't asked me if I love Randy yet.

'But, like, it's all good, yeah? You're really happy with him? You think this is going places, right? You're making plans for the future?' Daz may be the one asking the questions, but I can see all the journalists hovering intently on my answer. Even Caspian Latimer's beaky nose is leaning further forward than usual. Although the room is noisy around us, we are a tight little bubble of silence as they wait for me to speak.

'It's all good, Daz,' I say, thinking that if this is what passes for news, then I despair.

'I can quote you on that?' he says eagerly.

'If you like,' I say with a shrug. It's hardly the scoop of the century.

'Cool, yeah, great, later,' says Daz and instantly scuttles towards the door, bumping into several guests on the way. He's off up the stairs just two minutes later.

With his departure, the crowd of journalists seems to lose its focus. Everyone melts into the crowd with polite murmurs of 'great party' and 'nice to see you'. I look out across the room again. Rochelle's quiff is bent low over Nina the Cleaner and the two of them are speaking animatedly to Nolan, who roars with laughter and slaps Rochelle's thigh, to her evident surprise. Nina's half-empty packet of biscuits sits on the table next to them. Barry is engaged in conversation with one of the barmen, whose flirtatious manner suggests he is not unaware of Barry's reputation for generous tipping. Camilla is still talking to Jamie from African Vision, but their companions appear to have gone elsewhere. I don't know what he can be saying, but Camilla's eyes don't leave his face. Randy . . . Randy . . . where the fuck is Randy? He's unmistakable in that hat and unmistakably not here.

I know exactly where he's gone – he can't hide it from me. I storm up the stairs to the landing, two at a time, and push open the door to the men's toilets.

I knew it.

The door to one cubicle is closed, and I can hear stifled giggles from inside it. So he's got a partner in crime, has he? What kind of friends does Randy have that they'd jeopardize everything by doing this in public? If any one of those journalists had come in here instead of me, Randy could lose everything. I tiptoe towards the cubicle, but they must know someone's here as I hear a muffled 'shhhh'. Just in case I had any doubt that Randy was inside, the knotted ends of his leopardskin scarf trail out from under the door.

I go into the next cubicle and lower the toilet lid as slowly and as silently as I can. Taking off my shoes, I step on to the lid and lean over to look into his cubicle, ready to catch him in the act.

But I'm wrong.

Randy Jones isn't doing coke. He's doing Jemima Morgan. From behind.

25

I really should state, for the record, that I'm not proud of myself for throwing a kiwi fruit at them, but there they are at the bottom of my handbag, which is still slung over my shoulder, and before I know what I'm doing I've hurled one to splat with a shockingly loud thump on the cubicle wall. Two horrified faces, satisfyingly spotted with tiny black seeds, stare up at me. So I throw another one for good measure before getting a grip of myself and running out of the room. Despite Jemima's later accusations, there is no way I could have anticipated that the next person to enter the gents that night would be Declan Costelloe, nor that the sight of the splattered kiwis would be enough to set him off on a dramatic panic attack that meant an ambulance had to be called.

Unknown to me, this rather effectively disguises both my exit and Randy and Jemima's indiscretion.

Truly the universe moves in mysterious ways.

Even though it's warm outside, I feel suddenly freezing. Perhaps it's shock, but I shiver on the steps of Savoy Street as the photographers begin to circle, scenting a story.

'Everything okay, Lizzy, love?' one shouts. 'Where's Randy?'

'Just need a breath of fresh air,' I mumble. 'So hot in there.' I fan my face as nonchalantly as I can, but a suspicious volley of shouts and screams rises up from downstairs, and the photographers begin to move closer. Later I will learn that this is Declan in a kiwi-induced frenzy, but, not knowing this, I begin to panic. I don't know if I'm more afraid that Randy will chase after me, or that he won't. All I know is that I have to get out of here fast.

Ignoring the shouts of the photographers, I walk as speedily as I can in my high heels, head down, towards the warren of little side streets that lead from Savoy Street to Embankment station. I know they won't follow me for more than a few steps – the big story is clearly still going on inside, and a picture of me without Randy is practically worthless. Especially if it's a picture of my back. In the dark and quiet streets of tall Georgian townhouses I allow myself a few hot tears now that no one can see them. But it isn't until I find myself on Villiers Street, surrounded by Saturday-night crowds, that I realize I have nowhere to go.

The keys in my bag are to Randy's house, and for all

I know he's heading there himself. With Jemima. I feel sick. The keys to my own flat are on the dresser in an upstairs bedroom in Belsize Park; I haven't touched them for weeks. I can't face telling Lulu the whole story yet, especially so soon after her warning about Randy, and anyway, it's gone eleven on a Saturday night – if she's not out herself, she's going to be busy with Laurent. I just want to get as far away as possible from all of this. To somewhere no celebrity can find me. To somewhere Randy would never think to look.

Guildford.

My brother takes my somewhat incoherent phone call with surprising calm, despite the fact that I'm only capable of gibbering 'Randy Jones' and 'need to come tonight', and that it's past eleven and ten o'clock is considered a bit of a late one at Ben and Jenny's. Sometimes I'm so grateful my brother isn't one for meaningful conversations. Tonight is one of those times. He doesn't ask what's happened, he doesn't tell me to get a grip, he doesn't say I told you so – he just tells me to call him from the train and he'll pick me up from the station. He even says he's glad I'm coming.

As I cross Hungerford Bridge towards Waterloo, I finally let myself properly cry. The approaching lights of the South Bank are a wavering blur as I hiccup and sob my way to the station. With my back to Savoy Street, to Belsize Park, to Soho, to Mayfair, to Regent's Park, to Randy, I feel I'm turning away from the London I've been living in for the last few weeks. Who was I to think that I, sensible Lizzy Harrison from Guildford, lately of Peckham, could ever make it as the girlfriend of Randy Jones? Mine is the world of the suburbs, of planning in advance, of Ocado deliveries and middle-class gastropubs, of monogamous relationships and fixed-rate mortgages. Of course I never meant anything to Randy Jones, superstar Shagger of the Millennium. How could I have let myself believe that any of it was true? I sob. He was just using me. A tiny part of me thinks perhaps you were just using him too, Lizzy Harrison. But I swiftly silence it; if you can't feel sorry for yourself when you've just caught your boyfriend shagging your Lego-haired nemesis, then when can you?

When we get back to Ben's house, it's past one in the morning. He closes the front door behind him, wrestles with a series of Chubb locks and flicks on the hall light as I stumble noisily over Graham's buggy. Next to the buggy lie three pairs of wellies, one pair of slippers in the shape of rabbits and two battered shoes that resemble a pair of crimped Cornish pasties in earthy red. They're adorned with thick gold and green laces, and, though I can't detect it from here, I know that if I bend down lower they'll smell of joss sticks.

'Mum's here?' I say, turning to Ben in shock. I'm not sure I can handle any more surprises. 'But . . . but she's not due back until next week.'

'Change of plan,' says Ben with a maddeningly calm shrug. 'Now go to bed.'

So I do.

I'm woken at seven-thirty by an insistent tapping on my forehead which, when I open my eyes, turns out to be coming from the plastic arm of a small plastic bunny wielded by my nephew.

The door of the study opens a crack and Jenny pokes her head round it. Even at this hour she looks as healthy and fresh as a shiny apple, her cheeks scrubbed, her hair pulled back in a colourful scrunchie. 'Oh God – sorry, Lizzy. I thought he must have come in here. Is he bothering you?'

'No, no, it's fine,' I say, sitting up and pulling the duvet towards me to cover up the fact that I'm wearing only my expensive, Randy-bestowed and, frankly, rather slutty bra and French knickers. I push my tangled hair off my face, suspecting that I'm probably exposing the smeared remains of the make-up I didn't wash off last night. I feel as if we're a Hogarth sketch in which she represents Motherly Purity while I am Urban Vice fresh off the pavement at Gin Lane.

Jenny sits down on the side of the sofa bed and Graham launches himself into her lap with a shriek.

'Is everything okay, Lizzy? Ben said something about Randy Jones.'

If this was anyone else, I'd think they were after

gossip. But Jenny, for all her reading of *Woman's Own* at the hairdresser's, is no more interested in celebrity gossip than she is in astrophysics. In fact astrophysics is probably far more her thing. She wouldn't even recognize half the people in *Hot Slebs*, and I know she's asking out of genuine concern for me rather than for something to tell her friends later. As it begins to dawn on me that this isn't going to be true of everyone in the coming days, I feel the tears start up again.

'Oh, Lizzy – don't cry. I'm so sorry – I didn't mean to upset you,' she says, alarmed, and reaches out to hug me to her fleece-clad chest. Graham forces his way into the hug, squeezing me so tightly I fear I might have a bunny-shaped indentation on my chest for ever.

'I'm . . . I'm okay,' I sob into Graham's blond curls.

'Bloody Randy,' says Jenny with a fierce loyalty that surprises me, seeing as she doesn't even know what's happened yet. 'Well, you stay here for a bit,' she says, getting up with Graham in her arms. 'We're all going to take Graham out for a walk, and maybe when we're back we can all have breakfast together. Okay?'

'Okay,' I sniff, wiping my eyes.

'Buh-bye,' says Graham with a wave from the door.

'Bye, Gray,' I wave back, and then collapse on to the pillows with my eyes closed. I can only have been lying there for a few seconds when I smell the distinctive whiff of Nag Champa incense.

Mum.

My eyes fly open to see her leaning over the bed with a frown of concern, wrapped in what appears to be several layers of blue and purple cloth indistinguishable as individual items of clothing. Her grey hair is cut close to her skull in a crop that thankfully owes more to Judi Dench than the shaven-headed monks she's been spending her time with lately. She flings her arms wide and envelops me in a tight hold, squeezing my face into her joss-stick-fragranced wrappings. I can feel her slow, steady breaths as she holds me without saying a word, and I suspect she's trying to do something self-consciously spiritual and odd like heal me with the power of breathing. I suppose I should be grateful she isn't chanting over me or whispering positive affirmations in my ear. I don't know if the special ashram breaths are working their magic, or if it's just the presence of Mum after these crazy few months without her, but I do actually start to feel a bit better. Randy and Savoy Street and Camilla and Jemima all feel a long way away from Ben and Jenny's sofa bed and the presence of my family.

'Mum, I—'

'Shh, darling,' she says, finally letting go. 'All in good time. You go and have a shower while we go for a walk. We'll all have a talk over breakfast.'

She kisses me once on the forehead and glides out of the room so smoothly it's as if there are little castors under her Cornish-pasty shoes.

After a few moments I hear the front door slam and the house is silent. Silent except for a beep from my phone. I know I should have turned it off, but I have a perverse desire to see if it's a message from Randy. Not that any of the others have been. I texted Camilla from the train, just an innocuous message that I'd decided to go home, and she's sent a few anxious messages since. Apart from that the phone's been tauntingly mute since I left Savoy Street. I leap on it and open the text. It's from a number I don't recognize.

> Sorry u had 2 find out lyk dis, i tryed 2 tell u B4. Sun Reporter p 4,5,6, + sidebar p7 + Hot Slebs Weds. Jazmeen.

As if things couldn't get any worse. I turn my phone off. I don't want to hear what anyone else has to say about this.

By the time the others come back from their walk, I've had a shower and got dressed in a pair of Jenny's combat trousers and a long-sleeved British Trust for Conservation Volunteers T-shirt, although I drew the line at the pair of yellow Crocs that had also been left outside the bedroom door. I'm still feeling sick enough to think I may never eat again, but for the others I've set the kitchen table with cereals, bread and jar after jar of Jenny's home-made preserves. I'm attempting to force down a cup of milky Earl Grey tea when they all burst through the front door, Graham clutching a handful of leaves which he deposits in my lap before dragging Mum off to the living room and the television.

Ben approaches the table cautiously as if fearing I might burst into tears at any moment.

'All right, Lizzy?' he says.

'Well, go on,' says Jenny, appearing from the hallway. 'Show her.'

'I thought we said—' Ben turns to his wife, trying to silence her, but I've already seen the copy of the *Sunday Reporter* poking out from behind his back.

'It's Jazmeen Marie, isn't it?' I say wearily.

'So this is what last night was about?' says Ben, laying the paper on the table in front of me.

'I don't exactly know,' I say, reaching for the paper and turning straight to page four.

I'M CARRYING RANDY JONES'S LOVE CHILD,
SAYS STUNNER JAZMEEN

With my brother and sister-in-law breathing heavily over my shoulder, I learn for the first time that Randy is due to become a father in four months. No detail is spared: the nights they spent in a London hotel, Randy's five-times-a-night appetite, his penchant for a rose-quartz dildo with a fox-brush tail (so that's where it went). How he'd told her she was different from all the other girls. How Randy was in rehab when she found out she was pregnant. How he'd ignored her desperate messages. How she'd even tried to contact

Randy's new girlfriend for help. But Jazmeen, posing in nothing but a pair of knickers, and what I believe the lad mags call an 'arm bra', in which one's nipples are barely covered by one's forearm, is proud to be pregnant. Indeed she has already named the child, a daughter, Tiffany Blue.

The sidebar on page seven turns out to be an exclusive interview with me, conducted last night by Daz 'Dazzler' Davies, in which I tell him that, despite Jazmeen's news, 'it's all good' between me and Randy. Which I do remember saying. And 'I love him and stand by him no matter what'. Which I don't. A 'source', by which I assume they mean Daz himself, is quoted as saying that Lizzy Harrison is telling friends no love child is going to get between her and her man.

My shoulders start shaking.

'Lizzy,' says Ben. 'Oh God, Lizzy, this is awful.'

Jenny pats my back awkwardly. 'Lizzy, I'm so sorry.'

'Oh God,' I say, clutching on to the table for support. 'Oh my God.'

'You're . . . laughing?' Ben says.

But I can't help it. Jazmeen's baby, Randy and Jemima's kiwi-splattered faces last night, the idea that I ever thought I was in control of this situation for a moment – it's too ludicrous. All the anxiety and stress of trying to keep Randy within the bounds of media-acceptable behaviour, of helping Camilla without her even knowing, of keeping the relationship secret from my friends and family; how did I ever think I'd get away with it? How did Randy? I laugh myself into weeping, hiccupping hysteria.

Later, Mum takes me out for a walk. As she's already been on one today, I suspect it's really a ruse to bestow the wisdom of the ashram on me, but I let her do it anyway. We take the muddy path that leads from Ben and Jenny's cul-de-sac up to the woods behind their estate. Although it's still August – just – the leaves are already beginning to lose their glossy greenness. Conkers hang from the heavy branches of the horse chestnut trees, preparing to fall. The brambles around us glisten with blackberries. In a few weeks it will be autumn.

'You know, this time of year was always Daddy's favourite,' she says.

'It was?' I ask. I don't remember. 'Even though school was about to start?' It sounds so unlikely that my teacher father would have looked forward to the beginning of term. Wouldn't the summer holidays have been more appealing?

'Oh yes,' she says. 'I think he never lost that feeling of new beginnings and a clean slate that you get at the start of the school year. He always used to say it was a chance to start over.' She links her arm with mine and looks up into the canopy of leaves above us. 'And autumn is so beautiful, too.'

'It is beautiful,' I say.

'Did you love him?' she asks suddenly.

'Daddy?' I say, in surprise.

'No, darling, of course you loved Daddy. I mean Randy.'

'I – I think I thought I did. For a while. I think I really wanted to – because, well, it's been so long since Joe, and I think I just—'

'You wanted it to be real,' says Mum.

'I did. I got scared that I was too closed off to being in a relationship, or love, or anything. Lulu said—'

'Oh, darling, you didn't take relationship advice from Lulu, did you?' Mum laughs. 'You two are so different!'

'I know, Mum, but she said I was too uptight and in control, and I think I wanted to prove to her that I wasn't. But then when I got involved with Randy, I kind of wanted to prove to *myself* that I wasn't. So I let myself fall for him.'

'And do you think he fell for you?' she asks.

'I thought he did, but now I look back, it was one of those relationships where nothing was actually said. I . . . I suppose I just filled in the silences with what I wanted to hear. It – it was all in my head.' My voice starts to wobble.

'Maybe you thought if you spoke to him properly you'd hear something you didn't want to hear,' says Mum thoughtfully as we walk on through the woods, our strides falling into a gentle rhythm. 'Maybe by not talking about it, you kept the illusion that you had some control over where it was going.'

'No, Mum, that was the point – I was *losing* control with Randy,' I say; it's like she's misunderstanding me on purpose.

'You weren't, darling,' says Mum firmly. 'You thought this was a safe way of falling in love; one that you could be in charge of and, well, if it didn't work out then it didn't matter because it wasn't real anyway.'

I can't answer straightaway and Mum doesn't press me. We walk on silently, listening to the sounds of the woods: the drill of a woodpecker, the dry rustle of leaves as an animal moves through the undergrowth. The branches of the trees meet over our heads, forming a leafy tunnel as the path climbs upwards.

'So,' I begin, 'you think that I never really did risk anything with Randy?'

'Only you know that, darling,' says Mum. 'It just sounds to me like you didn't really risk yourself. What do you think?'

I leave a long pause before answering.

'I think you're probably right,' I say slowly, knowing Mum will hug this small victory to herself for days. It's so rare that Ben or I allow her to be the enlightened sage she tries to be.

'The thing is, Lizzy, we can't control the things that really matter. People die, people fall out of love with us, people go away, people let us down. But that's all part of—'

'Mum, if you make any kind of reference to "the rich tapestry of life", I'm going to have to discount anything else you say,' I warn her, laughing.

'Stop it, you – I'm still your mother and you have to listen to me,' Mum says, squeezing my arm. 'All I mean is that real life, real love, means you have to risk yourself. Or it's not worth anything. Would you rather never have known Daddy than to have lost him how we did?'

'Of course not,' I say, feeling my throat tighten. Even though it's nearly twenty years since he died, sometimes it can feel, for a moment, as shocking and horrific as if it has only just happened.

The path opens out into a clearing at the top of the hill. A bench has been set against a row of beeches, and a small brass plaque tells us it's dedicated to the memory of Bill, 1925–2003, who loved this place. We sit down, and Mum reaches to put her arm around my shoulders, even though she's far shorter than me. I shuffle down in my seat to let her do it; I want to feel small and protected again.

'I miss Daddy,' I say.

'So do I, darling,' she says.

We sit like that for a long time.

26

I don't think I've ever been so grateful for a bank holiday Monday – a further day of grace before facing the mess back in London. But on my way back to Peckham that night, unattractively attired in clothes borrowed from Jenny, I start thinking of my flat, dark, unwelcoming and unlived-in. And suddenly I realize that it is even more unwelcoming than I had feared, since my keys are still at Randy's and I have no way of getting in, short of shinning up a drainpipe.

I decide to make a detour to Lulu's, where my spare keys hang on a hook by the front door in case of emergencies. I've already spoken to her today and confessed everything, and I know she's meant to be in tonight. But still, calling in unannounced is a riskier strategy than it may first appear. Everyone knows it's not the done thing to just drop in on friends in London, not even your very best friends. Evenings together must, by common agreement, be decided upon by at least fifteen emails batting to and fro offering various dates at least three weeks in advance, and then, once a date is agreed, it is expected that one party will have to cancel at short notice. With such a carefully planned schedule of events, an unexpected ring on the doorbell in London is to be ignored, not welcomed – only the hopelessly socially inept or undesirable, such as Jehovah's Witnesses or door-to-door salesmen, would visit without warning.

Even so, I'm not expecting a reception quite as frosty as the one I get.

'What are you doing here?' asks Dan, frowning, when he opens the door on my third ring. His hair is even more tangled than usual, as if he hasn't brushed it for days, and stubble shadows his jaw.

'Hi, Dan,' I say with an attempt at a smile, which he doesn't return. 'Is – um – is Lulu in?'

'No,' he says, keeping the door half closed across his body.

'Right. Okay. Can I come in and wait for her?' I ask, taking a step towards the door, but he doesn't move. 'It's raining.' I point upwards stupidly, as if he might have forgotten where rain comes from.

'Look, now's not a good time,' he says with a backwards glance into the corridor.

'Sorry, I didn't realize—' I say.

'What do you want anyway?' he interrupts, his eyes unfriendly.

'I just – I'm locked out. I came to pick up my spare keys,' I stammer uncertainly.

Without a word Dan reaches behind the door. He holds the keys out to me, pinched between his finger and thumb as if he might catch something from them; or me.

'And – and I was hoping to see Lulu, too,' I say, taking the keys and clutching at the door so he can't close it on me. 'Just to catch up.'

I'd never imagined that I would have to beg for entry to Dan and Lulu's; I thought their door would always be open for me. It's too weird to find myself standing on the doorstep, barred from coming in.

'Yeah?' he says mockingly. 'Want to catch up on your latest fake relationship, do you? Who is it this time? Tom Cruise?'

'Dan, that's not fair—' I start. He suddenly opens the door wider, and it crashes against the wall. With the hall light behind him, he seems hugely tall and intimidating – his broad shoulders tower over me.

'Not fair?' he hisses. 'I'd say it's not fair to take the piss out of your friends by lying about your relationships. Who are you to talk about what's not fair?'

'But Dan, I'm sorry,' I protest, my voice choking on tears. 'It's not like you think.'

'Why do you care what I think?' Dan sneers. 'Why don't you just run off and cry your fake tears to your fake friends. I can't believe anything you say any more.'

'Dan, please,' I say, extending my hand towards him, but he takes a step back into the hall, out of my reach.

I hear a woman's voice call his name from inside the flat. Dan looks over his shoulder, and then back at me, eyes narrowed.

'I've got to go. I'll tell Lulu you called round.'

And he closes the door in my face.

I'm too shocked even to cry properly. How can this be the Dan I know? This big, angry, frightening man is like a stranger. I struggle to compose myself on the step, wiping my eyes and hoping that my tears might be disguised by the weather now that it's properly raining. I entertain a slight hope that Dan might relent and open the door, but when I see the net curtains of a curious neighbour twitch for the second time, I turn to trudge down the road towards the bus stop for Peckham.

As I put the key in my front door, I hear a man's voice shout, 'Lizzy!'

My treacherous heart leaps into my mouth for a second – Dan? Randy?

As I turn, I'm hit by four sharp flashes from a powerful camera, and a man runs away down the street. I feel like I've been mugged on my doorstep and instantly burst into tears. On top of everything else, I come to the horrible realization that Randy and I remain a big enough news story for some paparazzo to bother hanging outside my house on a wet bank holiday Monday. Far from being over, this story has in some ways only just begun.

Hassan from the downstairs flat opens his door a crack as I shut the front door behind me, wiping my eyes with the back of my hand. Inside I can hear the noise of the television.

'Okay?' he asks.

'Hi, Hassan – thanks for checking. I'm fine,' I sniff, and give him a wobbly smile.

'Okay,' he says.

'Are you okay? How are the children?'

'Okay.' Most of our conversations go something like this; I'm not sure he knows more than a few words of English, but he, his wife and their four almond-eyed children always exchange shy, polite greetings with me in the hallway.

'You been away?' he asks. 'Back now?'

'Yes, that's right, I'm back now. Back for good,' I say, and let myself into my dark, cold flat.

27

The next morning I'm nearly at the door of the office when my phone buzzes with a message from Camilla asking me to meet her at a café in Sloane Square instead of at work. It's not that I'm surprised she'd choose Sloane Square – this is Camilla we're talking about, after all: her sisters are called Caroline and Sophie, and I know there's more than one velvet headband in her wardrobe – but I don't understand why she wants to see me out of the office. My stomach lurches with sick anticipation.

Until I received that message, I'd convinced myself I was clawing back some semblance of my old life. I'd welcomed my morning routine like an old friend after the weeks with Randy. Hello, morning run around Peckham Rye. Hello, Radio 4 in the background. Hello, own bathroom, own bedroom, own wardrobe. Shoving Jenny's old clothes in the laundry basket, I'd dressed with great care, as if each item was a piece of bullet-proof clothing that would protect me from attack: studded strappy heels, a pencil skirt, a shoulder-padded blazer over my T-shirt, immaculate make-up. I'm not going to let anyone see this has got me down. I've replied to all the texts on my phone and declined kiss-and-tell offers from two national newspapers. The slate is clean. My life begins again today.

Camilla hasn't arrived yet, so I order a cappuccino from the slick-haired young waiter and look around the room, which is tiled from floor to ceiling, making it feel like we're all sitting at the bottom of a rather glamorous swimming pool. Three coltish schoolgirls giggle over their coffees by the window, flicking their blonde hair over their shoulders. Whatever are they doing up so early in the last week of the school holidays? An ancient lady with a Margaret Thatcher helmet of hair sips tea, staring into the distance as her black pug lies snoring under the table. She sees me looking and purses her red-lipsticked mouth. I smile at her and she inclines her head in gracious acknowledgement.

When Camilla arrives, I see immediately that she carries nothing with her other than her red patent-leather handbag. For some reason, this deviation from her normal pack-horse routine alarms me more than the meeting itself. As she allows the waiter to pull out her chair, I see she's even had a manicure. Something is definitely up. With brisk efficiency, she takes out a small hot-pink leather notebook from her bag and pulls a silver pencil out of its spine. She opens the notebook and looks at me with a grave expression. I feel as if we've swapped roles but no one's told me. Now she's all organized and capable, while I'm the clueless bringer of chaos. Perhaps even now there is an undetected smear of baby food on my skirt.

'So,' she says finally. 'Would you like to tell me precisely what's been going on?'

'Regarding . . . ?' I say uncertainly. I seem to incriminate myself every time I open my mouth at the moment, so I'm not about to volunteer anything Camilla doesn't know.

'Let's start with Randy Jones,' says Camilla, reading from a scribbled list in the notebook. 'Followed by kiwi fruits, Declan Costelloe, Jemima, and the fact that you ran out of Randy's after-party on Saturday without a word to anyone.'

'I'm sorry I ran out,' I begin. 'I just found myself in a situation I couldn't handle. I'm afraid I panicked. I should have told you.'

'Perhaps you should also have told me that you were having an affair with Randy?' says Camilla, coolly sipping her coffee and replacing the cup in the saucer as I stare at her, open-mouthed.

'Er, right – yes, I probably should have,' I say, squirming in my seat with embarrassment.

'Really, Lizzy,' says Camilla briskly. 'I thought much better of you than that. I thought you were a professional, not one of those silly girls who'd fall for Randy's tired old lines. Let me guess – did he tell you that you were different from all the other girls?'

'I, er . . .' I stammer, allowing my hair to drop forward and hide my burning face.

'And so you thought you'd have a little fun, did you? You thought you'd risk the company's relationship with its star client just so you could get a big celebrity notch on your bedpost? I'd expect this of someone like Mel, but not of you, Lizzy.'

'Camilla!' I exclaim. 'It wasn't like that! I never jeopardized anything. You have no idea what I had to do to make sure Randy stayed in line.'

'Oh, I have a pretty good idea what you did,' says Camilla with a brittle laugh. 'I thought I could trust you to behave appropriately, no matter what the situation. I'm very disappointed to find out that's not true.'

'What about Jemima?' I burst out furiously. It's not like I'm the only one at Carter Morgan who's fallen for the Randy Jones charm offensive.

'Jemima,' Camilla huffs, casting her eyes to the ceiling. 'Jemima Morgan is even more of a fool than you are. She thought sleeping with Randy would make him want to be her client instead of mine.'

'So that's why—' I say. 'But he wouldn't—'

Camilla lets out a harsh burst of laughter.

'You should know as well as I do that Randy has a fierce Madonna/whore complex. Now that he's slept with Jemima, there's no way he'll consider her as someone who might represent him. And the same goes for you.'

'Are you – are you calling me a whore?' I ask, hardly able to believe my ears. For a moment I think Camilla is about to burst out laughing – her eyes have a peculiar glint to them. But her face remains serious.

'Well, you're certainly not a Madonna, are you?' she asks tartly. First Dan, now Camilla. Is everyone going to turn on me?

I don't reply. I can't.

'Lizzy,' she says, snapping shut her notebook. 'You can consider this a formal warning.'

'Just a minute,' I say, suddenly enraged. I no longer care about the consequences. 'None of this would have happened if you and Jemima hadn't put me in this situation in the first place. You told me to act like Randy's girlfriend. I did. And I would have thought, after everything I've done for you, that you could cut me a bit of slack for getting – well, carried away.'

'Everything you've done for me?' says Camilla in a dangerously calm tone. 'Would that include making out that I am some kind of incompetent who can't be trusted to make a decision without being saved by the sainted Lizzy Harrison?'

'I haven't—' I splutter.

'Yes you have,' says Camilla. 'I'm not saying I'm not grateful to you, but you should have demonstrated a little faith in me as your boss. Have I ever let you down before?'

'No,' I mumble, 'but—'

'But nothing. *You* have let *me* down, Lizzy, and you need to seriously consider your position at Carter Morgan.' She glances at her watch. 'I've got a conference call at eleven. We need to get back to the office.'

'But I—'

'Now,' says Camilla, standing up.

We don't speak a word on the way back to the office; in fact Camilla strides ahead while I trail five paces behind her like a dutiful Muslim wife. I am seething. I can't believe she would turn on me like this. She isn't who I thought she was. This job isn't what I thought it was. First I'm forced to be the fake girlfriend of a celebrity, and then I get a formal warning for taking my role a little too seriously.

When we get to the office it's nearly eleven and there's a distinct scent of cigarette smoke in the corridor. The door to Jemima's office is closed, as if we won't know it's her, back on the tabs again. Whenever Jemima falls off the cigarette wagon, it's like a smoke signal to the rest of us: keep your head down, avoid eye contact, be prepared to fling yourself under your desk in a commando roll rather than face her wrath. There is even a rumour that, on one such smoking day, she threw a stapler at a work-experience girl, but no one's ever been able to prove it. (Though that sixteen-year-old who'd been doing the photocopying did leave very abruptly, come to think of it.) There's a tangibly hysterical atmosphere, and even the usually sanguine Winston is anxious.

'It's a Health and Safety violation, Mrs Carter,' he calls as we pass reception.

'It certainly is, Winston – I'll sort this out,' says Camilla.

She strides through the cubicles towards Jemima's office. Every head turns to watch her pass. She flings open the door and a cloud of smoke emerges, as if she's entering the lair of a monster. And then she slams the door behind her. It feels like the whole office is holding its breath.

And suddenly everyone is overcome with the urge to make a cup of tea or coffee in the small kitchen opposite Jemima's office. It's like one of those how-many-people-can-you-fit-in-a-phone-box competitions as secretaries jostle with account execs and the surprisingly aggressive work-experience boy to get a spot near enough the door for the best view of Jemima's office, but close enough to the kettle to be able to pretend to be busy in the kitchen should either she or Camilla emerge. I pretend to be reading the laminated "What to do in Case of Fire" leaflet that's stuck on a pinboard just outside the kitchen. Everyone is hissing at everyone else to shush.

The kitchen falls silent as everyone strains to hear any suggestion of a raised voice from Jemima's office, but there's nothing.

'Lizzy,' hisses Mel from within the kitchen scrum.

'Yes,' I answer mildly, still pretending to be engrossed in Human Resources literature.

'You were out with Camilla this morning – what's going on? Is this about Randy Jones and that Jazmeen slapper?'

'Your guess is as good as mine,' I say, thankful that self-obsessed Mel's first thought is for office politics rather than how I might feel about it as Randy's nominal girlfriend.

There's a muffled thud from behind the closed door. Everyone gasps.

'Do you think that was the stapler?' whispers Lucy, eyes wide.

'Definitely not,' says Mel. 'I removed all heavy objects from Jemima's desk when she went to the loo earlier. It was obvious how this day was going to go.'

'So what do *you* know?' Francoise asks Mel from underneath the armpit of Josh, the work-experience boy, who has claimed pole position in the doorway.

'Nothing,' says Mel, rolling her eyes, 'but *something*'s going on with her and Camilla.'

There's another thud from Jemima's office, and this time Josh, who's a good foot taller than the rest of us, swears he can see, over the top of the frosted glass, Jemima slamming her hand down on her desk for emphasis.

'What's Camilla doing?' asks Francoise eagerly.

'I can't . . . quite . . . see . . .' says Josh, eyes goggling as he strains higher.

The handle to Jemima's office door turns sharply and the stack of people in the kitchen doorway collapses into its component parts: Francoise and Lucy busy themselves by the kettle, Mel picks up a mug and intently examines its cleanliness, Josh flees to his desk. Two terrified assistants actually duck behind a partition as if a stapler might be hurled at any moment. But Camilla emerges with a serene, 'Morning,' to everyone as she passes the kitchen. Jemima is glimpsed for a brief moment, and closes her door again, shutting herself back into the gloom. Tendrils of smoke curl in her wake.

'I don't think it's fags, I reckon it's the steam from her cauldron,' hisses Lucy as she makes her way back to her desk. 'Eye of newt . . .'

As the morning progresses, it brings further revelations about Randy. Rochelle, it seems, got spectacularly drunk at Randy's party on Saturday and let slip to a journalist that she has sunk her leopardskin claws into Randy on several occasions. She didn't hesitate to confess that one of those occasions was as I waited downstairs before Lulu and Dan's party. I remember her flushed face and messy hair as we waved goodbye. God, I even offered to help her with her stupid bags. But more embarrassing still is the fact, revealed in stark black and white on the *Hot Slebs* website, that Randy told her I was just a fake girlfriend, purely PR, and that I didn't really mean anything to him. My humiliation is complete.

But at the same time, it's all over. There are no more secrets to hide. I've no doubt that there will be other revelations – that bitchy girl from the underwear shop is surely saving her story for a rainy day – but for me it's finished. I know, once and for all, that I never meant anything to Randy. Surely nothing further can hurt me.

As I sit at my desk, email upon email piling up in my inbox, I'm overcome by a peculiar feeling. I don't care about any of it. I really don't care. Sorry, Caspian Latimer, but I can't be arsed to reply to your email about picture credits. Nope, Isobel Valentine, I am not going to find someone to look after your dogs while you have a pedicure. As for Declan Costelloe's request for a written apology for the kiwi fruits: denied. Why am I spending my life pandering to the whims of spoiled celebrities? I could be doing something that actually matters, something that makes a difference. Why should I sit here and get a formal warning for doing what I was told to do in the first place? It's clear that Camilla has changed over the last few weeks. She's back in charge. She doesn't need me any more. And

I don't need her. It's like a fog has lifted and I can at last see the horizon ahead. Afterwards. For me, it will have nothing to do with Carter Morgan.

Full of resolve and confidence, I push open the door to Camilla's office. She looks up in surprise, her expression cold.

'Yes?' she snaps, covering the papers on her desk with her hand.

'Camilla, I've been thinking about what you said,' I say, hovering in the doorway. 'And I've decided I have no choice but to resign.'

Her face softens a fraction, but there is a peculiarly triumphant smile on her lips.

'Lizzy,' she says calmly. 'That is positively the best news I've had in weeks.'

28

It's not that I was expecting tears and rending of clothes, nor that Camilla would fall on to her knees and beg me to stay, especially after this morning's discussion in Sloane Square, but I did think that at the very least she would be a little sad to see me go. After all, it's been more than four years. I've booked her holidays, bought her pregnancy tests, wiped baby sick off her clothes with tedious regularity. I thought we were more than just colleagues. I thought we were friends. It seems that about this, as about so many things, I have been wrong.

'Pack up your personal belongings,' says Camilla, standing up and collecting the papers in front of her with purpose. 'I'd like you to put your resignation in writing and be ready to leave immediately following the twelve-thirty meeting.'

'What twelve-thirty meeting?' I ask, confused.

'The one I'm about to announce just as soon as I've spoken to Jemima,' she snaps.

As she passes me in the doorway of her office, she stops for a moment and squeezes my arm with baffling chumminess.

'You did the right thing, Lizzy,' she says, smiling as if we are the best of friends again, and then heads down the corridor to Jemima's lair. Heads turn to watch her pass like a mini-Mexican wave.

And then I'm on my own, rooted to the spot with my mouth hanging open. So Camilla has finally completely and utterly lost it. Or – my stomach clenches at the thought – is this what she wanted all along? To get rid of me? I guess I've saved her the trouble of firing me. Fine! Fine, if that's how she wants it. Let her see how she copes without me. I allow myself a brief fantasy of torching the office with a can of paraffin, burning all evidence behind me and destroying forever my peerless filing system before I pull open the drawers to my desk and begin the much more mundane task of packing up.

By the time we are all called into the boardroom for the twelve-thirty meeting, my handbag is bulging incriminatingly, stuffed with a Rolodex, my personal stash of Muji office equipment (so much more attractive than that stuff from the Viking catalogue), and a selection of emergency snacks, painkillers and nail files that were floating around in my desk drawer. I prepare for my last meeting at Carter Morgan.

We crowd into the boardroom, jostling for chairs around the table. You can tell this meeting is a hastily arranged one because there's not a biscuit to be seen. Usually no one at Carter Morgan would think of turning up without first checking that sufficient Marks & Spencer's Extremely Chocolatey Mini Bites had been purchased. I place myself as far from Jemima as possible, but it's impossible to escape her cold stare. It's as if she's one of those Dementors from Harry Potter, sucking all warmth and happiness and joy out of the room until everyone loses the will to live.

At last everyone is settled. Jemima sits at one end of the table, Camilla at the other. They stare at each other coldly. Jemima waits for the room to fall silent before she stands to speak.

'I'm sorry to have to announce,' says Jemima, 'a series of departures from Carter Morgan.'

There is an audible intake of breath, and everyone glances at each other with silent questions. Jemima waits again, like a professional actress, for the room to be still.

'Randy Jones has left Carter Morgan. With immediate effect he will be represented by the McCormack Agency in New York and Los Angeles.'

This time people don't bother keeping silent. The McCormack Agency is one of the biggest in the world, a behemoth with offices in every major city. No wonder Camilla was in such a terrible mood this morning.

Randy has betrayed her – all of us – for his shot at world domination.

Jemima clears her throat to speak again. 'All media queries regarding Randy's departure are to be directed to me, and me alone.'

All heads swivel to the end of the table where Camilla sits. Why would Jemima take it upon herself to handle the fallout from Camilla's former client? Camilla smiles implacably, but a small muscle pulses vigorously at the base of her throat. As Jemima begins to speak again, the heads swivel back in her direction as if we're all watching an extremely slow game of tennis.

'Camilla Carter will also be leaving the company today,' Jemima says stiffly.

I almost fall out of my chair with the shock of it. I turn to look at Camilla along with everyone else, but she sits as still as if she were made of stone, and her smile never wavers. 'Her personal assistant, Lizzy Harrison, leaves with her. I regret that circumstances mean we don't have the chance to give them a proper send-off, but I'm sure we all wish them well for the future.'

I'm not sure how Jemima has managed to make these few brief words imply that Camilla and I are both leaving in shame and disgrace immediately following Randy's departure, but it's clear from the way hardly anyone will meet my eye that the staff thinks we must have done something appalling. Only Lucy stares at me openly from the other side of the boardroom table, mouthing, 'Did you know?' I shake my head and look down into my lap.

'I will be sending out a press release this afternoon announcing these departures, and that Carter Morgan will henceforth be known as Jemima Morgan PR,' says Jemima with a victorious glint in her eye, though I note she's not able to look in my direction for a moment.

'That's all for now,' she says, standing up and smoothing her Lego hair with both hands. 'Thank you.' She glances at Mel, who leaps to her feet and follows her out of the meeting room with the unquestioning obedience of a lapdog.

You can see that none of the remaining staff knows quite how to act with us. Do we carry the taint of failure? Might it be catching? Will Jemima punish anyone who's seen to regret our departure? Lucy breaks the silence and grabs me into a hug.

'I've got no idea what's going on here, but I'll miss you. You'll stay in touch, won't you? And let me know where you end up?' She breaks away with an anxious look in the direction of Jemima's office.

'Course I will, Lucy. I'll miss you too,' I say, and she steps towards Camilla to say her farewells.

That breaks the deadlock, and for a few minutes we're surrounded by cautious well-wishers carefully expressing their regret at our departure without in any way appearing to take sides or say anything which may be used against them by Jemima later. It's like a Communist purge – no one dares to ally themselves with the dissidents, afraid they might be next. Only Josh, the work-experience boy, who has nothing to lose but an unpaid job, confides that, if we ask him, we're well out of it.

Five minutes later we're standing outside on the steps of the building, and the Carter Morgan PR Agency is no more.

'Lunch?' asks Camilla brightly.

29

At first I decline Camilla's offer of lunch; breakfast wasn't exactly pleasant. But it's as if she's had a complete change of personality since the meeting, and she cheerily drags me off to a small sushi place in the back streets behind our office. She picks plates off the conveyor belt with huge enthusiasm, seemingly oblivious that I'm not joining in. When she finally notices that I'm sitting in stony silence, she bursts out laughing.

'Don't look so worried, Lizzy,' she says, tearing open a paper packet of chopsticks. 'This has all gone absolutely beautifully. Couldn't have gone better.'

'What?' I ask in disbelief. I've feared it for a long time, but now it's clear that Camilla Carter has truly lost it. 'Randy's left, you've lost your job, so have I . . .'

'I sacked Randy, darling,' says Camilla as I goggle at her in confusion. 'I said I would, and in any case, I can't represent him any longer. I've spent the last month trying to break up the company so I can leave. Jemima – well, Jemima hasn't exactly made it easy for me.'

'Break up the company?' I echo, parrot-like.

'Yes, darling, I have a new job. And so do you, if you want one. With African Vision.' Camilla spears a slice of sashimi and dips it in soy sauce.

'Wh-what? You're going to Africa?' I say. 'What about the babies, what about Jeremy?'

This all seems ridiculously improbable: Camilla exchanging her Chelsea tractor for a rickety jeep in a refugee camp? Setting out to charm dodgy warlords instead of newspaper editors? Surrounded by small children in the manner of Bob Geldof? Handing out bowls of rice with flies crawling all over her three-hundred-pound Jo Hansford highlights?

'Good God, no!' says Camilla, roaring with laughter. 'Not Africa! Jamie Welles wants someone to set up a celebrity department – in London, darling, in London. Oh dear, did you really think they'd send me out to Darfur? I think I can do much more good here. And that's where you come in.'

'Me?' I'm still taking all this on board.

'I've been asked to establish a department to coordinate all the personality-driven PR and events for African Vision. There will be four of us, and I want you to come with me. My original start-up agreement with Jemima meant I couldn't take any staff with me when I left.' She smiles at me warmly. 'That's why I had to force you to resign. I'm so sorry about this morning. I knew you wouldn't go if I didn't push you, and I couldn't leave you there to face Jemima after Saturday night.'

'You mean you're not cross with me?' I asked.

'With you?' She laughs. 'Oh, darling, I couldn't give two hoots if you slept with Randy or the full Carter Morgan client list, for that matter. You work hard and you're loyal, and that's what matters to me.' She casts me a shrewd look. 'But I do hope you've realized Randy is not at all the right kind of man for you.'

'Er, yes,' I mumble.

'So, will you come with me? To African Vision?' she asks.

To my surprise, I hesitate. Two months ago I'd have thought that I'd follow Camilla anywhere. I'd refused promotion after promotion that would have taken me away from the comfortable security of a job I could do standing on my head. But now things have changed. I resigned for a reason, after all: hiding behind Camilla might once have been what I did best, but after the last few months I feel I can't go back. This is an opportunity for change; I can't let it go.

'Camilla, you know I love working with you,' I say slowly, and a little frown appears between her eyebrows as she listens. I take a deep breath. 'I think it might be time for me to move on. I've been a PA for too long. I need to have my own responsibilities, my own projects, not to hide behind someone else all the time.'

I can hardly believe I'm saying this.

'Oh, is that all?' says Camilla, leaning back on her stool in a relaxed fashion. 'Well, that's not a problem, darling – of course I didn't think of you coming as my PA. In fact I've already hired my assistant. Naturally you'll be an account executive, and of course you'll have your own projects from now on. Haven't I spent the last two years telling you it was time you challenged yourself?'

But still I say no. I'm too bruised and battered from the last few days to make any kind of a lasting decision about my future. I promise I'll think about it. After all, hadn't I wanted to do something that would actually make a difference in the world? Maybe this is my chance. But maybe it isn't. I feel as if my world has tilted on its axis, and a whole new array of possibilities is spread out for me to choose from, like cakes on a plate. Camilla tells me she's negotiated six months' salary for me as a leaving present, in exchange for my silence on Jemima's indiscretion, of course. God knows what kind of deal Camilla must have negotiated for herself, but she seems quietly content, so I can only imagine it's something substantial.

When I say goodbye to Camilla after lunch, I watch her stride purposefully up the road, heading back to her family at home in Chelsea. She has somewhere to go, a new job to prepare for, the children to look after, a husband expecting her. But here I am, rooted to the pavement by indecision, with absolutely nothing to do. For the first time in my adult life, I'm freed from the steadying moorings of the nine-to-five. It's three in the afternoon, and I can do anything I like. I don't feel like going home to my flat by myself, but everyone I can think of will be at work right now. Maybe I could run away?

Thanks to my unexpected windfall, I could get on a plane right now and go to Morocco, stay in a riad, tour the souks and sip hot, sweet mint tea from a coloured glass. Come to think of it, why be so modest in my ambitions – I could go travelling for a year! Diving in Malaysia, trekking in Thailand, touring the wats of Cambodia. Or what about volunteering for a charity – maybe I could go and build new homes for families in Guatemala? Teach English to street children in Rio? Save the whales on one of those Greenpeace boats (though that sounds a little chilly; aren't there always icebergs in the backgrounds of those pictures)? I'm quite taken with the idea of myself as a selfless volunteer worker, preferably somewhere warm so that I end up with a tan to complement my general do-gooder's glow. And think of the sense of well-being I'd get from helping the needy instead of the famous. I'd return to London skinny from some exotic (but painless and brief) malaise, with stories of encounters with dishy French doctors from Médecins Sans Frontières and an attractive air of peace and tranquillity like a devastatingly sexy nun. People will ask in wonder how I've coped living amongst such poverty, but I will say, head modestly bowed, that my life has become so much richer from the experience.

'Oi, love, are you going to stand there all day?' demands a bald man in a fluorescent tabard who's attempting to weave past me with a trolley full of beer crates.

So I go home instead.

30

When I let myself into my flat, there's a courier note on the stairs saying that a package has been left with my neighbours. I knock on Hassan's door and hear the children inside squealing as they race to open it. There is much fumbling with the keys, and then Hassan's wife opens the door with children peering out from her skirts. I wave the note at her.

'Hi, how are you? I think you might have a parcel for me?'

'Okay,' she says, smiling politely and nodding. She doesn't move.

'A parcel?' I say again, miming a large box, and then a small one, as if I'm a raver from the Nineties.

'Okay,' she says again, perfectly still and smiling.

The eldest boy pulls at her skirt and says something I don't understand. She raises her hands in comprehension and says, 'Oh!' Then he turns to me.

'She says it's just here, innit,' he says in perfect

Peckham English, and reaches down behind the door to hand it over.

It's not a parcel, it's a small holdall that I've never seen before, in expensively distressed quilted leather. Two white interlinked Cs are embossed on the side. At first I think there must have been a mistake – this isn't mine. But a luggage label is attached, and my name and address are clearly written on it in capital letters.

'Thanks so much,' I say, taking it from the boy's outstretched hand. It's surprisingly heavy.

'All right,' says the boy very seriously. 'That is one sick bag. Later.' He closes the door behind me and I can hear the sound of children running back down the hall.

If he means sick as in 'makes Lizzy Harrison feel so' then he's spot-on. I know before I open the bag that this must have something to do with Randy, and that stops me from going anywhere near it for nearly an hour. I leave the bag in the middle of the living room and keep myself busy around the flat instead, spinning round every now and again to glare at it as if I might catch it unawares in a compromising position. When I've run out of distractions – I draw the line at cleaning the hob – I sit on the sofa and stare at it for ten minutes before realizing that the next step will be speaking to it, and then I will officially have turned into a crazy person.

I hesitantly pull open the zip, leaning backwards in case anything flies out. I'm not sure what I'm expecting to emerge – Randy himself, one denim-clad leg at a time?

The first thing I discover is a packet of HobNob biscuits, followed by a packet of ginger snaps and then some Breakaway bars. There's no accompanying note, but it doesn't take Sherlock Holmes to detect the hand of Nina the Cleaner saying goodbye in her own special language (and I don't mean Bulgarian). Then, as I peel back layer after layer of tissue paper, I find, individually wrapped, each item of underwear bought for me by Randy over the course of our so-called relationship. I pull out slippery silk knickers, balconette bras, embroidered camisoles and seamed stockings until the floor around me is littered with them. Underneath these, at the very bottom of the bag, lies a flat, square, navy blue box and a card. I know it's bad manners to open the box before the card, but seriously, who's watching? Inside the box, pinned on to the red velvet backing, are the earrings and bangles I wore to Dan and Lulu's party. The jewellery that was supposed to show how united Randy and I were as a golden couple. I close the lid of the box. The last item in the bag is *The Observer's Book of Grasses, Sedges and Rushes*.

Before I open the card, I look in every silk-lined pocket of the holdall to make sure there's nothing else there, but it's empty now. The card is addressed to me in handwriting I don't recognize. Maybe it's not from Randy after all? Though now I come to think of it, I never received anything from Randy in his own handwriting. Not even a scrawled note in the kitchen, let alone cards or letters. So it's not like the sight of his handwriting would make my heart leap.

The envelope isn't sealed, it's just tucked in at the back, and I push it open with my thumb. Inside is a postcard with a rather incongruous black and white photograph of a couple kissing. Nice, Randy, I think – why not pour salt into the wound. But then I remember the granny-pants and suspect that he probably didn't pick this one out personally in Paperchase. In fact it's perfectly possible this card isn't even from him.

But it is.

Babe. Thanks for everything. You're a great girl. The best fake girlfriend I could have had. I was a crap fake boyfriend but imagine how much worse if I'd been the real thing. Call it a narrow escape. I'll miss you.

I think these are yours.

Randy

I laugh despite myself. It's more than I expected, and yet it's exactly what I expected. Unreliable, unrepentant, entirely Randy. I never expected an apology from him, but, weirdly, this is enough. It's not the expensive underwear or the lovely jewellery – to be honest, I don't know if I'll wear any of it again. It's that Randy's card is an acknowledgement of – what? Friendship, I suppose. It's personal, and, in his way, thoughtful. For once

I don't see the hand of Camilla behind it, nor Bryan Ross's gruffness. It's all Randy, and it's all okay.

Later that night, I realize it's also a stroke of genius. Unlike a text or an email, a card limits you to only a certain number of words – no long and rambling self-justification or over-done extrapolation, just a brief window in which to convey your message. Even better, a card doesn't invite an immediate reply. The recipient actually has to stop and think before they answer. It makes them all the more likely to respond rationally. To keep their temper.

I realize it's just what I need to send to Dan.

31

Catching up with Lulu has proved to be ridiculously complicated. Although she swears she's forgiven me for not telling her the truth about Randy, and that she's not avoiding me, it's not until Sunday that we finally get together. And only then because I manage to pin her down to a snatched sandwich in the café next door to her salon, between appointments.

She bursts through the door, ten minutes late, in a cloud of tiny hair clippings that disperse, almost unseen, into the chopped salads of our neighbours.

'Harrison!' she exclaims in horror. 'A ponytail? What has Randy Jones *done* to you?'

Ponytails, Lulu has told me on many occasions, are for bathtime and face-cleansing purposes only. No self-respecting person would leave the house in one unless they had given up on attractiveness, fashion and, indeed, life itself.

'Oh, for God's sake, Lu,' I say, laughing. 'It's pouring

outside, it's a Sunday, I just couldn't be bothered doing my hair. My hairstyle is not a portent of doom, okay?'

'Ah, but this is how it starts,' Lulu says, wagging a warning finger at me. 'First you give up on doing your hair, next thing you know you've adopted six cats, haven't washed for a month and no one will sit next to you on a bus. You're worth more than this, Harrison. Come into the salon afterwards – I'm getting one of the juniors to sort you out with a blow-dry.'

'You don't need to do that, Lulu,' I say. 'It's fine. I'm fine. Honestly.'

'It isn't fine,' says Lulu firmly. 'I insist. Bloody Randy Jones. I hope his dick falls off.'

'Yeah, well, maybe it will,' I say, unable to muster up much enthusiasm for slagging him off.

'Come on,' says Lulu, 'get on with blackening his name – isn't that what we're here for? I've been practising my "all men are bastards" face all morning.'

'Not really,' I say, shrugging my shoulders. 'I've talked about Randy Jones enough, Lu. I'm over it.'

'Already?' she asks, frowning. 'It's only been a week.'

I can't blame her for not believing me, seeing as I've lied to her about pretty much everything concerning my emotional life for the last few months.

'I thought you'd be pleased,' I say. 'Given your break-up equation and everything. It's been a week – I'd call that excellent progress.'

'Darling, you always did take the break-up equation

too seriously,' says Lulu, rolling her eyes. 'A week is no time at all to get over being dumped by a celebrity and splashed all over the front pages of every red-top newspaper in the country. By my calculations, you should still be sobbing in a gutter.'

'I thought you were meant to be cheering me up!' I laugh. 'Look, I know it seems crazy, but I feel better now than I have done for weeks. No lies, no faking, no weirdness.'

'No job,' Lulu reminds me.

'But that feels fine, too,' I say calmly. 'Something will work out.'

Lulu looks at me sceptically.

'I can't explain it. I just feel like I spent all this time thinking I was in control and I never really was. So now it's all fallen apart it doesn't feel any less scary than it was when I was trying to keep it all together. Does that make sense?'

'Not really,' says Lulu, wrinkling up her nose as if she can smell something unpleasant. 'Frankly, it sounds like you've been spending too much time with your mother, Harrison. Don't go getting all weird and woo-woo on me.'

'Give me a break, I'm not going the way of the Cornish pasty shoe, I swear. I just mean that I really do feel fine. Truly.'

'Hmm, if you say so,' says Lulu, scrutinizing my face with suspicion. 'The ponytail still worries me, Harrison.

I'll give you the benefit of the doubt this time. But one more dodgy hair day and there'll be trouble, okay?'

'Okay. Now, let's drop it – it feels like we've done nothing but talk about me and Randy fricking Jones for ever. How are *you*? How's Laurent?'

'Oh, darling, he's tiring me out,' says Lulu, leaning back in her chair and raising the back of her hand to her forehead like a silent movie star.

'All that shagging?' I laugh.

'It's not the shagging, darling, though God knows there's plenty of that going on. I'd just forgotten how much *maintenance* there is in a relationship.'

'Maintenance?' I say. 'What, like shaving your legs every day?'

'Harrison, could you get your mind out of the bedroom for a moment? I don't mean that, although it has to be said that there hasn't been a single hair anywhere but my head for two months. No, I mean the phone calls, the having to tell someone where you're going to be, the *planning*. It's exhausting.'

She sips her Diet Coke. 'Exhausting, but actually quite great.'

'You're making *plans* with Laurent?' I ask, unable to believe my ears.

Planning? Lulu? I've lost count of the times I've heard her well-worn rant about the dangers of advance planning with a man. Apparently, committing to a dinner date more than a week in advance is the first step on a slippery slope that ends with the two of you arguing over melamine drawer-fronts in Ikea with a squalling baby strapped to your leaking bosoms. And, as far as Lulu is concerned, there can be no worse fate. Her rant usually concludes in a horrified shudder at the very idea.

'So, wait a minute,' I say. Even though Lulu is my very best friend, I do not dare to put into words what I really want to ask her. 'Are you saying you're Going To Ikea with Laurent?'

She isn't fooled. 'I'm saying, Harrison, that I am willing to consider looking at the Ikea catalogue with him.'

'That's quite a development,' I say, noticing that the two women to our left are eavesdropping with evident bafflement.

'I'm not ready to visit the Croydon superstore,' says Lulu. 'And nor is Laurent. Let's be clear about that.'

'No, no, of course not,' I say. 'But the catalogue is . . . promising.'

'Yes, it is,' says Lulu, twirling the straw around in her drink. 'It definitely is promising.'

'And . . . how's Dan?' I ask, as casually as I can manage. Which is clearly not very casually at all, as Lulu gives me a peculiarly shrewd look.

'Dan . . .' she says slowly. 'Dan is . . . weird.'

'Weird how?'

'Well, he's started seeing that girl Emma again. You remember the one from the party?'

'Oh. Right. Right, great,' I say, feeling a bit sick at the memory of that night. It must have been Emma's voice I heard when I called round on Monday.

'Yeah, it's odd. She's not his type at all, and he seems constantly irritated by her. It's hardly love's young dream.'

'No?' I ask, pleased despite myself. Ever since Randy and Dan nearly fought over her golden form, I have had a particular dislike of the ravishing Emma.

'I don't really know why he's with her. To be perfectly honest – ' Lulu stops twirling her straw and looks up at me – 'until quite recently I thought Dan was in love with you.'

She says it so matter-of-factly that for a moment I think I must have misheard.

'You thought he, er – I beg your pardon?'

'I know. Ridiculous, isn't it?' she says. 'But for a while there, I really did think so. He had total mentionitis – kept bringing up your name at the slightest excuse. He hated Randy with a completely irrational passion. He barely looked at another woman for a year, and then he kept acting all funny around you, picking arguments all the time. Didn't you notice?'

'Oh, ha! God, Lu, me and *Dan*?' I say, avoiding her eyes.

But I have noticed. I have. It's something I haven't wanted to admit to myself – after all, this is Dan, it's too strange – but I've been aware of it for weeks now. Like something that I've glimpsed, often, out of the corner of my eye but never looked at directly.

'Well, obviously I was wrong,' says Lulu dismissively as her BlackBerry buzzes on the table beside her. 'He changes the subject every time I mention you these days. Hang on.'

She picks up the phone. 'Burning? Burning how? Well rinse it off! Quickly! Offer her some free products immediately, and a glass of wine – two glasses of wine. If she's pissed she might forget about suing us. I'll be there in two minutes.'

Lulu grimaces as she takes the phone away from her ear. 'Sorry, Harrison, I'm going to have to go – slight disaster with a Brazilian keratin treatment.'

She kisses me on the cheek and races out of the café, leaving me alone with a half-eaten mozzarella and tomato sandwich, two Diet Cokes and some unsettling thoughts.

Of course I've noticed Dan's been weird with me. Maybe I was first aware of it that night at the comedy club. It was as if I'd never seen before how he always looked out for me; how tall he was; that I had to look up to see him properly; that he tilted his head to hear what I was saying, his dark curls falling across his eyes. The way his long, strong fingers wrapped themselves around his pint glass. But I tried not to notice, while I was playing at relationships with Randy, that the person who was acting the romantic hero – leaping to my defence, coming to my rescue, looking out for me – was Dan.

Lulu is right, not just about Dan having feelings for me, but in her long-ago assertion that I haven't allowed for the possibility that things might change. That my friend's brother might become something more to me. It has felt safer to keep Dan in the pigeonhole I've always had for him – safe, brotherly, non-threatening – even when it's been clear he's been trying to force his way out of it. Safer to lose myself in a pretend relationship than to take a risk on something big and real and scary.

But while I was flaunting my fake relationship in the pages of *Hot Slebs* magazine, Dan moved on. And now I've lost him. Not only what might have been, but the friend he has been up until now. I never appreciated how much a part of my life he is – his steady presence a constant in the background. I'm not saying I've realized I'm desperately in love with him or anything – don't be ridiculous; this is Dan we're talking about. But I never knew until now that he's someone I want to have in my life in his own right, as my friend Dan Miller, not just as Lulu's brother.

I still haven't sent him a card. Although I have an unwavering belief in the power of good stationery,

I know it's going to take more than a card to win Dan back as my friend. But it's a start. I'm sending one today.

When I step inside the tiny stationery shop off the Fulham Road, I sigh happily. I've always loved stationery in all its forms, from sensible brown envelopes in recycled paper to letterpress cards from tiny San Francisco collectives to notebooks for the writing of deep thoughts or, even better, shallow ones. But I pass the notebooks today. I pass the birthday cards, the cards of congratulation, the thank-yous and the invitations. There, next to the tasteful expressions of bereavement and loss, is a subsection devoted to apology.

'Sorry' says a mournful puppy looking upwards with appealing eyes from a tiled floor strewn with half-eaten spaghetti Bolognese. 'Forgive me' begs a pen-and-ink octopus clasping its tentacles pleadingly, though what seafood-related incident that card might be relevant for I cannot imagine. There's a preponderance of animals on these cards, as if it's easier to get a mute creature to make the apology on your behalf than to say it yourself.

Surprisingly enough, there isn't a rugby-themed card of apology. Nor one that features an apology for misleading one's friend over the nature of one's fake relationship with a famous comedian and legendary shagger. Sending one of the fluffy bunnies or puppies to plead for lenience would surely necessitate the sending of another card apologizing for being so wet. In the end I decide on a plain card with a typewritten Sorry in black on a white background. Simple, to the point, no beating around the bush.

As is the message I write in it when I get home.

Dan,

I'm so sorry for not telling you the truth about me and Randy Jones. I'm afraid that, at the time, I'd totally lost sight of what was real and what was fake. That's no excuse for lying to you, especially when you had gone to such trouble to warn me about Randy. I hope you can forgive me, and that we can still be friends. I miss you.

Lizzy

I post it that afternoon.

Two weeks pass. I don't get a reply.

32

I'm sitting in the French bar on Dean Street, fending off all attempts from after-work drinkers to encroach on the space I'm saving for Lulu. I've hung my coat over the back of the empty chair and left a copy of the *Evening Standard* on the seat, but that doesn't prevent hopeful table vultures from approaching every five minutes to ask, 'I don't suppose this chair . . . ?' I shake my head politely – 'Sorry' – and pour red wine into the empty glass to bolster the illusion that someone is actually sitting here with me. Any minute now I'll start conducting a conversation with my imaginary friend – that should put people off.

Although the Spinsters' Social Club has officially disbanded since Lulu has become fully loved-up with Laurent – I admit I'm still a spinster, but there's nothing social about being one by yourself – we've reinstated our Wednesday night drinks as of this evening.

It's the first time I've been back to this place since the fateful evening Lulu told me I needed to lose control. I think we can safely say I fulfilled her remit beyond either of our hopes. I might be the sole remaining member of the Spinsters' Social Club, but at least I'm no longer the accidental celibate of three months ago. So Randy turned out to be a bit of an idiot – I survived it. I'm not saying that if Randy walked in here right now I'd be thrilled, but when I saw in the latest issue of *Hot Slebs* that he has added Paris Hilton to his list of conquests, it made me smile rather than cry myself to sleep. And this whole experience is proof to myself that the end of a relationship doesn't mean I'm destined to become a hideous sobbing wreck like I was after Joe left me. I can walk away from my relationship with Randy, despite its fakeness, despite its attendant humiliations, and still be fine. And still be me.

'Sorry, someone's sitting there,' I say to another chair-stealing hopeful.

Lulu was right. I did need to lose control a bit to get out of the rut I'd accidentally fallen into. Randy was like electroshock therapy for the emotionally frozen – extreme and ridiculous and possibly essential. But over the last few weeks I've realized, as elements of my pre-Randy life have crept back, that being organized and a bit in control is just a part of me. I'm never going to be Lulu – as much as I would like to be the kind of girl who goes skinny-dipping in the Serpentine with the gorgeous twenty-four-year-old drama student in charge of the pedalos (Lulu's Mr May), that just isn't me – and that's okay. It's time I started being true to myself. I can open myself up to different experiences and still have a clean kitchen. I can adapt my routines, but there's a part of me that will always need a bit of routine to feel secure. I'm not about to go investigating it with a shrink or anything – they'll only make it all about my mother; they always do – I just know it's true. I can be the kind of girl who orders her shoes by colour *and* have a boyfriend. Though a tidy one would be helpful, I've got to admit.

'No, sorry, it's taken.' I smile a friendly but firm denial at yet another attempt to filch the chair. Where is Lulu?

And my life is already changing. I'm about to be really busy in my new job at African Vision – I start on Monday. Oh yes, I'm no longer going to be the sexy-nun charity worker. My idea of running away to an exotic environment felt much less attractive when I started to investigate it all. Let's just say that there's a time in one's life when cold showers, hammocks and long-drop toilets are acceptable for months on end, and I believe that time is under the age of thirty. I allowed Camilla to believe that it was her powers of persuasion that changed my mind; she need never know that she shares this victory with the appeal of indoor plumbing.

'I'm sorry, someone's sitting there,' I say for what feels like the fortieth time, but this particular chair-stealer is a bold one. He's got his hand on it and he's pulling it out from the table in a determined fashion.

'Excuse me, I *said*—' I say, looking up crossly.

'Dan!'

'Hi, Lizzy,' he says, looking down at me with the ghost of a smile on his lips. 'Can I sit down?' His hand hovers over the chair.

'Er, yes, of course you can,' I splutter, entirely taken aback at his appearance. His appearance in the bar, I mean – he looks just the same as usual: work suit, check. Messy hair: check.

'I mean, that's to say,' I continue, 'I'm saving it for Lulu – she's due here any minute. So you'll have to give it back when she gets here.'

Oh, hurry, hurry, hurry, Lulu – don't leave me here with your brother on my own. It's all too weird. Or maybe he's here to meet Emma, and I'm going to have to sit with the two of them while they passionately snog and paw at one another.

'Lulu's not coming,' says Dan, hanging his coat on top of mine on the back of the chair. He slides himself into the seat, his shoulders hunched up in a way that makes him seem far too big for it and for the flimsy table that separates us.

'But she never said—' I say, picking up my phone to check it for messages.

'I told her not to, Lizzy,' says Dan with a look of grim resolution that rather frightens me. 'I wanted to see you on your own.'

'You're not meeting Emma here?' I ask nervously, expecting her to appear at any moment.

'No,' he says, his eyebrows knitting together in a frown. 'That's finished; it didn't work out.'

'I'm sorry,' I say.

'Don't be,' he says, helping himself to the wine I'd already poured for Lulu. 'I didn't come here to talk about her. I came here to talk to you.'

I wish I could say that this statement, and Dan's unexpected appearance, fills me with a feeling of delirious happiness and a realization of true love; I know how this kind of story is supposed to end. The truth is I feel the same sickening dread as when I found myself standing on the top high-diving board at the Guildford Spectrum Leisure Centre circa 1987. On that occasion I was able to beat a shameful retreat back down the steps after being unable to jump. Here there is no escape – believe me, I have already surreptitiously checked out my potential exit routes, and the only possibility that doesn't involve physically pushing past Dan is throwing myself down the trapdoor behind the bar and ending up in the wine cellar. As that would involve leaping across the bar in the manner of an Olympic high jumper, I have regretfully ruled it out. For now, at least.

'Dan, I'm so sorry I didn't tell you about Randy,' I say as fast as I can, trying to get it over with quickly, like ripping off a plaster, before he can shout at me.

He just looks at me, saying nothing, twisting the stem of his wine glass round and round.

'I – I just got myself into this stupid fake relationship,' I continue, words tumbling out far too fast, 'and I couldn't tell anyone because I'd promised and, well, you were being so kind and protective to try and warn me off, and I didn't want to lie, but I couldn't tell you the truth. I mean – well, there's no excuse. I'm sorry, Dan, I'm really sorry.'

He's still looking at me silently, his lips pressed into a line. It's impossible to tell if he's trying to prevent himself from losing his temper, or from bursting out laughing.

'I behaved really badly,' I persevere doggedly. It seems he really does want me to crawl on my belly. 'I should have been honest, Dan. I just lost sight of what was important, and . . .'

'So what is important?' asks Dan suddenly, his head tilted slightly to one side as he awaits my answer.

I eye the height of the bar speculatively. Would it really hurt so much to propel myself over it and escape down the trapdoor? Might it not be less agonizing than this conversation?

'Er, what's important?' I repeat, feeling butterflies start up in my stomach. What does he want, blood?

'Yes. You said you lost sight of what was important,' says Dan, unsmiling. 'So what is important, then?'

'Well,' I begin, feeling like I'm at a job interview for which I'm entirely unprepared. 'Er, friendship is important – our friendship, I mean – and being truthful.'

'Yes?' says Dan.

'Umm, and being honest? Honest with myself as well as other people.'

'Yes?'

'Jesus, Dan, I don't know what else to say!' I protest in exasperation. 'If you want me to wear a hair shirt, then just hand it over and I'll put it on. I'm sorry and I've said so, and I don't know what else to say.'

This whole apology thing is not going quite how I expected.

'I'm afraid I'm all out of hair shirts,' says Dan, his lips twisting into a wry smile.

'Have you got a big stick for me to beat myself with then?' I ask grumpily. 'Maybe one with thorns on for maximum punishment?'

'Nope, no sticks,' he laughs.

'Well, if you're going to deny me any mortification of the flesh, Dan, then you'd better be prepared to forgive me without it,' I say, looking at him hopefully. If he's laughing then surely he can't be too angry with me.

'You don't have to beat yourself up, Lizzy,' says Dan. 'Not with a big stick and not any other way. Of course I was angry with you – I didn't like telling you about

Randy. I thought it would really hurt you, but I thought it would hurt you more not to know.'

'Dan—' I start.

'Just let me finish,' he says, frowning and twisting his dark curls with one hand. 'So discovering it was all some big joke, some huge set-up, it – it felt like you'd been laughing behind my back with that arsehole.'

'Oh, Dan, no!' I say. 'I never, ever discussed you with Randy. I'd never laugh behind your back, not with him or with anyone else. But listen – this isn't about him; it's about us.'

'About us?' says Dan, his eyebrows rising in interest.

'You know what I mean,' I bluster, allowing my hair to fall over my face as I look down at the table top with great interest, as if there might be another escape route scratched there by a previous customer.

'Do I?' he asks, leaning forward on the table, which lurches alarmingly so that he has to grab his wobbling wine glass and sit back up.

'I mean, Dan,' I say, looking him in the eye as steadily as I can, which is not very, as my eyes keep being drawn down to his lips to see if he's smiling or not, 'that Randy is in the past—'

'So's his wardrobe,' mutters Dan. 'That fucking double denim . . .'

'Dan! Stop talking!' I lean across the table to push his arm for emphasis. 'I mean that whatever happened between me and Randy is finished – over. I mean, our friendship – yours and mine – is far more important to me than anything that might have happened in the past. Okay?'

Dan smiles, his eyes crinkling in a way that I hope means forgiveness. He picks up his wine glass and lifts it towards me.

'Here's to friendship, Lizzy Harrison,' he says, and reaches, with his other hand, for mine.

And suddenly, just like that, with the touch of his hand, I am back on the top diving board at the Guildford Spectrum Leisure Centre. Swooping dread and nervous excitement. A sense of terrifying anticipation. A dizzying feeling that the ground is far, far away. There is something there, something between us, and the fear of doing nothing about it has become bigger than the fear of doing something.

My heart pounds in my ears until I can hear nothing else. The room goes blurry around the still point of Dan's face as he looks at me quizzically.

I'm going to jump.

I reach over the table, steadying it with both hands, and press my lips to his for one brief moment.

I don't know what I was expecting to happen – in fact, that's the best thing about it: I didn't weigh up the pros and cons, I didn't worry about the consequences – but it's safe to say I didn't expect Dan to start laughing. So there we have it. I took a risk and look where it got me. I have just kissed my best friend's brother and he thinks it's all a huge joke. I feel as exposed and embarrassed as if I were sitting here in my underwear. How will I ever live this down? Laughter echoes round and round the bar, and although I know it's just the general sound of people enjoying themselves (I hate them all), it feels to me as if everyone is joining Dan in ridiculing me.

'Oh God – sorry, Dan,' I say, blushing furiously. 'I don't know what came over me.'

'Lizzy Harrison, you're a woman of surprises,' says Dan, still smirking.

'Yes, yes, whatever,' I say, picking up my handbag from the banquette seat. It's time for me to get out of here, and not via the trapdoor. 'Sorry to embarrass you, I should go . . .'

'Sit back down,' says Dan, reaching over to push my bag back on to the seat.

I look him full in the face. I feel as if I could close my eyes and still remember every part of it. His navy blue eyes, so dark when he is angry or emotional. His stupid hair, always falling across his forehead in resolutely unstyled curls, a few silver hairs at his temples. The faint beginnings of stubble on his jaw. His gently mocking expression; one eyebrow raised.

'Lizzy Harrison,' he says, with great seriousness. 'Are you putting the moves on me?'

I wish for the earth to open up and swallow me whole.

'Er, no, that was a mistake. My – my, erm, my face just fell on yours accidentally, Dan, ha-ha,' I say, sitting on my hands to stop myself from physically writhing with shame. 'Sorry about that.'

'Yeah, right, totally understandable,' he says, leaning closer. 'These things do happen.'

And then he reaches over and takes my face between both of his hands, twining his fingers in my hair. His lips fall on mine in a way that is not even slightly accidental. I feel as if all my bones have turned to spaghetti. I couldn't move my limbs if I tried.

'Whoops,' he says, his eyes twinkling with amusement as he pulls away. 'My mistake. Must have slipped.'

It seems like everything has gone into slow motion; that if I tried to speak my words would be all stretched out and slurred. I can't stop myself from smiling in a manner that is actually beginning to make my cheeks hurt. Dan's dark eyes meet mine with a force that feels like it should be visible, fizzing and sparking between us. His fingers are now laced with mine across the table. I can't let go.

'So,' he says finally.

'So,' I murmur, hardly able to form an 'o' sound, so fixed is my ridiculous grin.

'What next?' Dan asks, squeezing my fingers with his.

'I don't know,' I say. 'Is that okay?'

'You don't know?' teases Dan, throwing his head

back in laughter. 'Lizzy Harrison doesn't have a plan? Surely you've at least booked a minicab to pick you up in five minutes?'

'No minicab,' I say softly. 'No plan.'

Dan grins and kisses me again, pulling me close towards him. I distinctly hear someone next to us say 'get a room'. Maybe we will.

I know I'm meant to tell you what happens next. But here's the thing. I don't know.

And it's wonderful.